Dark Finds

Gary Colton

First published in 2024

~

Copyright © Gary Colton, 2024

This novel is entirely a work of fiction. All characters in this novel are fictional. Any resemblance to a real person, alive or dead, is coincidental.

Trade Paperback ISBN: 987-1-80517-363-2
E-book ISBN: 987-1-80517-364-9

For Bubba, you are everything I wouldn't change...

Part One

Chapter 1

Toronto, May 2019

The air felt damp as homicide detective Eve Salah emerged from her black sedan, adjusting the rim of her Blue Jays cap before breathing into her hands for warmth. Eve was the youngest member of the Toronto Homicide Department, an attractive twenty-nine-year-old with a petite frame, dark eyes, caramel skin, and black wavy hair. She was a self-confessed overthinker with a tenacity to match. The sort of person who refrained from googling words she couldn't remember. The kind of personality who would fixate on finding the end crease on a roll of Sellotape and not stop until her fingernail peeled back the lip. Great traits for detective work, but not so great for relaxing or trying to fall asleep, where her thoughts would bounce around in her skull, her neurons lighting up like the bulbs of a pinball machine.

Eve took a deep breath, anticipating the night ahead. The wind that moved through Toronto's financial district always felt colder to Eve, picking up pace as it swooshed between skyscrapers, planting a cold kiss on her cheek before scampering on again like most of the men she had dated over the past few years. Flings mainly. But Eve didn't want flings. She wanted real love, the sort of love that would slingshot her out of Earth's orbit, turning the chemicals in her brain from cold to hot. Or maybe it was just a little excitement Eve wanted. Some adventure, some mixing of molecules that would allow her to feel as though she sat behind the wheel of a whirlwind, waltzing on to God-knows-where without a worry in the world. But Eve didn't have time for any of that. Her job was hectic. She had a lot to prove, and having fun just got in the way of her ambition.

Eve slipped on a pair of protective shoe coverings before ducking beneath the yellow police tape bordering the crime scene. Forensics were already canvassing the area, snapping photographs, and collecting evidence. A white tent had been erected around the victim's body, its canvas walls flapping in the breeze down a dark alley close to Clearwater Plaza. Eve's gaze was inexorably drawn to the victim's face, a pulpy mess without shape, teeth mixed with brain matter, his eyeballs split open like over-boiled beans. A two-kilogram lump hammer lay close by, smeared with blood and bits of the victim's beard. Eve had attended other murder scenes where people had been stabbed, shot, and even speared, but never bludgeoned with such force. She tried to imagine the rage it must have taken, raising her shoulders slightly, the little hairs stiffening on the nape of her neck.

'Who called it in?' Eve asked one of the forensic technicians.

'Some late-night runner,' the technician said. 'She's over with Officer Lee now.'

'Okay, thanks,' Eve said, ducking beneath the police tape and walking towards the half-dozen cop cars parked outside Clearwater Plaza. Journalists and news crews were arriving like vultures at the scent of blood. Cameras flashed, excited figures moved impatiently for a front-page story. Some reporters tried pushing through the police cordon on Bay & Wellington, but the cops directed them back, threatening to arrest an overzealous journalist who attempted to breeze by, flashing an imaginary badge.

Officer Lee nodded when he saw Eve approach. 'Are you looking for the woman who called it in?'

'Yeah,' Eve responded, trying to control the slight tremor in her hands.

'She's in the back of my cruiser,' Lee said, nodding to his car. 'Be careful where you stand; she vomited all over the sidewalk.'

'Roger that,' Eve said. 'Any sign of Mitch?'

'No,' Lee answered with a slight roll of his eyes. 'Probably just as well, eh? We don't need him messing up the scene again; the last time was a nightmare.'

Eve nodded before turning around and clutching her chest. She felt close to another panic attack. The ambient noises around her began to distort and fade, drumming strangely in her ears as if coming from underwater; as if she was caught in a rip tide, the pressure on her chest felt crushing, her lungs felt as tight as a wrung cloth.

Not tonight. Stay calm, just breathe.

She ran her hands down her face and felt her balance falter.

'You okay?' Lee asked.

'Aw, too much coffee,' Eve said, trying to force a smile.

The scene stirred up a whirlwind of memories. A girl crying in the back of a cruiser. Police lights blinking blue and red. Onlookers whispering to one another, their eyes greedy for gossip. Each image felt more visceral than the last, all leading back to a traumatic event that happened to Eve at age fourteen when her father attacked the boy she was dating. What a drag that had been, a time when she wished the ground would open up to swallow her, where her humiliation tore at the seams of her teenage years like a mole scratching at the earth.

Just focus. You got this.

Eve took calming breaths, swallowing deeply as if to rinse away the bad memories. Officer Lee's cruiser was parked haphazardly by the curb, its back door ajar, a jogger's pink trainer dangling out. Eve tapped gently on the window and smiled at the young woman in the back seat. 'I'm Detective Eve Salah. Can I have a word?'

The woman nodded meekly as Eve bent down to appear less threatening.

'How are you doing?' Eve asked.

'I feel like I'm going to throw up again,' the woman said, wiping away wisps of black hair from her tear-stained cheeks. 'Every time I close my eyes, I see the man's face.'

Eve put a warm hand on the woman's shoulder. 'Let's go get some air. If you don't feel like talking tonight, that's okay; we can sit in silence.'

'Okay,' the woman said, emerging from the cruiser. 'My name's Samantha. I'm from St. John's. I only moved to Toronto last year. My pops warned me this would happen, you know. He said the big city is full of crime and heathens, but I wouldn't listen to a dang word.'

'You're safe now,' Eve said, as they sat on a nearby bench.

'I don't feel safe. I was just out for a run, like, why did I have to see that?'

'What did you see?'

'The man in the alley. The man without a face,' Samantha said, her pupils dilated, the blue veins pulsating heavily in her hands. 'I thought it was a homeless man asleep at first, but something didn't look right. It was the way he was lying on the ground like he'd been crucified. I was about to run on, but something in my head told me to go look.'

'Was there anyone else around?' Eve asked.

'No. The financial district is a ghost town on Friday nights.'

'And did you notice anything unusual?'

'No, it was just really quiet,' Samantha said before pausing to think. 'Well, there was a note on the man's chest. That looked a bit weird, like someone had placed it there.'

'What sort of note?'

'A handwritten one,' Samantha said, pulling nervously at a frayed thread on her sleeve. 'I don't know. I just ran back out onto the street and called 911.'

'Okay,' Eve said, standing up. 'I'll get an officer to bring you home. Give them your contact details, and we'll be in touch with any other questions.'

Once Samantha was back in the cruiser, Eve slipped on a fresh pair of shoe coverings and latex gloves. She ducked under the police tape again and called over to the female forensic photographer.

'There was a note left at the scene?' Eve asked.

'Yeah,' the photographer said. 'A poem, and you know what that means.'

'Can I see it?'

'It's in evidence,' the photographer said. 'Hold on a moment; I'll grab it for you.'

Feelings of unease and excitement moved through Eve. Adrenaline flooded her body like tons of dynamite exploding out in all directions. Could The Poet really be back? Eve hadn't worked any of the other murders, but her partner Mitch had worked all four, and they were no closer to catching him. Maybe Eve could crack the case. She indulged the idea for a moment, the glory of it, imagining herself on CTV News announcing to the city that they had caught the serial killer who had terrorized Toronto over the past three years.

When the photographer returned, she handed Eve the evidence bag with the note inside. Eve's eyes scanned over the text as she read the note aloud.

And Tantalus stole the nectar's seed...
There goes the home where I was born!
      For death, not life, must punish greed,

Must feed, his wicked deeds & burn!

Do you believe in Evil?

Liar!

Dark Finds

Eve's eyes softened to focus, reading the note again. 'I wonder if he's back?'

'Who?' Mitch asked, appearing behind her.

Eve could smell the alcohol wafting from Mitch's breath. He appeared drunk, inhaling half his cigarette in a single drag, then flicking it onto the ground.

'You reek of booze,' Eve said. 'And don't go littering the crime scene.'

Mitch ignored her. 'Who's back?' he asked, grabbing the evidence bag from Eve before scanning the note.

'It's him,' Mitch said. 'Signed the same way. *Dark Finds*, written in the victim's blood.'

'Why now after all these months?' the photographer asked. 'And why here? It's such a public spot.'

'We can't be sure it's him,' Eve said. 'Only one victim this time – a lone male.'

'But that's not The Poet's MO,' Mitch said. 'Something doesn't feel right here.'

Chapter 2

'I just spoke with forensics,' Mitch said, walking into the atrium of Clearwater Plaza. 'I have them widening the crime scene area. If this is The Poet, then there must be another body close by.'

The atrium was empty at this hour. It rose like a vast expanse of shimmering glass and polished metal, stretching skywards, illuminated by the cool, sterile lights from within. Above, escalators, walkways, and glass bridges connected the floors. The distant hum of the city buzzed outside; the soft rustle of a forgotten newspaper page and the gentle flow of a cascading water feature could be heard near the entrance.

'He could've changed his MO,' Eve said. 'Bundy changed his. In his first two attacks, he broke into women's houses. The ones after that, he lured them to his car before abducting them. Anyway, we'll have to wait until forensics review the note. It could be a copycat.'

'The poems were never released publicly,' Mitch said. 'A copycat wouldn't know that The Poet signs off as *Dark Finds*. The poem looks legit, but the victimology is way off.'

'Maybe this victim is special.'

'Maybe,' Mitch said.

Eve's voice softened as she put her hand on Mitch's shoulder. 'I'm going to talk to you as a friend here, Mitch. You can't show up drunk to a crime scene. Chief Cutler won't put up with it, she'll fire your ass, and none of us want to see that, eh?'

'I'm not drunk,' Mitch said, wiping sleep crumbs from his eyes.

'I can smell the booze on your breath.'

'You've no right to judge,' Mitch said. 'A few months ago, you were messed up all of the time; remember that?'

'I got help,' Eve said, holding his stare. 'I got my shit under control. You need to do the same. You've been through a lot, take some more time off.'

When Mitch ran his hand through his hair, Eve's eyebrows raised. 'What happened to your hand?'

'Nothing,' Mitch said, shuffling his hand into his pocket. His knuckles were swollen, and he had scratches all over the back of his hand. He'd been blackout drunk that day and couldn't remember what had happened or where he'd even been.

'I need some air,' Mitch said, walking away.

He sat on the steps outside Clearwater Plaza and lowered his face into his palms. Mitch felt like he was losing control again, like he had all those years ago. The Toronto Police Service didn't know that Mitch had overdosed on heroin at seventeen. He was found in a shopping centre toilet with a needle still upright in his arm, lying dead on a piss-stained floor for over a minute before a paramedic brought him back to life. For twenty-three years, Mitch never touched drugs or accepted pain medication, even after a shootout with a city gang when he took a bullet to his left thigh. He always chose alcohol-free mouthwash and limited himself to one cup of coffee a day, bought at the same café each morning and sipped slowly on his twenty-minute drive to work.

Relapsing was something Mitch thought would never happen, and most wouldn't think it possible either. His tanned complexion, muscular body, and stoic nature all hinted at the hallmarks of a man who'd never once stumbled at a single crossroads. But everything changed when his five-year-old daughter, Betty, was killed in a hit-and-run three months ago. Mitch fell back into the arms of his old ways, and his life was starting to fall apart and crumble like pastry in a child's hands.

Mitch took a flask of bourbon from the inside of his blazer pocket, raising the flask to his lips, shuddering at the sweet, piercing smell of bourbon. In one swift swallow, he felt the boozy liquid sting his taste buds, swim down his oesophagus, and blaze in his belly like a bonfire. Mitch sighed with relief, but he hated himself for drinking again, and for the impact it was having on his marriage. He hoped the booze would rid the image of Betty from his mind, her body mangled on the road outside their house, her little blonde pigtails stained with blood, her eyes still open when he found her.

Mitch was holding back tears when Eve appeared behind him. 'Forensics got a name from the victim's driver's license, and the CCTV footage is ready. Come on.'

The security guard shook his head as both detectives walked back into the atrium. 'You won't get much off the CCTV footage. The cameras haven't been cleaned in weeks, and the dust around here muddies up the lenses.'

'We'll still need to see it,' Eve said.

'Follow me,' the security guard said, motioning them towards his back office.

'The victim's name is Paddy Fitzgerald,' Eve said. 'He had an Irish driver's licence in his wallet.'

'Irish?' Mitch quizzed.

'Yeah. But we won't know more until forensics run his prints.'

The demons that had driven Mitch to drink were growing uncontrollably louder, and slouching forward in the security guard's office, he watched a man who looked like Paddy Fitzgerald leave Clearwater Plaza at 10 pm. The man appeared to be walking toward a nearby taxi when something caught his attention down the dark alley between Clearwater Plaza and another tall office building.

'Rewind that a few seconds,' Eve said to the security guard. 'Why would Paddy have walked down that alley?'

'I don't know,' Mitch said.

'The killer must have been waiting down there for him.'

'Even so,' Mitch said. 'You wouldn't just wander down a dark alley at night in a quiet part of town.'

'Unless the victim knew the killer,' the security guard said, leaning forward on the chair behind them. 'Otherwise, I ain't walking down no alley at night. Crazies and crackheads everywhere these days. I'm getting in that cab and getting back to my hotel as quickly as possible. Especially if I'm Paddy Fitzgerald.'

'You knew Paddy?' Eve asked.

'Dude owns this building,' the security guard said. 'Well, kinda. He was one of the Clearwater co-founders. The watch on his wrist goes for like three-hundred grand. I ain't walking anywhere in Toronto with that drip on me. The dude should've had bodyguards and shit. I guarantee you this was a robbery. Easy money if you feel me.'

Both Eve and Mitch raised their eyebrows at each other.

'The watch was still on his wrist,' Eve said.

The security guard laughed. 'Some fool missed an easy payday.'

'What else can you tell us about Paddy?' Mitch asked.

'Not much,' the security guard said. 'Dude seemed nice. He was over here all week from Dublin. I think that's where he lives. He has a thick Irish accent, and that's where Clearwater's HQ is located.'

'Anything else?' Eve asked. 'Did you see anyone hanging around that looked out of place?'

'Nope.'

'Can you pull a list of the meetings Paddy had this week?' Eve asked.

'Not sure if I have that access,' the security guard said. 'But I'll take a look.'

For the next few hours, Mitch and Eve viewed the CCTV footage from eight other cameras. They drank cups of coffee trying to stay awake. Most of the footage was grainy. There was nothing out of the ordinary: businessmen and women leaving Clearwater or other nearby offices, some homeless men rambling around the sidewalk, runners pounding the pavement on their nightly jogs.

It was close to 4 am when Eve's cell phone vibrated in her pocket.

'Hey,' Eve answered.

'It's Officer Lee. Can you meet me out front? We have a woman here who says she saw something strange.'

'Give us five minutes,' Eve said. 'We're just finishing up with the CCTV footage.'

'I need a smoke,' Mitch said. 'I'll meet you outside.'

Mitch's drunkenness was wearing off. He felt sleepy, hollowed out, like a balloon with a small hole, slowly deflating. The cool outside air made Mitch feel a little woozy. He sat on the steps again and lit a cigarette, inhaling deeply and breathing the smoke out through his nose. The crowd at the police cordon on Bay & Wellington had grown larger, and the street emitted a heavy hum of conversation and staticky voices coming over police radios.

Mitch stubbed out his cigarette before rustling through his jeans pocket and pulling out two OxyContin tablets. Booze was one thing, Mitch thought, but taking Oxy could ruin his life completely. The memory of his opiate days sent a shiver down Mitch's spine. All at once, he felt plunged into the ice-cold recesses of his youth, seeing himself in the third person, smoking heroin, wandering the streets, stooped over and grossly malnourished.

The thought of an opiate release seemed to open a portal in Mitch's memory, old circuitry prised free from stasis, repressed sensations alive again, leaping from neuron to neuron at the speed of light.

When Eve appeared behind him, Mitch closed his hand quickly.

'You good?' Eve asked.

Mitch nodded, putting the Oxy back in his pocket.

Throw them away.

Officer Lee nodded at Eve and Mitch when he saw them approach. 'This is Glenda,' Lee said, motioning to the middle-aged woman beside him, a thin-faced Torontonian with a narrow upper lip, who had formed the habit of speaking with her teeth clamped shut. 'She came down when she saw the news.'

Eve took out her notepad and smiled at the woman. 'I'm Detective Eve Salah, and this is my partner Mitch. We'd like to ask you a few questions if that's okay. We just want you to tell us what you saw.'

'And remember,' Mitch added, 'even the slightest detail can be important.'

'Okay,' Glenda said, smiling at Mitch. 'I was late leaving the office, probably around ten. I usually finish at nine, but sometimes I like to stay a little longer and sit at the computers pretending I'm not just a cleaner and all. I know it sounds odd, but I always wanted to work in a big office and wear those nice dresses the women flaunt around in. Anyways, it was really quiet, it always is on Friday nights, so the scream sounded really loud.'

'Scream?' Mitch probed.

'Or maybe it was more like a cheer,' Glenda said. 'The sort of noise someone makes when their team scores a touchdown.'

'And did you see who let out the scream?' Eve asked.

'Kind of,' Glenda said, her eyes narrowing. 'He was down that alley where the tent is set up now. I couldn't see what he was doing; he was hunched over something, like bags of trash.'

'Trash?'

'I hope it was trash,' Glenda said, shaking her head softly. 'I know it could have been a body, but my mind doesn't want to think it was.'

'And what was the guy doing?' Eve asked.

'I don't know,' Glenda said. 'It's weird; it was like he could sense me standing there. He turned around slowly, but he didn't run or anything. He just stared at me until I got freaked out and walked on. It was only when I turned on the news that I realised it might've been the killer.'

'What did the man look like?' Eve asked.

'I didn't get a good look; it was too dark. But he looked Caucasian, probably in his mid-twenties with an athletic build. This sounds crazy, but he looked like that actor who plays Superman.'

'Would you mind sitting down with a sketch artist?' Eve asked.

'Sure, but I don't know if it will help.'

'Would you do it now?' Mitch asked. 'It's best to do these things when the image is still fresh. I know it's late, but I can have one of the officers drive you to the station.'

Glenda agreed, and Mitch walked her to a parked cruiser.

'I'm not in danger, am I?' Glenda asked. 'You know, being a potential witness and all.'

'No,' Mitch said. 'Don't worry about any of that, and if you feel scared or anything, here's my card. Call me any time you want.'

'I'd like that,' Glenda said, a soft, flirtatious look settling in her eye. 'Any time, right?'

'Any time,' Mitch said, nodding.

He was startled when Glenda suddenly reached out and hugged him. He felt confused at first, but the longer they shared

13

heat, the more Mitch didn't want their hug to end. He hadn't properly grieved Betty's passing and it felt good to be held by someone. As they pulled back, their eyes locked, and the space between them felt charged with the possibility of something more, something deeper.

'Speak soon,' Glenda said, her eyes searching Mitch's before turning to leave.

Mitch hadn't felt like that in years, the rush of some forbidden excitement, his heart pounding in his chest like drumbeat. He didn't look at the sea of spectators; he didn't see the killer smiling to himself, his eyes as big as saucers, imagining the murder over and over again.

Chapter 3

Jack Lawson looked like another shadowy figure lingering near the police cordon. The neon swirl of police lights illuminated his face in intermittent blues and reds as he watched the cops move with grim efficiency, speaking in hushed tones, their breath visible in the chilly air.

Tonight was the night, Jack thought. Toronto felt taut with terror again. A name had been scratched off his list like a bad debt. *The Poet* was back. Jack tried not to smirk too hard as he remembered Paddy Fitzgerald's final words. *An eye for an eye leaves the whole world blind. I'm sorry for what happened. I'm so sorry.*

Jack's smirk widened.

Paddy doesn't have eyes anymore; he doesn't have a face.

There must have been over two hundred people gathered at the police cordon. Their empathy felt nauseating to Jack. All the false pretence, the soft sniffling, the animal inside of them sick and bloated from feeding on its own rotten conscience. They were all bound together by common feelings: fear, sadness, and sorrow. Those grief hogs wanted to be seen as earthly in a world that had mistaken empathy as the jewel in the crown of evolution. Empathy had only one purpose in Jack's refrigerated world: it was camouflage, like a costume he wore to cloak his true nature, a sort of shroud he wrapped around his *shadow-self* to appear more sincere.

Jack led a double life, and the duplicity excited him the most; how he could walk through the meadow as the wolf and the sheep would smile at him because he didn't growl or bare his teeth. Jack considered himself transcended in that regard. A new breed of evolution. A cultural mutation spawned from the materialistic excesses of modernity, combining strains of suffering, selfishness, and rage into a being comparable to God. No one was aware of the danger that walked among them, calm as a monk, handsome as Hollywood's latest heartthrob.

'I heard on the police scanner that a poem was left at the scene,' Jack said to the influencer standing beside him. She wasn't like the others, Jack thought. She was more of a gore hog, rooting around the edge of a crime scene at 4 am hoping to catch sight of a dead body.

'A poem?' the influencer said. 'Is The Poet back?'

'I don't know,' Jack said, with a subtle smirk. 'It doesn't really fit The Poet's MO, does it? It's too public here.'

The Poet, Jack thought. What a lame moniker. The media were so easily fooled by intrigue. They didn't know he only left a poem at the scene to make it all about himself and not the victim. It was like taking their life twice. **Dark Finds** was a more fitting name, but the cops never released his signature – how he found a thread of darkness running through the vein of every conversation, the horror he harboured, the disgust and detestation he projected onto happy people. Sometimes, he'd see their lips blister and boil as they talked, imagining his hand rooting through their windpipe, like a crackhead tickling coins in an empty coffee cup.

'Who cares?' the woman said, opening Instagram on her phone. 'Gossip sells, and The Poet is about as hot as a topic gets online.'

'Really?' Jack asked, beaming on the inside.

'Yeah,' the influencer said. 'I run a true crime account on Instagram. Any videos I post about The Poet drive five times more engagement. Serial killers sell, especially the active ones.'

Jack rolled his eyes to the side. The term serial killer was so cliché, he thought, so unimaginative, something the media loved to use to boost their ratings. Jack considered himself more of a gamesman, like a chess grandmaster, toppling things and taking lives just to prove how good he was at doing it. He enjoyed the wonders of his own dogma, an embryo psychopath who concealed an intrepid murderous streak; a calm killer who, from an early age, imagined himself in ownership of a dark superpower.

At age ten, living in the slums of Toronto, Jack peered out his bedroom window one gloomy afternoon and breathed on the glass pane. He drew a hammer in the condensation, then watched a young couple walk directly towards the lump head. Jack experienced his first erection at that moment, imagining the couple bludgeoned to death on the sidewalk, believing himself to be love's executioner. He pictured the couple bleeding out on the pavement, all the darkness rising from their bodies, like a plume of smoke he could breathe in to nourish his own dark desires. And baffled by the whole experience, Jack ran to his bedside locker, scribbling this poem on a tattered piece of paper.

Rat-a-tat-tat,
  Watch this couple go splat,
    And with my hammer,
I make their face go splatter,
    I don't feel bad,
I just feel glad.

  Dark Finds

The influencer broke Jack's dark reverie. 'Do you want to be in my Instagram video?' she asked excitedly. 'I have half a million followers, you'll be like, famous.'

'No thanks,' Jack said, slinking through the crowd again. He knew how reckless he'd been. Rule number one: never go back to the crime scene. The cops are sneaky. They sometimes photograph the crowd knowing that killers often return to the scene. But Paddy Fitzgerald was special. Jack had learned everything he needed to know about what happened to his family. Paddy had confirmed his suspicions, and Jack needed to feel the energy at the scene, to trample around the tragedy and watch the cops bumbling about like imbeciles as the killer stood a few feet away from them. Jack glared at all the spectators like they were streams of atoms, something his rage could split and blow apart. They didn't know what it felt like to bludgeon brains into a pale, tepid gravy; that when brain matter hits the pavement, it shrivels, momentarily, making it look alive like a maggot on a bed of salt.

It didn't take long for the rumour of the poem to wash through the sea of spectators. A communal hum of shocked, sad, and excited chatter flurried in people's throats. Jack took a couple of steps forward, closer to the barrier, and looked down at the ground where a bunch of flowers lay. He stepped on the head of a rose and walked on, relishing the greasy feel of the crushed petals underfoot.

It was then Jack noticed her. The woman standing fifteen metres away, all the dark emotions bubbling up inside her; the grain of some psychic sadness devouring her like leprosy. Jack wanted to reach out and touch her. To feel her darkness. He liked to watch people. To look into a person's eyes and know every part of their personality. Traits intersecting with memories, feelings developing like mutating cells; the intricacies and complexities of consciousness in manifest. It was all there, dilating in the woman's pupils, shifting in the fine muscles orbiting her eyes.

Death and darkness and desperation. Jack sensed her world was much like his own.

'Who is she?' Jack asked an idle cameraman.

'Detective Eve Salah,' the cameraman said, smiling. 'She might be a rookie, but she broke the Freeway case and her profile is on the rise.'

'Eve,' Jack said slowly, walking on again. Stalking the perimeter of the scene, following the play of Eve's lips as she spoke, saying her name over and over again in his head like a spell of sorts.

Eve, the first woman. The sinful one. I want to be the dark apple she bites into.

Chapter 4

It was close to 5 am when Jack entered an all-night café around the corner from the crime scene. He ordered a filter coffee and sat in a corner booth, stirring his brew with his finger. The café was a relic of old Toronto, nestled between gleaming modern buildings but refusing to bow to the march of time. Its neon sign flickered intermittently, casting a dim glow that barely reached the now rain-slicked streets.

'Detective Eve Salah,' Jack muttered to himself. 'I want to unleash your darkness onto the world.'

The soft hum of a worn-out ventilation system mingled with the murmur of a television tuned to the late-night news. The headline flashed across the screen – **Is The Poet back?**

'Can you turn that up?' Jack asked the female server behind the counter.

'Sure,' the server said. 'It's scary to think what happened around the corner, eh?'

'Spooky,' Jack said.

'I guess, we never really know what's going on in someone else's head,' the server said. 'To think the killer could have been in here, drinking coffee before he did it.'

'It's enough to make your skin crawl,' Jack said before shifting his attention to the TV.

'Is The Poet back?' the female news anchor asked in a clear voice. 'That's the question on everyone's lips this morning. We have multiple reports that a poem was left at the scene of a murder in Toronto's financial district.'

'But the Toronto Police Service has yet to comment,' her male co-anchor added.

'The Poet,' the female anchor went on, 'has killed eight people across Toronto over the past three years. His victims have been wealthy couples living in affluent areas. His first victims were Roger and Emma Carmady...'

Jack's thoughts drifted off as he thought of Emma and Roger. What a blast they had been, wealthy middle-aged entrepreneurs who owned a successful chain of organic grocery stores across Ontario. They married soon after college and longed for a large family, the sort of picturesque suburban dream with white picket fences, a modest SUV, and nightly cookouts in the summer where their children's laughter floated in the air like the diffusion of happiness itself. But at twenty-four, Emma Carmady miscarried twice in the same year due to a problem with her ovaries. They decided to adopt soon after but never did. Later, they realised, like a brawler losing a fight in the final rounds, how they wished they'd tried harder in the beginning – how Emma Carmady chose materialism over motherhood, how Roger had become the world's best dad to organic produce.

The Carmadys told Jack all this personal information on the first night they met him, at an indie festival, drinking craft beer and smoking pot beside the glow of tiki torches in a wood outside Toronto. Jack barely spoke that night. He just listened, nodding his head reflectively as though he understood the very soul of their struggles. And when the tears flowed, which they often did that night, Jack embraced Emma and Roger tenderly, curling them into his chest, kissing their foreheads, saying, 'It's okay. God has sent me here to make it all better.'

Jack, who went by the name Aaron Arweller at the time, told the Carmadys he worked in real estate, selling hotels and old

21

industrial buildings around Ontario. He claimed he donated seventy per cent of his salary to homeless charities across Canada. 'I just can't bear to see people suffer,' he told them over lunch a week later. 'Capitalistic greed has turned men and women into monsters, don't you think?'

Roger agreed, grimacing and gently laying down his fork. 'We used to be different, Aaron. We used to hate the people we've become.'

'Used to?' Jack asked, leaving the conversation hanging there like a raw nerve.

As the weeks wore on, Emma was not quite herself around Jack. Scrubbing her hair one morning in the shower, she realised how his words felt almost psychical, like a hand slipping up her skirt, tickling along her inner thigh. She'd never felt so enraptured, and with steam rising in the shower and a lather of soap flowing down her legs, Emma slid her hand down along her tummy, past her pubic area, curling it underneath, applying mild pressure. She masturbated for over ten minutes, imagining Jack leading her to the back office of their Spadina grocery store, spreadeagling her across the office desk and heaving his seed into her womb. She wept and moaned throughout the fantasy. Guilt looming like a spectre, its presence drowned out by the wet squelch of her fingers.

Roger Carmady felt enamoured by Jack but in a different sort of way. Rapt by his righteousness, Roger regarded Jack as an accomplice who would revolt with him against the greed of Western culture. And slowly, Jack's charm appeared smeared across their lips like the sugar glaze from a doughnut. Jack made sure they became inseparable, and naturally enough, this constant exposure segued into regular sexual encounters. Reality seemed to completely distort when they began taking LSD, living naked for days in the Carmady's plush Kingsway home. Roger started making large donations to charities and soup kitchens, and it seemed to the Carmadys that Aaron Arweller was a saint sent by God to set them straight.

Their friends later recounted that it was as though Emma and Roger were under a hypnotic spell, possessed by some mysterious man few had ever seen or met. Jack lived in the background of their lives, pulling the strings like a puppeteer personifying his mindless marionettes. Then, one night during an acid trip, Jack claimed that God had spoken to him directly, insisting that the Carmadys should buy a hotel and transform it into a hostel for the homeless, and if so, a baby would miraculously sprout in Emma's womb. Two days later, Jack brought them to the front of an abandoned hotel in Mississauga. He'd picked the lock before their arrival and proceeded to give them a tour, suggesting, 'Years from now, they'll say this is where the revolution began. Where kindness triumphed over greed. Four million dollars, and it's yours.'

The Carmadys never suspected the deal to sour as it did. A week later, as requested, they handed Jack four million dollars in two duffel bags. The couple never felt so alive, born-again, 'soon to be parents.' Emma ran excitedly to the toilet with a pregnancy test, emerging sometime later, baffled that the test had registered negative.

Jack bludgeoned Roger to death with a seven-pound Himalayan salt lamp while Emma sat frozen in the corner of the room, shaking out of fear and desperation and producing a humming sound that resembled a mother whale's deep ocean lamentation. She went to speak, but her head shook uncontrollably, and the last sensation Emma Carmady felt was the cold, damp feeling of a Himalayan salt lamp pounding her skull apart.

Jack studied the Carmady's bodies afterwards, trying out different tableaus for the sake of artistry, eventually posing them kneeling with their hands joined in prayer. He spent a further few hours rearranging them in exact symmetry, waiting for rigour mortis to set in so their bludgeoned faces joined like the apex of a temple he had built.

Jack scrubbed every inch of the house afterwards, erasing any fingerprints or fluid he might have left over the prior weeks. At midnight, he snuck around the block to his car and retrieved two large black sacks from the trunk. The first sack was filled with thousands of used cigarette butts that Jack had collected over the prior year. He scattered them in every room, on bedside lockers, in pillowcases, under couches. Next, he tore open the second sack and tossed hairs and fibres throughout the house before sitting at the kitchen table and writing a poem for the cops.

Detectives, Hi

While I slithered through the glades of Eden,
and death was an unknown fear,
I met two lovely love-birds,
And whispered the prospect of a child into their ear.
Greed, guilt, grief & hope,
I spun those torments around their dreams,
Folly sailed through the evening like a fin,
Brains burst from skulls; hope slithered from the seams.

No hard feelings,

Dark Finds

Lawson lived in the Carmady's home until the stench of decaying flesh became unbearable. Speeding back towards downtown Toronto with four million dollars on the back seat of his car, Jack knew two things about himself.

He enjoyed killing, and he was only getting started.

24

Chapter 5

Mitch stood at the front of the briefing room with an array of images, maps, and notes plastered on the walls around him.

The images showed a gruesome tableau of crime scenes: couples bludgeoned, posed religiously, a poem left close by their bodies.

'All right, listen up,' Mitch said, demanding the attention of every cop in the room. The restless shuffling of chairs and murmurs ceased. The dimmed overhead lights cast a cold glow on Mitch's chiselled features, emphasising the lines etched by countless sleepless nights. His piercing blue eyes looked tired, glassy, and a little drunk.

'Forensics has come back,' Mitch went on. 'The poem left on the latest victim matches the other four poems left by The Poet. But the victimology is different this time, and we need to figure out why. The Poet isn't just a killer. He's an artist of death, a performer. He's telling a story, and we must figure out the narrative before more bodies start showing up.'

'To help with this,' Eve said, standing to the side of Mitch, 'we've brought in a forensic linguist to analyse the meaning and word selection in The Poet's latest poem. She'll brief us either tonight or tomorrow morning.'

'We need this solved ASAP,' Chief Cutler said at the back of the room. She emerged from the shadows, her hair peppered with grey and black. She wore it short, not just for convenience, but because of the intense way it framed her face and eyes. 'Twitter has already turned into a powder keg,' she went on, 'and Mayor Adams is pilling on the pressure. I want everyone working around the clock for the next few days. We can't let him slip away again.'

'We're on it, boss,' Eve said with a subtle nod.

'This is Paddy Fitzgerald,' Mitch continued, clicking his remote so a picture of Paddy's LinkedIn profile appeared on the projector screen behind him. 'He was a co-founder of Clearwater Capital. He lived in Dublin, Ireland, and his colleagues have confirmed he was in Toronto on a five-day business trip. He was due to fly home at lunchtime today...'

'Could this be worked related?' a rookie interrupted.

'We don't know,' Mitch said. 'There's a lot we don't know. And I suppose, until we know more about Paddy, we might as well focus on what we do know about The Poet.'

Mitch clicked his remote again, so the picture of a young couple smiling on a beach in Hawaii flashed on the projector screen.

'This is Jess and Ajay Kirby,' Eve continued. 'Ten months ago, The Poet murdered this couple in their Annex penthouse condo. We believe he gained access through a communal rooftop garden just above the balcony. It was a hot night, and we believe the balcony door was left ajar. Crime scene investigators suggest that The Poet jumped down from the rooftop garden sometime after 2 am and entered through the balcony door.'

'Jess Kirby was tortured and bludgeoned,' Mitch said, locking eyes with every officer in the room. 'Her hands and feet were hammered pre-mortem. Her face and neck were hammered so severely, I can only describe what was left as soup.'

'Was she the main target?' an officer asked.

'We don't know,' Mitch answered. 'Ajay was found in the kitchen. Almost every bone in his body had been hammered. And similar to Jess, his face and neck got the worst of it.'

'So, The Poet spent more time with Ajay?' another officer asked.

'We don't know,' Eve said, 'but his injuries were more severe.'

'A canvassing of the area revealed no footprints or fingerprints,' Mitch said. 'Neighbours recall no unusual activity. The sole clue was found pinned to the fridge by a magnet.'

Mitch clicked a button on his remote, and a poem appeared on the projector screen.

Many years later,
As the firing squad sets their guns to aim,
I remember softly,
  with triumphant smile,
 the sweet eternal note of a woman's name.
What I have not yet said,
And perhaps should now confess,
 (as ten bullets pace towards my hard beating chest)
Was how my cold hands hammered and beat
   that poor, sweet woman's face and neck.

 Hi detectives. You won't find me. I'm long gone.

 Hope you like the poem.

 Dark Finds

'Jess was the target,' an officer shouted out.

'He wants to get caught,' another added. 'He already knows his fate; he wants to confess.'

'Why the hammer?'

'Why leave a poem anyway?'

'And why does he call himself Dark Finds?'

'Quiet down,' Eve said. 'We know nothing for sure.'

'Do we have a profile?' asked an officer at the back of the room.

'We do,' Eve said, nodding at the male profiler in the front row.

Luke Ramirez stood up and poised himself at the front of the room, a halo of light shining down upon him from the projector overhead. He was tall and slim, his dark hair slicked back, his face emotionless. 'As we've seen from the evidence,' Luke began, 'The Poet has had a very specific taste until his latest victim. Young couples, seemingly in the prime of their life, blessed with fortune. But it's not just about their wealth; it's about what that wealth represents, and I believe this is where there's a connection with Paddy. As we've heard, Paddy co-founded the investment company Clearwater Capital and helped grow it into one of the largest investment firms globally. He was a multi-millionaire who seemingly had it all.'

'So, wealth is the real target,' an officer interrupted. 'It's not just couples.'

'Maybe,' Luke said, changing the slides to images of the Paddy Fitzgerald crime scene. 'Wealth seems to be the main constant in his crimes. Or maybe it's what wealth symbolises – freedom. What is also consistent is the way he kills his victims. Bludgeoning,' Luke continued slowly, 'is an intimate form of violence. It requires proximity. Strength. A degree of rage. The Poet wants to feel the life slip away from his victims. There's an element of envy, a need for dominance, and perhaps some twisted sense of justice in his mind.'

'He's not just killing them,' an officer shouted out. 'It looks like he's punishing them for their success, for their freedom, for everything he believes he's been denied.'

'Yes, maybe,' Luke said. 'His motivations, his chosen MO, seem to emanate from a deep-seated resentment, possibly anchored in a personal trauma or loss related to wealth.'

'He's intelligent,' Eve added, 'methodical. These murders aren't spur-of-the-moment. He plans meticulously, stalking his prey, learning their routines.'

A map of the city appeared on the projector screen next, with red dots marking the spots of each crime. 'He strikes in affluent areas,' Luke said, pausing. 'Kingsway, Forrest Hill, Willowdale, the Annex and now the financial district. These are high-risk areas where people have Ring doorbells and CCTV cameras on their property. And yet, we don't have a clear image of him. This suggests he's able to blend in. He'll look ordinary, just like anyone else you'll pass in the street. The suspect sketch from the Carmadys Spadina store manager suggests he's a white male in his early thirties. He's six-foot-tall with an athletic build and a thick beard. He has intimate knowledge of Toronto's affluent areas, but we believe he lives in a poorer neighbourhood. He may be a delivery driver or work in a job that lets him travel freely without raising suspicion. He'll be a loner, living on a low income, maybe still with his parents...'

Mitch felt his mind drift off as Luke delved further into his profile. He put his hand inside his blazer pocket and rolled the Oxy around with his fingers. What power those small white tablets possessed, like a doorway to another world, like the onset of a dream where pain did not exist and his daughter was still alive again, laughing, filling his world with joy.

I just want to take them once. I just want the pain to go away. I won't touch them again after that. I promise.

In Mitch's mind, he saw himself, though a different version, a man stood before a judge, wrists manacled, his body donned in an orange jumpsuit awaiting sentencing. It began as a simple thought, but as Mitch felt the first, second, and third rush of heat flush his body, he regarded it as a premonition. The eventuality of things to come, wrangled into being by his next words. 'I need to step out for a minute,' he whispered to Eve.

Eve nodded as Mitch walked on with his head down. The room around him seemed to blur as he contemplated his next move.

Don't do it. Please don't do it.

He opened the washroom door and held the Oxy in the palm of his hand. Every cell in his body seemed to morph and spiral into a scene he'd spent twenty-three years avoiding. Then, in one swift jerk his palm met his mouth, and Mitch felt the Oxy tumbling down his throat.

Chapter 6

It was close to midnight when Eve reached for the butt of a freshly lit cigarette, inhaling deeply before blowing a cloud of smoke through her clenched teeth. She sat in the smoking area of Benny's Disco Bar, in a far-off corner, amidst the glow of neon lights and the distant hum of a bassline. Alone. Isolated. As if distance could ward off the world's contagion. As if other people were the cause of her own unhappiness.

Eve hadn't slept in over forty hours. She was scared to go home and face the pillow. To disturb the fact of her loneliness. Her mind wouldn't settle anyway. It would be thinking of the case. Mulling over the profile of the killer. *It always starts in childhood*, Eve remembered the profiler saying, *monsters aren't born, they're created, and the first five years of childhood do the damage.* Eve thought of her childhood; her father's anger, the cool flicker of a fluorescent light, broken plates and cups smashed all over the kitchen floor. His paranoia almost unravelled the borders of Eve's sanity. Her mother died in childbirth, and Eve was blamed and shamed every day of her childhood. Without a sane guardian to protect her, Eve endured years of interrogation and ridicule at the hands of a father who rationalised a tragedy as either extra-terrestrial or supernatural interference.

A strobe light flickered from the doorway of the bar. Eve tried to focus on the black silhouettes, the figures rimmed in silvery light. She took a small pocket mirror from her handbag and gazed at her reflection. *I'm an animal. Emotionless. Eve Salah. Nothing will ever break me. Fucking nothing, Eve. You hear me, nothing will ever break us. Oh, Lord! Look, I'm speaking to you as though you're someone else, but you know what I mean. You know, come on! Don't look at me like that.*

Eve slammed the pocket mirror shut, shuffling it back into her handbag, ashamed of what she'd seen and supposedly said. She gnawed at her lower lip, scraping the soft flesh against her upper teeth. The hypnotic hum of house music thumped against her chest, causing Eve to feel anxious and awkward. Ever since her first day of school, her anxiety recurred and recurred throughout her life, like malaria. Most girls in her class wanted to be lawyers, nurses, CEOs or pilots sailing the skies, but Eve wanted to be able to ruin all those girls' lives at some appropriate time when they failed to indicate out into traffic or were pulled over for a DUI. Once, when a teacher asked Eve what she wanted to be when she grew up, she replied. 'Someone else, somewhere else.'

The definition of Eve Salah started with the word *confused* and ended with the words, *Help. I thought I didn't give a fuck, but I do, and I'm scared, I'm alone and don't know what to do!* It was safer to imagine herself as chaos, a hot mess, a tamale too hot for Toronto's taste buds. And that night, sitting in the smoking area of Benny's Disco Bar, Eve did not go unnoticed. As she lit another cigarette, Jack Lawson edged closer, asking her for a lighter. His aftershave smelt expensive; rich, woody notes with a hint of sweet musk. His clothes looked expensive too. Tight, cream-coloured chinos, a fitted white shirt with the top two buttons open, and a cream-coloured sportscoat. His white trainers dressed down the look, Eve thought, but people that dressed like him didn't belong in Benny's.

'Got a lighter, darlin?' Jack asked again, speaking with a clear Kentucky accent.

Staring into Jack's intense eyes, Eve moved between states of excitement, paranoia, and mischief. She took a lighter from her handbag and handed it to Jack. His confidence bordered on arrogance, she thought. He was conventionally handsome. Disarming dark eyes framed by dark lashes, thick eyebrows, and a chiselled jawline dusted with a hint of stubble.

Jack never took his eyes off Eve as he lit the tip of his cigarette. For a moment, Eve considered brushing him off and retreating into the comfort of her thoughts. But something in Jack's eyes held her back.

'Do you ever feel you need to get so drunk that you forget about living?' Jack asked with a smooth southern drawl. 'That you forget about the eternally tragic and ludicrous sequence of events that hammer you down into some incoherent experiment you call – you.'

'Fuck off, psycho.'

'You see,' Jack said, 'from time to time, I like to stare up at the guillotine. I like to bare my teeth and grin at my reflection. We fall backwards and forwards, but it doesn't matter, we're walking on a razor edge anyway.'

'You got your lighter,' Eve said sternly. 'You can leave now.'

'You're colder than the ice I'm trying to break.'

A subtle smirk broke out on Eve's lips. 'I'm the Arctic fucking circle.'

'Nah, that's only what you want people to believe,' Jack said, staring intensely into Eve's eyes. 'It's almost midnight, and you're sitting alone in the smoking area of a dingy bar with three empty tumblers around you. Double bourbons by the looks of it. The servers haven't even come to collect the glasses. You give off that energy – back-the-fuck-off energy,' Jack said before nodding at the unopened water bottle on the table.

'You've been picking the label off that water bottle the last hour I'd say, piling up the debris on the table, molehills mentally shifting into mountains. You haven't taken one sip of water, but you know you should. Like you know you should have gone home hours ago. But you don't really sleep. Your mind is constantly scribbling. Dreams mixed with nightmares. The past creeping into the present. You probably had a horrible childhood; some unresolved trauma is still swimming through your psyche like a shark on the supper trail. Daddy's fault no doubt. You wanted to shoo me away the minute I got here, the same way you want to shoo your pops from your thoughts. You called me a psycho in your first three words. That's how you see men, isn't it? As various projections of your father.'

Jack took a drink of his whiskey before continuing. 'There are six half-smoked cigarette butts in that ashtray. You crave a dopamine rush that never comes. Your eyes suggest frequent Xanax use. How you applied your lipstick implies a slight tremor in your hand, possibly due to Xanax withdrawal. Hmmm,' Jack said, staring deeper into Eve's eyes. 'No, you're cutting back on the Xanax. There's something big going on in your life, and you can't afford to be zoned out and numb all the time. Something with work.'

Eve sat stone-faced but she felt close to tears.

'Well, whatever the big thing is,' Jack said, turning to leave, 'best of luck with it, and thanks for the lighter and all.'

'How did you know all that?' Eve asked hurriedly.

'I've been stalking you,' Jack said, turning back to smile. 'I'm joking; let me state that right now before you get creeped out and call me a psycho again. I know all that because I've been there, sitting in the same hell as you, trying to hammer my way out with bad decisions. I don't even smoke,' Jack said, stubbing out his cigarette, 'but when I saw you sitting there, I saw an image of myself. I would've loved for someone to pull me out of my thoughts and break the cycle. Chin up, yeah. Things will get better.'

'They never seem to,' Eve said.

'They will,' Jack said softly. 'The most dangerous thing of all is the magnetic pull of our past – it's like a graveyard where everything comes back to life if we let it. Don't let it. Forget the past, move on and come into the present moment. It's the only way.'

'It's not that easy to forget.'

'It is,' Jack said. 'I found a way.'

'How?'

'You'll have to dance with me first,' Jack said, taking Eve's hand.

'No,' Eve said, giggling. 'I don't dance, especially not with strangers.'

'Take the risk,' Jack said.

'I don't do risks either.'

'Life's too short to not feel some excitement from time to time,' Jack said, smiling. 'Life's too short to sit there trying to smoke your way to happiness. Life's too short, period.'

'Life's too long in my eyes.'

'Have this one moment with me,' Jack said, pulling Eve up off her stool, 'allow yourself to forget all the other shit going on in your life. Allow yourself to be free and in the moment with me.'

Under a kaleidoscope of lights, they moved as one. Eve felt a flutter of butterflies in her tummy, and the hairs on her arms raised when Jack gripped her waist and hoisted her through the air. Nine billion neural connections pinged, lighting up inside Eve's skull like a pinball machine. All her pain and anxiety felt swept away by a man who demanded that all her attention be placed on him and not back on herself. His smile was like a stairway to another world, his voice dulled any thoughts of a boob job, but the strangest part of all, Eve felt beautiful in the spotlight of his stare.

Chapter 7

After drinking shots at the bar, Jack and Eve fetched a cab back to Jack's penthouse condo. Eve danced naked across Jack's bedroom floor, arms extended outwards, spinning on the balls of her feet like a small ballerina. She was a thing of beauty, Jack thought, lying on his side to admire her. It wasn't a circle of light glowing above her head, but a set of horns. Darkness scratched beneath her skin, like so many hours of suffering. She was like an animal pushed to the brink of survival – the way her eyes appeared alert for signs of danger, the way she sometimes paused to listen for noises, like a soldier facing shellshock. There was no getting around the fact that Eve had been damaged by some early childhood shelling – that she clung to an ice shelf and would experience intense anxiety no matter what direction she chose to climb. She hid a darkness that Jack could understand. She was a jumble of words he could rearrange, piece by piece, into a poem.

'I normally don't leave with strangers,' Eve said, lying next to Jack and staring up at the ceiling. 'You're not going to kill me, are you?'

'Only if you try to leave,' Jack said, laughing. 'That'll be an axe job.'

Meeting Eve felt like the quieting of a crowded room – Jack's mind traversing beyond the splaying darkness, and like sparks when the hammer strikes the anvil, there was just enough light to see the first glimmer of romance glow. The conversation coursed natural and easy. Goofy at times: their words often trailing off with a simple laugh or faint giggle.

'When I was young, I used to pray to a spot of mildew on my ceiling,' Jack said as Eve lay her head against his bare chest.

'Why?' Eve asked.

'Because, at least it was real. I could see it,' Jack said, 'like a worm crawling across my ceiling, growing larger by the day. I could believe in it more than I could believe in God.'

Eve laughed. 'You don't waste any time making a girl feel at ease.'

'Who's to say it didn't answer all my prayers.'

'You're dying for me to ask more, aren't you? Go on, what did you pray for?'

'A superpower.'

'Oh, a super...power,' Eve teased.

'That I could do bad things and never get caught,' Jack said. 'I was carrying around so much hurt back then. All I wanted to do was hurt other people so they would understand what it felt like and I wouldn't feel so alone all the time.'

'You still never told me how you were able to move on from everything,' Eve said a little distantly. 'At the bar, you said you'd tell me if I danced with you.'

'When the past is beating down your door, throw it someone else to eat.'

'What does that mean?' Eve asked.

'It means bundle up all your darkness and rage and let it loose onto someone else.'

'You excite me,' Eve blurted out before covering her mouth to giggle. 'Fuck! What am I saying? I don't even know you. I'm trapped between wanting to scream, cry, and laugh all at the same time. Have you ever felt like that? Like the wires in your head are all knotted up?'

'Not anymore.'

Eve punched Jack's shoulder. 'Do you feel anything at all, mister fucking robot?'

Guard down, Jack spoke truthfully, unencumbered, and couldn't fully understand why. 'When I was young, maybe I felt like that. Angry at everything and everyone. My mom and pops died young. I was sent to Toronto to live with my crazy aunt. She was one of those Old Testament types; believed that poverty and suffering brought us closer to God, and boy did she love to beat me with a broomstick she'd nicknamed *Penance*.'

'Yikes,' Eve said.

'When I asked why I got beat so bad,' Jack went on, 'I was told God wanted it that way. It was his design, and that a good Christian boy should never question God's work. He should say his prayers each night and thank God for the path he was given.'

'Sounds a lot like my father,' Eve said.

'God giveth and taketh.'

'Screw all that,' Eve said. 'Praise thy mildew. Cherish thy mould.'

'Forbidden words where I'm from.'

Eve jumped up and climbed on Jack. 'Forbidden things only make me want it more.'

Jack felt confused by the whole experience. Lies mixed with scrapes of childhood truths. Old nerves exposed to air for the first time. Jack wanted to rebel with Eve, but something stopped him. He had spent his entire adult life renaturing those rebellious impulses to portray the refined caricature of an ivy-leaguer, constructing a social mask with such detail and precision that not even the most observant psychologists or detectives could spot it as a fake. But there was no getting around the fact that it was crumbling.

'Fuck everything,' Jack roared. 'Break the rules. Fuck them all.'

Eve looked at him, neither frightened nor fazed but accepting (maybe even a bit excited by his sudden flare). She grabbed his face, breathed into his mouth and said. 'Fuck me, not them.'

Twenty minutes later, as the first streaks of dawn light stretched across Jack's grey bedroom walls, he knew two things. Something had changed inside of him. He didn't understand what or where it had occurred, only that it had. Secondly, Jack knew that Eve couldn't nourish two of him and lying back against the headboard, he spoke in his natural voice. 'I wasn't born in Kentucky. I was born in Ireland.'

Eve laughed. 'You hardly know Paddy Fitzgerald?'

'What?' Lawson asked, slightly unnerved.

'Nothing,' Eve said, appearing amused by her own remark. 'So go on, tell me, why the Kentucky accent?'

'I thought it would make me more interesting.'

'Is that how you pick up girls?' Eve asked. 'The smooth southerner?'

'Deeper than that,' Jack said. 'I thought if I played a character, people wouldn't see the poor little Irish boy shipped off to Toronto at four. The little orphan they pitied only to feel better about themselves.'

Eve softened at Jack's admission. 'I do stuff like that too. I pretend all the time. I pretend to be anything except myself. I'm like a car wreck, all you see is the damage.'

There was something undeniably beautiful in how they both looked at each other.

'I like car wrecks,' Jack said eventually.

'The flames or the twisted sheets of metal?'

'The tragedy,' Jack said, 'the irreversibility of all. Tragedy makes everything seem more beautiful and poetic. We're all so entombed in the monotony of everyday life that we so briefly feel anything new or interesting. But tragedy has a way of shaking people out of stasis. When I was younger, I used to go to random funerals just to watch the grievers, to see them mauled by emotion, to see reality drag them by the ankles, kicking and screaming into their sad little feelings. I wanted to be like them, I suppose; to feel like that, to experience real fucking feelings. Some nights, I'd stand on the roof of skyscrapers with my toes peeking over the edge, desperate to feel my heartbeat or my palms sweat. I just wanted to feel something, anything.'

'I used to do weird things too,' Eve said, her lips wobbling downwards. 'I used to cut myself hoping I could bleed the anxiety from my body.'

'What were you anxious about?'

'Everything. Nothing,' Eve said. 'It would attack randomly, like a sneeze, and I'd feel paralysed by it.'

Jack kissed her forehead and wiped away her tears. 'You're not the problem,' Jack said, appearing distant. 'It's society. The world feels so empty these days. Kids doom scrolling on their phones, lovers lying in different beds at night, dinner bought from vending machines, eaten with the eyes, not even tasted by the tongue. Everything just gets emptier and emptier; from the calories we eat to the people we fuck, the fun we have, and the emotions we try to plunder from one another to feel better about ourselves. Everyone seems defined by their next dopamine rush, and to hell with love, people don't have time for that commitment. Evolution has made a U-turn; our primal instincts have been severed off like gangrenous limbs. How is anyone expected to feel normal or connected these days?'

Eve looked lost for words. 'You're asking the wrong girl. I like hiding out in the darkness.'

'That was the first thing I noticed about you.'

'You're different,' Eve continued. 'I bet if I looked inside your head, all I'd see is scars.'

'And darkness,' Jack added wistfully, 'so much darkness, and a giant shadow slithering through me, pulling all the levers. The real Jack Lawson doesn't exist – he died at four years old. That's when the shadow entered me. I'm just the costume it wears to draw people in.'

'What happens then?' Eve asked, a little nervous.

'It's like the splitting of an atom,' Jack confessed.

Enthralled, Eve went to respond when her phone vibrated on the bedside locker. She ignored it at first, but on the fourth ring, she glanced over and picked it up. 'It's work,' she said before answering. 'Hey, what's up?'

'We need you to come in,' Chief Cutler said. 'The forensic linguist is ready to brief us.'

'Now's not a good time,' Eve said as Jack kissed her neck.

'Get here now,' Cutler demanded, ending the call abruptly.

Eve threw her phone against the bed and pushed Jack's head away. 'I have to go.'

'Why?'

'Work.'

'Who works on Sunday mornings?'

'Cops.'

'What?' Lawson said, feigning shock. 'You're a cop.'

'I'm a detective, homicide division. We have a briefing on a case I'm working on.'

'The Poet case?'

'Yeah,' Eve said, searching the floor for her clothes. 'All I can say is Toronto has a real sicko on the loose.'

Jack felt hurt by her remark, remembering the first time he'd been called a sicko, after asking his teenage crush if she wanted to hang out after school and *go kill something*. When she laughed it off as a joke, Jack insisted he was serious, and when he said they didn't have to kill a person, more like some rodent, she got scared and began crying. When Jack began detailing how fun it would be to watch it squirm and suffer, she ran away, her palms protecting her face, bumbling out the words *get away from me, you sicko*.

But that was all in the past, Jack thought, burying the memory under layers of glib optimism. *Eve will be different, she already is.*

'Should I be jealous?' Jack asked, forcing humour like many hours of constipation. 'Is he gonna steal you away from me every night?'

'Yep,' Eve said, slipping her jeans over her hips. 'This guy is a real psychopath. His balls are bigger than yours, babe.'

'Bet he's shit with his tongue,' Jack said, joking.

Eve paused to stare and smile. 'I shouldn't be talking to you about an active case.'

'I'm a psychologist,' Jack said. 'I could help you build a profile.'

'We've already got a profiler,' Eve said, turning to leave. 'Anyway, I gotta go.'

'I want to see you again soon,' Jack said.

Eve paused in the doorway and smiled back. 'I left my card in your wallet. Call me. Stalk me.'

Once Eve had left, Jack added her number into his contacts and sat for a while, staring out at Lake Ontario through his large bedroom window, watching the sun rise from the dark, inky water. A singe of excitement burned away inside him. Meeting Eve had exposed a hunger he never knew existed. He started a new message and wondered what he'd say.

Jack: Let's meet tonight, tomorrow night, the night after that, and the next and on and on and on. I miss you already. I've never felt so connected to another person.

A few minutes later, Jack's phone vibrated and he scrambled to open the message.

Eve: I felt the connection too. Not sure what time I'll be finished today but I'll message you. XX

Chapter 8

The Oxy Mitch had taken twenty minutes ago was starting to kick in. He felt his whole body calm. Purify. Perfect itself.

Mitch loved this feeling, where his thoughts floated by instead of exploding through his mind like munitions going BOOM in a mud pit. Everything felt flat again, his emotions threadbare, a smile appearing on his lips like a magic trick.

Mitch looked up as Eve tapped lightly on the briefing room door before stepping inside.

'Hurry up,' Chief Cutler said. 'We don't have all morning to be waiting for you.'

'Sorry,' Eve said, sitting beside Mitch, whispering. 'What have I missed?'

'Nothing yet,' Mitch said. 'Where have you been?'

Before Eve could answer, a communal hush descended as Dr. Lana Martinez, a renowned forensic linguist, stood at the front of the briefing room. Her thick, black-rimmed glasses reflected the projector light as she peered over them, a laser pointer in hand. 'Thank you for joining me this morning,' she began, her voice clear and authoritative. 'I know most of you haven't slept. Neither have I, so I'll keep this quick.'

She motioned to the projector screen behind her where The Poet's latest poem was displayed. 'Let me read it out before we break it down. *And Tantalus stole the nectar's seed... There goes the home where I was born! For death, not life, must punish greed, Must feed, his wicked deeds & burn! Do you believe in Evil? Liar! Dark Finds.'*

A few cops exchanged glances as Dr. Martinez paused for effect.

'*And Tantalus stole the nectar's seed,*' she began again. 'Tantalus is a figure from Greek mythology who was punished by the gods for stealing their nectar and ambrosia; food reserved only for deities. As punishment, Tantalus was condemned to stand in a pool of water with fruit-bearing branches above him. Whenever he tried to drink or eat, the water would recede, and the branches would move out of reach. It's a tale of perpetual torment and unquenchable thirst. This line may suggest that The Poet feels justified in his actions, seeing Paddy as deserving of punishment.'

Mitch leaned forward, interlocking his fingers. 'Are you suggesting that The Poet is well-versed in classical literature?'

Dr. Martinez nodded. 'Precisely. The style and composition of this poem, and the others too, suggest he's well educated with a deep knowledge of mythology. He flirts with abstraction and esoteric musings, which can seem strange at first. But make no mistake, The Poet is an intelligent predator. Like a cat with a mouse, it's not just about the kill, it's about the game.'

The room was silent for a moment as cops scribbled notes.

'The phrase, *There goes the home where I was born,*' Dr. Martinez continued, 'implies a personal connection or a vendetta linked to a particular location. It could be a metaphorical birthplace, indicating where the killer's dark urges first began.'

'Could he be referring to a childhood trauma or a grudge?' asked a cop in the front row.

'Keep your questions until after,' Chief Cutler said. 'Let Dr. Martinez finish.'

Moving swiftly, Dr. Martinez highlighted the third and fourth lines. '*For death, not life, must punish greed, Must feed, his wicked*

44

deeds & burn! The Poet sees himself as an agent of punishment. His choice of victims might be those he sees as greedy or sinful. The act of burning he mentions might represent a cleansing or purification of the world from these perceived wrongs.'

Dr. Martinez pointed her laser towards the line, *Do you believe in Evil? Liar!* 'These lines strike as confrontational. This is a challenge. A direct one. It's as if The Poet wants us to question our beliefs and moral compass. If we don't believe in the existence of true evil, we're liars in his eyes. The capitalisation of *Evil* might imply a fixation or an obsession with wickedness or Satanic worship. *Liar!* could be an accusation directed towards law enforcement or a specific individual.'

'Could it be an expression of internal conflict?' Eve asked. 'A hint that The Poet is battling with what he's doing.'

'I don't think so,' Dr. Martinez said. 'The Poet is a high-functioning psychopath. He can't experience emotion. Not like normal people. He doesn't suffer from anxiety or depression, sadness, grief or even guilt. In a world full of colour, he sees only grey.'

'He's just trying to taunt us,' Mitch said. 'He wants to play a game, and look at us, wrapped around his little finger.'

A few expletives swept the room.

'We'll see how much he wants to play,' a cop shouted, 'when my boot is on his face.'

'Quiet down,' Chief Cutler shouted.

Once the room was silent again, Dr. Martinez continued. 'The sign-off – *Dark Finds* – is interesting. The capitalisation suggests that Dark Finds may be an entity, an internal one, maybe how The Poet sees himself, as something capable of finding darkness in everything and everyone. It indicates a need for recognition. He wants us to see the depth and darkness in his crimes, to appreciate the *art* behind them. But the fact is, we're not sure what it means.'

Dr. Martinez gathered her notes, her eyes meeting each officer in turn. 'We're dealing with someone intelligent, possibly with a classical education. He's meticulous and may harbour personal grievances with the latest victim. One thing is for sure, The Poet won't stop. He'll keep killing, butchering and bludgeoning, trying to find a sense of relief that will never come.'

'Thanks for that,' Chief Cutler said as she walked towards the front of the room. 'Your analysis is always very insightful, Dr. Martinez. Everyone get back to work. I want every lead followed up. The financial district has cameras everywhere. I want you looking through every frame of footage.'

As the other officers began spilling out of the briefing room, Eve turned to Mitch. 'Do you want to grab a coffee?'

Mitch gazed at her slowly.

'Are you messed up again?' Eve asked when he didn't answer.

'No,' Mitch said. 'Give me a break, I haven't slept in three days.'

'Where are we with the suspect sketch?' Chief Cutler asked, standing above them with her arms crossed.

'That woman saw nothing,' Eve said, rolling her eyes. 'She probably just wants attention or something. The weirdos always come out of the woodwork when there's a serial killer on the loose.'

'Does the sketch resemble the sketch from the Carmady case?'

'No,' Eve said.

'Well, show the sketch to the Spadina store manager,' Chief Cutler said. 'See what he thinks. He got the best look at The Poet.'

'We don't know if he even saw The Poet,' Eve said. 'He saw some guy with the Carmadys one day. It could've been anyone.'

'Run it down,' Chief Cutler said, walking away.

As Eve went to leave, Dr. Martinez appeared. 'Detectives, I hope I'm not stepping out of place by saying this, but I don't agree with Luke's profile.'

'How so?' Mitch asked.

'It doesn't fit with the poems,' Dr. Martinez said. 'I went through all the poems again last night. The Poet isn't a loner working some mundane job. His poems exude confidence. He's more likely to be successful.'

'But how is he able to blend in?' Eve asked.

'I wrote up an alternative profile. It's all in here,' Dr. Martinez said, handing Mitch a thick, brown folder.

'We'll take a look,' Mitch said, briefly scanning the pages. 'And thanks again.'

'Happy to help,' Dr. Martinez said. 'I hope we catch this guy soon.'

'Keep that under wraps,' Eve said, once Dr. Martinez was out of earshot. 'The last thing we need is another profile confusing everyone.'

'I agree,' Mitch said.

As they went to leave, Mitch's phone vibrated in his pocket. Eve walked on as Mitch looked at his phone, letting his thumb glide across the smooth screen to unlock it. There was a message from a number Mitch hadn't saved in his phonebook. He clicked on the message and scanned the text.

416-555-0106: Hi detective, this is Glenda from the other night at the crime scene. The witness. Anyway, I felt we had some weird connection. Would you like to meet sometime?

Part Two

Chapter 9

Eve enjoyed Jack's company when she had it. Especially the Mondays when she counted down the hours, longing to get home for a cuddle or meet Jack at a nearby sports bar, downing a dozen beers and a basket full of chicken wings between them. They spent whole weekends exploring Toronto's sun-glazed streets. Visiting High Park or Toronto Island, watching families spread out on blankets, enjoying picnics, while fitness enthusiasts jogged and cycled along the winding paths. On Sunday nights, they often strolled, hand in hand, through the Distillery District. Their eyes soaked in wonder, watching street performers dance or do magic tricks, listening to the sound of a guitar being strummed in the distance.

How beautiful the world appeared to Eve. Five weeks of dating Jack felt more like five years. Five wonderful years. Where the woes of the past seemed secondary, belonging to foreign selves, rewritten by the opening gambits of flirtation and the involuntary ambuscades of meaningful connection. Jack's unwavering attention often unnerved Eve's adult self, but the teenager still lurking within her grew towards his affection like a flower struggling towards a beam of winter sunlight. She hadn't had a panic attack in over a month. It seemed her anxiety had melted away like grease from a hot spoon. She felt Jack was changing her in ways that seemed extraordinary. Everywhere she went, she could feel Jack lingering inside of her, reaching out, composing her, stroking her nature like an artist before his easel, and she lay hopelessly in those thoughts, awaiting the artist's touch.

But Jack had a dark side, too.

~~~

One night after work, Jack met Eve, and they walked hand-in-hand down Spadina Avenue. Jack had resisted asking anything about *The Poet* case. He didn't want to arouse suspicion, but on this particular night, as the scent of Asian food swarmed the sidewalk, the urge overpowered him.

'How's The Poet case going?' Jack asked. 'I never hear anything about it on the news anymore.'

'We've run down every lead, and nada,' Eve said. 'Three thousand hours of CCTV footage of that Friday night, and we didn't catch a single glimpse of him.'

'Are you sure The Poet is a male?'

'Ninety-nine per cent sure,' Eve said. 'We have two suspect sketches – both are male – but I don't know, they look nothing alike. Some cleaner thinks she saw The Poet the night Paddy Fitzgerald was killed, but I don't believe her. Her story checks out. On the CCTV footage, we can see her leave Clearwater Plaza at ten, and she does stop to look down the alleyway where Paddy was murdered.'

'I can sense a *but* coming,' Jack said, his mind racing. He remembered the woman, how she had looked at him with a cold terror in her eyes. He hadn't realised she'd sat down with a sketch artist. It mustn't have looked like him, he reasoned, otherwise Eve would've said something or brought him in for questioning.

'She thinks she saw Superman,' Eve said, laughing. 'Or the Hollywood actor that plays him. It's laughable, like some wish-

50

fantasy. She has that attention-seeking air about her. I've kept a wide berth, but Mitch seems keen on her.'

'What do you mean, keen?'

'He's met up with her,' Eve said, sighing loudly. 'Like do whatever you want but not with a witness. He's out of control lately.'

'Doesn't he have a wife?' Jack asked.

'It's complicated. Their marriage fell apart when Betty died. I think they've separated, but Mitch is still living with her and the kids for however long that will last. Mitch used to be the straightest arrow in the sleeve, but now he's messed up all the time, doesn't show up to work some days, and when he does, he reeks of booze. Chief Cutler mentioned something about his wife wanting a divorce.'

'Poor guy,' Jack said. 'He's been through the wringer, eh?'

'Ah, Mitch will pull through,' Eve said. 'He's cock-a-roach.'

'And some psycho just mowed down his child,' Jack said, a slight smirk appearing on his lips.

'I know, it's awful,' Eve said.

As they passed Chinatown, a group of hooded thugs edged a homeless man up against the side of a Seven-Eleven. People moved around the mob, afraid of being noticed, scrolling through their phones or aligning their stares toward the other side of the street. The sound of music booming from a nearby bar set the mob to move their heads and show their teeth. They laughed as the homeless man cowered. 'Go away, go away, I'll leave.'

Two punches later, the homeless man was lying on his back. Seeing this, Jack walked forward fearlessly, and as if greater than the sum of all his defects, he said. 'Have we a problem, gentlemen? How about you fuck off and leave this guy alone.'

Eve grabbed Jack's arm nervously as the thugs turned with their fists clenched. 'What you gonna do?' asked the tallest one,

Rocko, lifting his hoodie to reveal a Glock tucked into his jeans. 'Yeah,' he shouted. 'We got a problem...with you muthafucker.'

Eve motioned for her handbag but remembered she had left her badge at the station. 'Jack, let's leave,' she said, gripping his arm as tightly as she could. 'I'm a detective,' Eve said, glaring at the thugs. 'Leave before I call this in.'

'Shut the fuck up,' Rocko said, pulling out his pistol and resting the tip of the barrel against Jack's forehead. Lawson's heart rate was as flat as a triathlete's pulse in the dead of sleep. He laughed loudly into Rocko's face, into the eyes of a man itching to pull the trigger, to prove himself among his prison-bound peers. Eve seemed startled by the brisk, hearty shriek of Jack's laughter.

'Jack, let's go, babe. Come on.'

But Jack would not move a muscle. He liked to sharpen his talons on the throatiest of animals – on the sort of animal that barks loudest among its pack and sports a Glock close to his crotch. 'Nah, babe, I think I'll stay to see if this hotshot has the balls to pull the trigger.'

'What you say muthafucker?'

'He dead,' shouted one of the other thugs.

'Blow his brains out,' said another.

'Go on,' Jack said, tilting his head, curling his tongue upwards, and licking the gun's barrel. 'Pull the trigger, pussy.'

In Jack's mind, walking across a plank at twenty-thousand feet above sea level was no different than walking across the same plank flattened against the sidewalk. The battlefield was no more fear-inducing than a night at the ballet. A gun no more terrifying than a child's giggle. And there was no escaping the fact that Jack was an eerie fucker at times like this.

Rocko now looked awkward holding the gun to Jack's head. He swallowed deeply, and as the first glimmer of doubt skirted across his stare, Jack grabbed the gun, swung it like an axe and levelled Rocko unconscious. He hit the concrete with blood oozing from his hairline. Most of the mob scampered away but two stayed to scoff and scowl.

'Empty your pockets,' Jack said. 'Give that man what you took from him.'

The two thugs glared back at Jack; fear dappled in their eyes – Jack's as dark and large as lumps of coal. It was only when Jack motioned to strike them that they emptied their wallets before running off. A few spectators had gathered, whooping and hollering as Eve tried to keep her head down and her face hidden.

'That was like some Liam Neeson shit,' one spectator shouted.

'The gun is a fake,' Jack said, tossing the BB gun on the ground, relishing the attention. 'Just like those wannabes.'

'Come on,' Eve said, grabbing Jack's arm and walking on.

Jack felt buoyed with bravado, shuffling his hips and smirking wildly at Eve. 'This hellhound is heaven-bound,' Jack said. 'A good deed a day keeps the devil at bay.'

'What the hell was that about?' Eve asked. 'Seriously, that ain't normal.'

'Define normal?'

'You're not funny,' Eve said. 'What if someone posts a video of it on social media? You pistol-whipping some guy and me standing right beside you. I could lose my job over something like that.'

'I did a good thing,' Jack said. 'Those were thugs, bullies. And believe me, if no one was watching, not one of them would make it home.'

'I don't know a thing about you, do I?'

'I am whatever I need to be,' Jack said. 'Like a dream or your worst fucking nightmare.'

'Like God,' Eve said, the harshness in her voice softening, her lips curling into a smirk.

Jack then grabbed Eve by the hips, holding her close as people moved around them, kissing her feverously, eventually cupping

53

his hand around her throat. At that moment, both of them appeared to explore their own reflections, as mysterious as mountains, and in plain view of the public, the dark powers of romance rustled like leaves beneath the paw of a large, predatory cat.

'I fucking love you,' Eve blurted out.

It was the first time Jack had heard those words fired in his direction. He knew such words held a denser gravity than most, that such intent was as deliberate as premeditated murder, that such a simple slew of language could either ignite or extinguish the very nature of one's reality.

'Love you more,' Jack replied.

It was strange. In saying those words, Jack saw himself as a corkscrew flying through the air. Was that image a mere representation of love, he wondered. Were love and murder two strains of the same species? Was Eve a temporary intoxication, an inevitable hangover, a bottle waiting to be smashed?

Chapter 10

The weathered sign above the entrance read *Maple Café* in faded paint, as though the years had tried to erase it but couldn't quite succeed. Inside, wooden beams crisscrossed the ceiling. The walls, adorned with black and white photographs, told stories of old Toronto — trolleys on Yonge Street, children playing hockey on the frozen lake, couples strolling along the old waterfront. And there, Jack and Eve sat amidst the hum of conversation and the smell of blitzed bacon. What could prove more romantic than sharing food, Eve thought, smiling between sips of coffee. She whipped up her smashed avocado and smeared it over a triangle of toast. This was a little slice of time where she could stare into Jack's eyes and ask silly questions.

'Are you ever worried the mask won't come off?' Eve asked, a little frightened by her question. 'I mean, there are layers to you, Jack. That shit with the thugs was messed up. They could have done you in for sure.'

'I knew the gun was fake,' Jack said. 'And anyway, I don't go around living in fear. That's a sad way to live.'

'It mightn't scare you, but it scares me.'

'You seemed more turned on than scared afterwards.'

'Screw you,' Eve said. 'What is this? What are we, Jack?'

'Existentially speaking?' Jack asked coyly.

'It's the sort of question a bitch asks before cutting off your balls. So...'

'We're a thing.'

'What sorta thing.'

'The best thing I've ever felt,' Jack said, trapping a piece of crispy bacon between two slices of rye and chomping down. 'Life is one giant game of football, and you can either be the player or the ball they beat around the pitch. You make me feel like the MVP, babe.'

'Aww,'

'And speaking of games,' Jack said, looking around the café, 'let's play one.'

'What sorta game?'

'Do you trust me?' Jack asked.

'I probably shouldn't... but yeah, I do...ish'

'Good.'

'Don't embarrass me,' Eve said, looking sharply at Jack.

Jack leaned across the table and kissed her, making her toes curl and her hands ball into fists. 'Just watch,' Jack said, picking up his coffee cup and clinking it with his sugar spoon. 'Can I get some quiet,' Jack said loudly as some of the other diners half-glanced in his direction, mostly ignoring him between sips of coffee and stale conversation.

Eve sat as stiff as cedar. A thought had crept in.

Is he going to propose? Fuck, what do I say?

Like a teenage girl awaiting the last Tarot card to be turned, Eve stared at Jack, her heart nearly beating out her chest.

Jack clapped three times until the chatter hushed and everyone turned to stare in his direction. The occasional whisper and giggle elapsed, filtering through the café's strange, almost eerie silence.

'First off, I want to thank all of you for coming here today,' Jack said confidently. 'When Eve and I first conceived the idea of the Future Society, we knew it would not be an easy task. We received over fifty thousand applications across North America and less than fifty were chosen. Everyone, give yourself a round of applause. You've been officially accepted into the Future Society. By this time next year, you will be richer, more aware, and happier than you ever thought possible.'

First, there was silence, then someone clapped awkwardly near the door, and then almost contagiously, the next person clapped, and the next and the next until the whole café felt the urge to join in. Some whistled, others whooped. Eve couldn't believe her eyes or ears. Most people looked intrigued and ingratiated, all the while disguising their confusion at the fact that none of them had applied to be a member of any society and that the only reason for their attendance was due to a bout of morning hunger. And even those, Eve noted, who had caught on to the act seemed too embarrassed not to play along.

'We have big things planned for this year,' Jack continued. 'But first, I want to thank Rebecca for providing us with the space and hospitality to divine the future as we see fit.' Jack then nodded at the café manager, whose face was quickly colouring beetroot. 'Rebecca,' Jack said. 'Honestly, thank you so much. Give it up for Rebecca, come on now.'

A few people clapped. Rebecca appeared caught between a rock and a psychopath as her staff looked at one another, a little puzzled. 'We're happy to have the Future Society with us this morning,' Rebecca said nervously.

'What a time to be alive,' Jack said, clapping and slowly swinging his stare back towards his audience, who had grown increasingly excited by the thoughts of his next words. Some readied ideas on how the society should move forward, while a few had their feet aligned for the exit. One of the few, Denna Druery, shook her head, saying, 'I'm not sure what's going on, but I didn't sign up for any society.'

Her partner Dale, anxious and twitchy, kicked her underneath the table.

'What?' Jack said, scowling. 'This is invite-only.'

'Eh...,' Deena said.

'Leave,' Jack shouted. 'Pay Rebecca and get the fuck out of here. Initiates only.'

Denna looked nervously at Dale.

'Leave,' Jack shouted again. 'You can't just sneak in here and gorge your ears?'

Humiliated and verging close to tears, Deena stood up and walked to the cashier with her head bowed. One couple close to Jack and Eve's table even booed her. Deena tapped her card against the debit machine, and when she turned back around, Dale had fled. Alone and looking lost, Deena picked up her handbag and walked by Jack.

'Shame,' Lawson chanted, 'shame...shame...shame.'

Most of the morning mob joined in, with some staff chanting also, smirking at one another, eager to see what would happen next. Eve found herself beyond the borders of belief, opening her mouth like a snake, hissing out the words. 'Shame... shame... shame.' She could tell Jack's dark side was on the loose again, but rather than being fearful of it, she felt excited by its power, by a confidence she'd never felt within herself.

Jack now controlled the mob, Eve thought. From an initial act of applause grew obedience, conformity, and fear, so simple it had slipped their cognitive defences. And as the door shut in Deena's draught, Jack spoke again. 'My partner, Eve, will collect the fifty-dollar registration fee, as discussed. Remember, we're going to rewrite the future. We're the new Illuminati.'

Hands instantly shuffled into handbags or rummaged through jeans pockets. In a café full of strangers, Lawson smiled at Eve, motioning her to collect their plunder, and as natural as sunlight in summer, Eve was on her feet collecting fifty after fifty, stuffing note after note into the pocket of her short denim skirt.

Once the money was collected, Jack asked Rebecca and her staff to leave and give them a few moments privacy. 'Five minutes is all,' Jack said. 'I want to tell the *Futurians* the secret. What this is all about, and why they have been chosen going forward.'

Confused, Rebecca ordered her staff into the locker room and shut the door. They stood there giggling, staring at each other, wondering if it was some sort of YouTube prank, while out on the café floor, Jack walked by each table, gently touching some of the diners on their forehead, saying, 'I want all of you to change seats, change partners. The secret will change your lives, and I need you all to be completely open to it, to be divorced from the confining bounds of your customary reality. Move. Hurry up now.'

Moments later, the café transformed into a tapestry of demented servitude. Chairs were barged against the front door as a barrier. Couples swapped. Families had been siphoned off into odd clusters, and the words *Future Society* had been smeared on a window with tomato sauce. Eve looked around in disbelief. It had taken Jack less than ten minutes to renature and mentally dismember a band of hungry breakfast diners. He had blown like a dignitary into the megaphone of mystery, assembling obeisance like a master's hand around a servant's neck. And more than a thousand dollars richer, Jack spoke for the final time.

'I want all of you to join me, to join your fellow members, to close your eyes and lapse into a trance. Drift, show me your commitment to the cause, and when you awake, the secret will have been shared with each and every one of you.'

That said, Jack winked at Eve, motioning her to follow him. They tip-toed out through the kitchen, past the locker room where the staff were still huddled up, and out into the back alley.

Feeling daylight again, Jack exploded with laughter. Ten minutes had changed the nature of their relationship. Clyde met Bonnie, and Bonnie, in her own unbidden way, had got behind the wheel of a whirlwind, feeling the high-altitude jet streams of self-esteem for the first time. From that moment on, Eve would habitually consider her days in light of that event, a yardstick for measuring her proximity to maximal existence, and if the day's boundless opportunities failed to produce a similar intoxication, a sort of dial tone would beep in her ear. *Sorry, your smile is no longer in service.*

Eve could understand why people broke the law. The rush of danger made her feel alive in a way she'd never felt before. Eve felt every other moment in her life had been an act of crude imitation. That in those fleeting moments, as she collected cash from strangers, the ridicule of bullies, cruel fathers and judging peers had face-planted against the pavement of her past and would lie there, forever stiffened on the dark neural side-streets of forgetfulness. Eve felt forever free, running through the streets of Toronto, the whole event registering with a bloat of laughter in her tummy.

They eventually stopped for breath on College Street, a few kilometres away from the café. All the buildings were low-rise with a sandstone exterior – different from the tall, glass-faced mammoths that loomed eighty stories high in the downtown district. College Street was close to the University of Toronto, and even though it was a Saturday morning in summer, students passed them with coffee cups in hand, talking about last night's party and how they were late with their thesis.

Jack and Eve walked hand-in-hand down the leafy boulevard. Trees shimmered in the hot breeze. The sagging, overhead tram lines stretched into the distance as the morning sun spat wisps of vapour along the tree-flanked street. It was strange. When arranging things in her memory, Eve muddled up the facts. She remembered her role as different, more authoritative, as though it was her idea to collect the cash.

'Let's have some fun on their dime,' Eve suggested, looking at Jack excitedly.

'Absolutely, babe.'

Einstein's bar was dimly lit as they entered through the side doors. The main light source glowed from the fridges behind the bar, giving a ghostly aura to the space. A large mirror allowed Eve to smile at her reflection. She wondered if the café diners were still awaiting Jack's revelation, glancing over her shoulder, catching sight of Jack smiling back at her. She smiled and bit her lip, feeling her heart flutter in her chest. Her capture was as obvious as outlines, as grave as a crab wading in a bucket.

Eve pulled out a wad of fifties, handing the barman a fresh note before carrying two double bourbon and colas back to the booth where Jack sat smiling.

The barman called after Eve. 'You forgot your change.'

'Keep it,' Eve shouted back before snuggling in beside Jack.

They clicked glasses and smiled between giggles. 'That was the craziest shit ever, babe.'

'Hardly,' Lawson said, 'you work homicide.'

'I've still never seen anything like that. That's how cults are formed. You were like Koresh!'

'Nah,' Jack said. 'I didn't go screwing all the wives.'

Eve snorted with laughter.

'You like cult leaders?' Jack asked, lounging back in the booth.

'When I was young, I read about them all the time. Books, newspaper articles, and documentaries – anything I could get my hands on, really.'

'Why?' Jack asked. 'Disgust or fascination?'

'Envy,' Eve said between sips of bourbon. 'I wanted to be like them in a weird way. To not care about anything, to not feel anything, no remorse, no guilt, nothing. I wanted to be able to crush all the bullies like they were insects, but I never could. I couldn't even crush a fly. I hated spiders too, but when I'd see one on my bedroom wall, I'd trap it in a cup and let it out my window rather than kill it.'

'Is that why you became a detective,' Jack asked, 'to save all the helpless little spiders you hate deep down?'

Eve had never really thought about why she chose to be a detective. She figured she'd just wandered into it, like a doorway in a dream. 'Maybe I'm secretly a serial killer and want to be close to the case,' Eve said, laughing.

Jack laughed, too. 'Okay, psycho, tell me more about this case you're working on?'

'There's nothing to tell,' Eve said. 'We don't have any leads. The Poet is clever, he covers his tracks.'

'Are you ever worried he'll come after you?'

'No,' Eve said. 'Anyways, I don't want to talk about work; I want to have some fun.'

And so, an idle Saturday afternoon swung as loosely as a wizard's sleeve through the sunny streets of Toronto. Eve and Jack hopped from bar to bar, drank shots, and danced on tables as other revellers watched askance, whispering that Eve seemed to have something like love rattling in her bones.

As dusk descended, they sat in Sugar Beach Park, watching the last streaks of sunlight glaze over Lake Ontario. The sand felt hot beneath them as they lay back to watch a stream of a hundred coloured lanterns rise into the twilight. Eve thought it had a certain elegance as she snuggled into Jack's chest. Everything once blown asunder had reassembled. Everything that had once been predictable had changed its spots.

Eve felt sleepy as she counted the sky lanterns. On count forty-seven, something bubbled up within her, huge and eager. 'There's not a version of reality where I don't fall so deeply in love with you,' Eve whispered in Jack's ear. 'I wish your heart would just eat me so we'll never spend another day apart.'

'I feel the same,' Jack said, 'but more. Something I can't describe.'

Love was not a singular feeling, Eve thought. It was the whole universe exploding from her chest. Love had been described in a million different ways, yet all those words combined could not fill the echo of its roar. Their lips touched, and Eve felt her world spin. She felt the fumes of life, like the flicker of the first flame must have felt like to the darkness. Jack's lips explained the search for every meaning and the meaning of every search. It was a feeling of no worthy description but one of every worldly emotion.

'Save me,' Eve cooed breathlessly.

Jack's fingers combed through her hair like a god in caress of the globe. 'I love you,' Jack said, moving his fingers through the valley of Eve's breasts, up along her shoulders, sliding off the string of her kami top. Eve grabbed Jack's face and kissed him uncontrollably before mounting his hips and lowering her head so their noses touched. Pausing there, Eve's mouth opened as though to breathe her last breath, ingesting the atmosphere like a drowning girl who had finally accepted the flooding of her lungs.

Chapter 11

Most nights, Mitch sat alone in the garage attached to his house, lingering in the shadows, listening to an old ceiling fan spinning overhead. He never cared much for music, and TV had become a particular form of torture his wife and children enjoyed even more in his absence. He often heard the echoes of family time seeping in from the living room, their laughter and conversations, creeping into the garage like a spectre. Mitch couldn't understand how his eldest daughter Jessie, and his son Josh, had moved on so casually from Betty's passing. But worst of all was his wife, Judy.

How can she laugh at 'Modern Family' in there, sitting beside the empty chair where Betty always used to sit?

Maybe Mitch had loved Betty more. That's the only thing that made any sense. Betty had been a dream child, affable and mild; her laughter had a way of brightening up Mitch's world and releasing him from the darkness of his job. He just wanted to hold her again, to feel her warmth, and see her bright blue eyes shimmer in the summer sunlight. But those days were gone, and now Mitch preferred to sit alone at night, holding a bottle of bourbon with a homemade sticker pressed against the label: *Only to be opened in an emergency.*

Every night, when Mitch arrived home from work, he peeled off the sticker from the previous night's bottle and pressed it against the new one. And there Mitch sat, relaxing back into a cheap plastic deck chair, listening to the humming ceiling fan, a look of relief breaking out across his face.

Emergency averted.

It had been weeks since Mitch stopped for his customary coffee along his route to work. Things had changed, coffee replaced by hard liquor, his complexion screaming of some nutritional deficiency, like an open jar of mayonnaise left out in sunlight, the greasy yellow hue hinting at jaundice. Very seldom, when Mitch thought of himself existentially, he imagined Sisyphus pushing a large glass of bourbon up a mountain. And he only knew of Sisyphus because his wife regarded their marriage as equally toilsome.

Screw her and her divorce, and the kids, too. She can have them. They don't even care about what happened to Betty.

One morning in early July, Mitch stopped for a quart of bourbon from his local LCBO shop, rummaging through his pockets and searching for dimes and quarters. Instead of placing the change in the cashier's open palm, Mitch let the coins fall and bounce all over the cashier's desk.

'Asshole,' the cashier shouted.

Mitch didn't care. He felt too far gone to think about anything, to care about anything, to tighten the lid on the proverbial jar of mayonnaise and seal his suffering shut. He walked to his car, dreaming up a headline: *God is dead, but tins of tuna are buy-one-get-one-free.* Mitch smiled at the thought. Ever since his days as a beat cop, he liked to think in terms of underwhelming headlines as a way to escape the darkness of the job. Mitch felt he needed to escape more than ever this morning as he opened the driver's door, settled in behind the wheel and cracked his neck from side to side. He never bothered indicating as he veered into the stream of traffic. He disliked people who never used their indicators, who drove while texting on their phones and drank behind the wheel.

And yet there Mitch sat, with a quart of bourbon wedged between his thighs, unscrewing the cap with one hand, as he messaged Glenda with the other.

Mitch: Hey, are you still up for meeting later?

After sending that text message, Mitch paused at a red light and drank from the bottle. Glenda was a fun distraction. A fling just sort of happened. A door opened, and Mitch stepped through it, curiously, like a cat snooping through the kitchen cupboards. They met a couple of times a week, nothing serious, just two middle-aged people who enjoyed greasing each other's curiosity.

Horns honked, but Mitch didn't flinch. He sat at the green light drinking until the last drop of bourbon dribbled down his tonsils and the green light turned red again. Angry motorists shouted behind him, but Mitch didn't even look in his rearview mirror. He had outmanoeuvred the torments of the prior month, had sidestepped the niggling internal voice that started every morning's car journey with the words; *I should sober up. I should save my marriage. I should care more. I should...I should...I should.*

Arriving at the station, Mitch chewed two sticks of gum before entering through the main doors. He kept his head down, trying to walk straight and look sober. The station was alive with the hum of activity — a cacophony of ringing phones, rapid clatter of keyboards, and a constant flow of uniformed officers and plain-clothes detectives.

By the water cooler, Chief Cutler nodded. 'You finally decided to show up, Mitch.'

'I've been busy reviewing Dr. Martinez's notes on The Poet.'

'Anything of interest?' Chief Cutler asked.

'She's right,' Mitch said. 'We've spent the last month interviewing every delivery man in Toronto, and we haven't got a single lead. We're looking in the wrong place.'

'What do you mean?'

'The nature of his crimes and the poems he leaves behind all point to a man who believes he's playing a game – that he's several moves ahead. Dr. Martinez believes he has an insatiable need for recognition and validation. The Poet doesn't just want to evade us; he wants to be acknowledged by us. He wants to be seen as superior.'

'Get to the point, Mitch.'

'He'll want to be as close to the case as possible,' Mitch said. 'He'll follow the media reports closely and might even reach out to reporters offering tips or insights. He could pose as a concerned citizen, a witness, or even try to befriend us. Instead of running down delivery men, we should be looking into who's calling in with tips. Instead of looking at stupid CCTV footage of office buildings, we should be looking at footage of who was in the crowd that night. Eve doesn't want to listen, no one does, everyone is going around with their head up their own hole.'

'Are you drunk?' Chief Cutler asked.

'No?' Mitch retorted, drilling her with a look.

'Go home and sober up,' Chief Cutler demanded. 'This is your last warning, Mitch. If you need grief counselling, we can arrange it for you. But this has to stop. I turn a blind eye to the drinking sometimes. You detectives have a tough job, but I can't keep letting you away with it. You're a damn liability at this stage.'

'Oh, fuck off,' Mitch said. 'I'm the only detective here doing real work, thinking outside the fucking box.'

'Next time, it won't be a warning,' Chief Cutler said. 'I'll be taking your badge and gun, you hear.'

The consequences of this incident were not immediately apparent to Mitch. After leaving the station, he walked to his car, unlocked the door and sat behind the wheel. His precinct was located in Old Town, amid coffee shops, apartment blocks and dusty storefronts. The warm breeze smelled of exhaust fumes and burning clutch oil from a motorbike. Mitch tightened his grip on the steering wheel, waiting for some internal combustion to move him forward. He turned the key in the ignition, shifted into gear and pulled out into a slow-moving traffic lane.

Ten metres away, Jack Lawson revved his motorbike lightly, indicated out, and followed Mitch's car.

Chapter 12

Mitch spent that afternoon in Castor's Bar, drinking bourbon and staring over at Glenda's apartment, waiting for her arrival home. Between sips, Mitch thought about his father, praying in their living room that the repo man might choose to knock on the neighbour's door instead. The thought seemed to tighten around Mitch's throat like a noose. Those wretched memories. The suffocating flashbacks. A house alive with rats rummaging along the floor, ants in myriad marching over scraps of food, roaches crawling out of kitchen drawers, crows whizzing in and out through broken windowpanes. The sound of his father safely snoring. Then, the screams, his mother's wailing, trapped in the corner of her bedroom, trying to dodge her husband's rage.

Mitch felt equally dead as he did alive. He looked down into his glass of whiskey. It was empty again. Mitch half-expected to see Betty's eyes looking back at him or hear her laughter bubbling up through the fizzy cola. He felt like crying but couldn't force a tear, and the next thing Mitch felt was a hard slap across his face.

'What the hell, Mitch?'

Eve stood glaring at him like a bull before a matador, dressed in tight denim jeans and a loose-fitting white t-shirt.

'Go away,' Mitch moaned. 'The last thing I need is you lecturing me as well.'

It broke Eve's heart to see her partner downed like that. Mitch appeared tortured and dishevelled, with shaggy hair, a rugged beard, and a gaunt, wrinkled face. All of Mitch's muscularity had faded, and the enormous bags underneath his eyes added years to the man Eve had once admired more than any other.

Eve shook her head and called out to the server. 'Two more bourbons.'

'Doubles,' Mitch added.

Eve sat down and smiled at Mitch. A part of her couldn't help it. 'Might as well kill ourselves together, eh?'

'Knew I could count on you,' Mitch said dryly.

'I should've punched you in the face instead,' Eve said. 'It might have knocked some sense into you.'

'Wouldn't have made a difference.'

'Then what will?'

'You got your gun?'

'Yeah,' Eve said. 'Why?'

'Put a bullet in my head.'

'Is that what you really want, Mitch?'

'Yeah.'

'Then just wait another damn week or two. Your wife will be driven to it soon enough. And what's this about you screwing around with that weird witness? You love Judy. Who are you anymore?'

'I'm the same guy I've always been.'

The server arrived back with their drinks and a bowl of peanuts.

Eve handed her a fifty. 'Keep the change.'

'Serious?' the server asked.

'On one condition,' Eve said, pointing towards Mitch, 'don't serve this fucker anymore today.'

The server smiled. 'Deal, he never leaves a tip anyway.'

Eve's stare softened. 'The state of you, Mitch. This has to stop. Chief Cutler is losing her shit. If you don't make some effort to sober up, you'll be suspended, or worse.'

'Good. I don't care.'

'No, not good, Mitch. Have I to talk to you like a child? Being fired, not good. Being a drunk, not good. Losing your family, not fucking good.'

'I lost my family when Betty died.'

Eve folded her arms across her tummy and shook her head. She usually enjoyed riffing back and forth with Mitch but now felt sorry for the man he had become. A depressive with only a cobra inside his head for company. It was clear that Mitch had plunged deeper into some idea of himself, into the full possession of the past, into a distortion of reality so cruel it could only be lived through bloodshot eyes and numbed nerves. Eve could feel Mitch's madness – the anger orbiting his head, days of trench warfare where every bullet is aimed at oneself, and the white flags of surrender are knotted into nooses.

'You won't scare me away, Mitch.'

'Well, you always were a moron.'

'Who are you anymore?'

'This is me,' Mitch shouted, his voice a mixture of rage and alcoholic fervour. 'You're looking at the real me, and you've no right to judge. No one has. I lost my little Betty and everyone has just moved on without a care in the world. You all make me sick.'

'I didn't come here to lock horns,' Eve said. 'I came as a friend, to help.'

'Help,' Mitch mocked.

'I've had low moments too.'

'I don't care.'

'Listen,' Eve shouted. 'The Poet is out there bludgeoning people for sport. Where's the passion for catching these guys gone? You're the best detective in the squad. Stop being so selfish. Pull yourself together and let's start catching the bad guys again.'

'I don't care.'

Eve shook her head, catching sight of a familiar figure from the corner of her eye. Jack Lawson strolled into the bar, dressed in a navy suit, carrying a black leather briefcase – an alarming sight for Eve. 'Shit,' she muttered.

Mitch followed her gaze to where Jack stood leaning on the counter, ordering a whiskey sour. 'What?' Mitch asked. 'You know that asshole?'

'Do you?' Eve asked, growing more alarmed.

'He's a regular here,' Mitch said. 'He used to go to the gym I went to. He's like a fucking shadow.'

'What else?'

'He's a loudmouth.'

Jack instantly spotted Eve and Mitch in the booth by the window, sitting across from each other like two warlords trying to negotiate a treaty that would never hold. A moment or two passed, and Eve swallowed deeply as Jack walked over to their booth, placing a kiss on her cheek.

'Let me guess,' Jack said, smirking, 'you two are discussing The Poet case?'

'What are you doing here?' Eve asked, deliberately ignoring his question.

'My practice is close by,' Jack said before directing his gaze to Mitch and extending his hand. 'Dr. Jack Lawson. You must be Mitch. Eve's told me lots about you.'

Mitch stared into Jack's eyes, refusing to extend the courtesy of a handshake. 'What are you?' Mitch asked. 'Some shrink?'

'A clinical psychologist working corporate,' Jack corrected, placing his business card in front of Mitch. 'I've seen you here before, staring into that glass like it's a door to another world.' Jack tapped his business card three times. 'If you ever need to talk, you know where to find me.'

Mitch glared at Eve instantly. 'Is this your fucking doing? Brought your boyfriend along to get into my head?'

'Screw you,' Eve said.

'He's a snake,' Mitch roared, regarding Jack as not only repulsive but also deaf. 'Mark my words; he'll eat your heart and stare into your eyes as he does. I've chased freaks like him before. He has that psycho-deadness in his eyes.'

Eve ignored the remark, but she'd often noticed that same deadness in Jack's eyes, and all the charm in the world couldn't hide it. All the romantic fervour couldn't drown out the little voice in her head telling her to be careful.

'Steady on,' Jack said, putting his hand on Mitch's shoulder.

Mitch boiled and slapped Jack's hand away.

'What's going on over there?' the manager shouted from behind the bar.

'Nothing,' Eve shouted back. 'Jack is just about to leave.'

She looked at Jack apologetically, lipping the words, 'Please, babe.'

Jack smiled back before bending down and picking up his briefcase. 'I'll see you later, dinner at mine, say eight o'clock?'

Eve nodded as Jack downed his whiskey sour. 'Good luck catching The Poet,' Jack said, walking back into the busy street.

'Jesus Christ, Mitch, you're out of control. Jack was only trying to be nice, and you wouldn't even shake his hand.'

'When guys like him grin,' Mitch said, 'a forked tongue pokes out between their teeth. He mentioned The Poet case twice. You read Dr. Martinez's profile; The Poet will try to get close to the case. For all we know, your smirky boyfriend is slithering between your legs one day and out bludgeoning people the next.'

'You know what,' Eve shouted, 'you've turned into a real asshole, Mitch.'

'And your instincts have been coddled by that fucker's charm,' Mitch said, slamming down his glass. 'I saw him smack someone with a dumbbell at the gym just because the guy accidently took his bench. He's dangerous, Eve. Why are you with someone like that? He might dress up in a fancy suit, but you know what he is deep down. His lies will pile up soon enough and smother you.'

'I love Jack.'

'Yeah, maybe it's his handsome looks,' Mitch said. 'I can't help but see the resemblance to Glenda's sketch of The Poet. Same strong jawline and dark, intense eyes. You need to wake up, girl.'

'And you need to patch things up with your wife,' Eve said, 'instead of screwing the witness who provided the sketch. That's messed up, Mitch. It could harm the case.'

'When he gets bored of you,' Mitch said, pointing into Eve's face, 'we'll be zipping up your body bag. I don't see a soul when I look into his eyes. I'm at this game longer than you, Eve. I know the eyes of a killer.'

~~~

Later that evening, Mitch turned Jack's business card over in his fingers while driving home. A plot had begun to develop, and if working homicide had taught Mitch anything, it was that coincidence often slept in the same bed as guilty men and women. He put Jack's business card down on the passenger seat, uncapped a fresh bottle of bourbon and took a thoughtful swig.

Glenda would know.

Mitch jammed on the brakes, his car screeching to a halt as he pulled onto the sidewalk in the sleepy suburbs close to his house. Fumbling with his phone, Mitch pulled up Jack's LinkedIn profile photo and took a screenshot. He grimaced slightly. Jack looked different in the picture, he wore glasses, had a thick beard and his hair was tighter on the sides.

It's worth a shot.

Mitch typed a message to Glenda and shared Jack's picture.

Mitch: Is this the man you saw the night Paddy was murdered? Please, it's urgent.

Mitch could feel his adrenaline surge, his fingers drumming on the dashboard as he waited for Glenda's response. He could feel the tension building, drinking mouthful after mouthful of bourbon, trying to loosen the knot of nerves in his stomach.

Then his phone buzzed.

Glenda: I don't know. Similar eyes, maybe, but I can't be sure, sorry. It was so dark that night, Mitch. Do you want to meet again soon?

Chapter 13

Jack's receptionist, Jess Polizzi, knocked lightly on his office door the following evening.

'Come in,' Jack said, writing notes at his desk.

Jess opened the door slowly and peeped in. 'Sorry to disturb you, but there's a detective in reception saying he needs to speak to you ASAP.' Jess lowered her voice and looked over her shoulder to check if the detective was listening from the lobby. 'What are we gonna do? You said they'd never be able to trace any trades back to us.'

Jack smirked, not a line of worry wagging above his eyebrows.

He'd met Jess three years prior in a nearby sports bar where she worked the floor instead of client schedules, using her smile like an oyster knife. Jess wielded a different sort of gravitas, a punchy cocktail of beauty and elegance, a femme fatale type usually spotted wearing large horn-rimmed sunglasses and stepping onto a billionaire's yacht on the Riviera. That night, Jack watched her charm every table she served, reading people like they were picture books.

She's the one, Jack thought, calling her over and asking for the bill.

'Was everything alright with your food, handsome?'

Jack grinned, offering her a job in a new business venture, a high-end corporate wellness clinic, using his forged clinical psychologist documents to exploit the egos of wealthy financial professionals for a thousand bucks an hour and bleeding them of insider knowledge he'd use to balloon his investment portfolio. Jess would, as was her talent, charm each client, making sure those stock market mavericks kept coming back with their dicks swinging between their legs.

'I've heard that before,' Jess had said. 'Anyway, I like this job; what you're offering sounds boring.'

A wry smile played on Jack's lips as he pulled out his car keys. 'I'll throw in my Porsche to sweeten the deal, a seventy-thirty split of the profits and a view of Toronto so high God will look up at us in envy.'

A week later, using money he'd made from the Carmady murders, Jack rented office space on the seventy-third floor of Berkley Plaza. As the years went by, the money flowed in, and the ruse ran without a wrinkle – until, Jess noted, a detective showed up flashing his badge.

'What's the detective's name?' Jack asked, looking up momentarily.

'Mitch Bauer,' Jess replied. 'What should I do? You have a client scheduled for five-thirty.'

'Cancel the appointment and send Detective Bauer in.'

Jess shook her head. 'Jack, you can't cancel it. It's Bernie.' Code word for we're fucked.

Lawson winked and mimed the words. 'Don't worry, it's a little game I'm playing.'

'Okay,' Jess said, closing the door behind her.

Moments later, Mitch appeared in the doorway of Jack's office. His eyes scanned the room slowly. The colour scheme was black and white. The large, airy space hinted at some kind of pathological minimalism, consisting of little more than a white desk and chair, white bookshelves, and a black leather couch with a matching black chair positioned close by. The only other decoration was a large charcoal drawing, depicting monstrous waves collapsing along the bow of a broken ship.

Jack looked up and smirked. Mitch was so obvious, Jack thought. Standing with his hands wedged into his stained trouser pockets like an awkward teenager. Jack could tell that Mitch imagined he'd find more. That he expected his presence would produce such heat that guilt would break through Jack's lips like a lizard hatching from an egg. But instead, in the stillness of the scene, everything settled like dust before a gunfight, so evocative it seemed both men wore cowboy hats and donned names like Billy and Wyatt, Doomed and Deadly. Seconds shrugged and scampered off. Jack persisted in scribbling notes, making Mitch feel small and meagre, like an ant before the orbit of an elephant.

'I didn't expect to see you so soon,' Jack said, looking up briefly to smile. 'Not until your funeral. With the way you've been drinking, I'd predicted late November.'

'You like to think about death?' Mitch asked.

'As much as you like to think about a drink,' Jack said, still drawing clouds of circles in his notebook. 'Death is the closest approximation one gets to absolute reality. Evolutionary biologists like to reduce everything to food, sex, and survival. Christianity reduces everything to suffering, and the Buddhists reduce everything to attachment. But a true realist reduces everything to death. The final state. The absolute.'

'I don't get it,' Mitch said.

'Ah, you wouldn't,' Jack said, smirking. 'The animal inside of you is too tame, detective. I've watched you drinking alone in Castor's Bar, all sad and emotional, your eyes puffed up with pain. You're like one of those scratching poles a cat uses to sharpen its claws. Life just tears away at you for sport, doesn't it?'

When Mitch went to respond, Jack interrupted. 'Always the wick, never the match. Take a seat, detective.'

But Mitch had other ideas. He walked over to Jack's qualifications hanging on the wall and squinted to read the print.

'I finished top of my class,' Jack boasted.

'Is that so?' Mitch asked.

'So real it squirms.'

Mitch walked back and sat down in the black leather chair as Jack continued to doodle in his notebook. 'That's my seat,' Jack said without looking up. 'My pets lie on the couch.'

'I'm not your pet,' Mitch said.

'Well then, why are you here, detective?'

'For some advice on a case I'm working on,' Mitch said. 'I thought you could help build a profile since you're a shrink and all.'

'It's not really what I do.'

'It's about The Poet,' Mitch added quickly.

'Oh, The Poet,' Jack said with a smirk. 'He seems to have captivated the city. CTV ran a report last week. They reckon he's envious of the upper class, that the couples he kills are surrogates for some personal trauma he's trying to cure, or that it's sexually motivated, that he likes control and dominance. But they have it all wrong.'

'Really?' Mitch probed.

'Maybe he just enjoys killing,' Jack said. 'But, society demands you have a quirk, some signature, a personal brand, so he leaves a little poem to seem all deep and meaningful.'

'And why the couples?'

'Because the cops in this city are so incompetent they might not connect the murders if he didn't leave a pattern.'

'I have another theory,' Mitch said.

'I didn't pick you for the theorising type, detective.'

'See,' Mitch said, 'the coward that committed these murders, I bet he's a real fucking loser. He was probably never loved or held as a child, he never quite fitted in, a real oddball. One of those guys who can't please his woman, whose cock is always soft. You know the type.'

'I can't say I do, but you seem to be an expert,' Lawson said, gritting his teeth, fighting the rage brewing up within.

Mitch smiled. 'Now Eve, she thinks differently. She thinks this loser is sophisticated or something, that he's real clever, one step ahead of everyone. But what the hell would Eve know,' Mitch mocked. 'The poor girl is just two brain cells hauling around a set of breasts. An infant smiling at the next piece of shit that passes.'

Jack sucked his lips and put his pen down. 'Shots fired,' he said, feeling the urge to strangle Mitch, to wrap his hands around his neck and watch the life vanish from his eyes.

'I'm no gunslinger,' Mitch said, pausing. 'More of a prize-fighter in the last round.'

'Same thing, really,' Lawson said, walking towards Mitch, his eyes as black as onyx. 'The only difference is the prize-fighter's family gets to watch him fall apart slowly. How are Judy and the kids? Such a shame what happened to little Betty.'

Hearing the mention of Betty's name, Mitch stood up, spat on the floor, washed his tongue against his upper teeth and met Lawson face to face.

'Oh, oh! Here comes the combo,' Jack mocked, breathing down on Mitch. 'Boom, bang, wallop.'

'Mention Betty's name again and I'll empty a whole clip into your head, you hear.'

Lawson smirked, staring deeply into Mitch's eyes. 'You found her, right? All mangled and mutilated. And the monster that mowed her down still hasn't been caught. I don't know how you get through the day, knowing he's still out there living his life as yours falls apart. Poor little Betty.'

Mitch grabbed Jack by the neck and slammed him back against the wall. 'Don't say her name again.'

'Betty,' Jack mumbled, before forcing Mitch's hands away from his throat.

Mitch shook with rage. 'Don't close your eyes,' he said, slapping Lawson's face. 'I'll be watching, waiting for you to slip up, and you will. Your office is conveniently located beside the alley where Paddy was murdered. That's no coincidence. I'll catch you. The Carmadys, the Kirbys, Paddy Fitzgerald, and all the others. I'll find the little thread and pull and keep pulling until your whole world unravels,' Mitch said, turning to leave. 'You don't scare me, not one fucking bit.'

'You've let the tarantula escape from underneath the teacup,' Jack shouted after Mitch. 'Don't chase it into dark corners, detective. It might like it.'

Chapter 14

After Mitch had left, Jack sat at his desk wondering why he'd been so audacious.

Maybe I'm bored.

And maybe boredom to a psychopath is like an itch to a leper. The game thrilled Jack, but he knew he'd messed up this time around, that Mitch would come for him, guns blazing, like a soldier on the front line. He drained the half cup of coffee on his desk and lay back in his chair. The room seemed to close in on Jack as he breathed heavily through his nose. He looked calm as he drew circles in his notepad again, but inside, a storm was brewing. For the first time, Jack felt he had underestimated someone, that he had pushed Mitch too far, that their fight would have no referee – their brawl, no-holds-barred.

Since the Carmady murders, Jack had followed Mitch around in the shadows. He searched online, but Mitch didn't have any social profiles. Jack only found shreds of information, some dozen news articles where Mitch's name was loosely mentioned as the detective on a murder case. Desk research flowed into obsessive fieldwork. Jack followed Mitch for months and was shocked to discover how anyone could live such a sterilised life. The routine and monotony seemed monastic, if not masochistic. But after Betty's death, everything changed. Instead of going home to his family after work, Mitch spent his nights drinking in a nearby cop bar. Jack watched him some nights, staring into his glass, his eyes mushy with grief, his soft sniffles as delicate as rose petals.

Then, a week after Paddy's murder, Jack observed another sudden change in Mitch's behaviour. Instead of driving to the nearby cop bar, Mitch turned right rather than left on Front Street. Jack followed him through the throng of traffic, through blinking taillights, honking horns and a fog of cold exhaust fumes. Five minutes later, Mitch parked his car outside Castor's Bar, lowered his baseball cap and locked his car with a double-click of the key fob. Jack followed Mitch inside, where football highlights played on large TV screens and the smell of buffalo chicken wings sifted through the air. He considered sitting in the booth beside Mitch but didn't want to risk exposure. Instead, he sat on a bar stool and ordered a pint of Moosehead. Mitch ordered a double bourbon and cola, staring into his glass and then out the window in a meditative trance.

What's he up to? Jack wondered. *Why here? Why tonight? Why that booth with a view of that apartment block?*

Jack washed down the possibilities over another pint of Moosehead. Then, minutes later, as Jack scrolled through Instagram on his phone, a revelation occurred. A bedroom light flashed on in the apartment block on the far side of the street. A woman threw her handbag and coat on the bed and yawned into a mirror, stretching her arms overhead before letting them fall flatly to her sides. Mitch's lips seemed to break into a subtle smile. His body straightened from its slouched position, and Lawson could just about make out the slight movement of Mitch's Adam's apple. Jack recognised the woman. She had seen him the night of Paddy's murder and Mitch had led him right to her.

That's the bitch who gave the cops my sketch.

Throughout all those months of watching, Jack learned that Mitch was like him in a way: obsessive, damaged, and dangerous

83

when cornered. They moved through the world unpredictably, like dreidels spinning out, like flames over gasoline.

It was dark when Jack left his office, dressed all in black, with a baseball cap pulled down low against his brow. How had it come to this, Jack wondered. One moment of weakness, one lapse in judgment, and he had given Mitch a way in. His arrogance had opened a door his charm couldn't close.

The neon lights from bars and late-night cafés cast eerie, dancing shadows on the sidewalk. The city buzzed with activity, music echoing through the streets, the CN Tower piercing the skyline, its red light pulsating softly at the top.

Jack's darkness was on the loose again.

They're all laughing at you, looking down on you, you fucking pussy. And you just let them, you little soft boy. Do something about it. Take the life they took from you. Paddy gave you your proof and you've done nothing about it, Mr. Big Killer. Soft boy. Show them all who you really are. Make them feel what you feel, pussy.

Jack screamed to himself.

Shut up.

Check. Check. Check. The pain is real, allow yourself to feel it.

Jack burst out laughing.

Pain is sane. Think about it. Don't be stupid, they'll let you down. They always do. Eve is fodder. Why bother? Devour her whole.

Jack shook his head. Seething. Slipping further.

Kill Eve, you know you want to.

'Fuck off,' Jack said, his knuckles white with rage as he pressed his fist into his mouth and bit down hard. He made his way through Chinatown, scanning the crowds and searching faces. A young couple walked by, laughing, holding each other close. No, they weren't right. Spadina was too public anyway. He continued on, the energy inside of him turning nuclear. His mind scribbling little poems about every passer-by, dark stanzas, gory graphics, his thoughts poking around in their lives like a fork poking around in a mincemeat pie.

> There is no place for love to nest,
>   rage has slithered into every crawling
>   and bats hang on the door of every thought;
>   the shape of every smile is a bright rainbow falling.
> My darkness stills and sinks beneath a murky current,
>   into the abyss, it struggles, rolls and tussles,
> far beyond the reach of sunlight, drooling down,
>   and waiting at the bottom are bludgeoned faces and fast-panting muscles.

Jack's anger pulsed through his veins. His darkness drove him forward, his shadow-self seething to split the atom; his rage, like a warhead looking for a world to wreak. He imagined the bright light flashing out in all directions. The sonic boom. People exploding into clusters of pink mist. All the shapes of buildings suspended briefly in particles of dust. He could feel the power building up inside him, the dark, destructive energy that left no room for mercy or remorse.

As Jack reached Harbord Village, the city bustle slowly gave way to darkened sidewalks and empty streets. Jack slipped on a pair of running gloves and took off in a jog. He had coursed this route many times before. It was mostly residential. Old townhouses with some student accommodation. Jack took a left turn and increased his pace, running through Palmerston, then up through Seaton Village and into Davenport. There were no CCTV cameras in this part of town, and the streetlights were dimmed to a pale orange.

As Jack reached a more desolate stretch, he spotted her. Alone, sitting on a step, smoking a cigarette in an alleyway at the rear of a restaurant. Her silhouette was illuminated only by the dim moonlight. She seemed lost in thought, the cigarette burning away between her fingers.

'Hey, you're Sarah, right?' Jack said approaching her down the alleyway, scanning for cameras.

The woman appeared startled as she looked up. 'No,' she said. 'I think you've got the wrong girl.'

'It's definitely you,' Jack said. 'You served me and my sister here last week. You go to the university, right?'

'Wasn't me, buddy.'

'I could've sworn it was you,' Jack said. 'I'm normally so good with faces.'

The woman never responded as Jack walked closer. 'Hey, could I be a pain and bum a cigarette?'

'Sure,' the woman said, rolling her eyes.

As she went to hand Jack a cigarette, he sprung, wrapping his arm around her neck and lifting her up in a rear guillotine choke. She went to scream but only managed to heave out a few mumbles. Jack felt eagerly alive, feeling the woman's struggles, almost materialising the orgasmic outcome with each toss and jerk. He used all his strength to tighten his grip around her neck, dragging her over to a large dumpster of dirty kitchen oil on the other side of the alley. He applied deadly pressure until her struggles faded.

'Shush now,' Jack said, opening the lid of the dumpster and dipping her in headfirst.

The woman struggled for a few seconds, her submerged screams rising to the top in little bubbles. When she stopped moving, Jack closed the lid and walked on, moving through the streets of Toronto, through the aisles of life, differently, more determined, imagining how he could suddenly appear in a stranger's life, like a black hole, charming them into his all-consuming presence, ingesting their entire agency before annihilating them with the bone-crushing callousness of inverted space.

Jack felt relief again; the day's anger drained like a lanced boil.

Chapter 15

The first time Eve saw Jack's condo, she found it slightly spooky, as though the space suffered from some weird form of pathological neatness. Everything was arranged in pristine order – not a speck of dust to be seen – with no real sign that human life had ever traversed across the threshold. A scene, Eve thought, where some robotic ritual might have taken place just hours before. From the front door, she could barely see any colours other than white and grey, moving through the high-ceilinged hallways like fodder for some synthetic lifeform that slithered through the circuitry.

Eve had similar thoughts about Jack during the early days. She wondered if he was as synthetic as his home or if anything loving lay beneath the charm he'd used to hack her intrigue. It was difficult to detect any genuine emotion in Jack back then. His affection often felt flat, his kisses too; something in his eyes was not entirely loving, not wholly human, the sort of nature that could lick its conscience clean. But lately, Eve noted, her doubts had receded like storm tides. Splashes of colour had begun to appear. The distant look in Jack's eyes seemed washed away, his glacial stare thawed by some internal passion that was absent at the start. There was a genuine warmth now when Jack held Eve in his arms. His affection no longer felt store-bought. Their future no longer felt like a fantasy, something overworked into exhaustion, something that, at the start, Eve feared would be spotted fleeing in a wig.

Eve was sitting at her desk thinking of Jack when Officer Lee sat down in the chair beside her. 'Another body was found a few nights ago,' Lee said with a grim smile. 'Drowned in a dumpster of dirty kitchen oil. What a way to go, eh?'

'What's the deal with that?' Eve asked. 'Drowning someone takes time and lots of force – it sounds personal.'

'Well,' Lee said. 'The vic's colleagues said she had just split with her boyfriend. Fassnidge is questioning him now. He has no alibi, and he fired a crossbow at Ramirez when he called to his condo. Hopefully, this one could be closed soon.'

'Fingers crossed,' Eve said. 'We need a quick win. We have the highest unsolved rate in the country. Chief Cutler is piling on the pressure, especially with The Poet case. We need an open and shut case.'

'All these unsolved cases and suicides,' Lee said. 'Do you think there could be two active serial killers?'

'Why do you think that?' Eve asked.

'Over the past year alone,' Lee said tentatively, 'five wealthy men have committed suicide when they seemingly had everything to live for. Last year, there were seven, including that rapper, SabyBah. It strikes me as strange.'

'SabyBah was my first case working homicide,' Eve said. 'We ruled it a suicide; he overdosed on pills.'

'Or maybe it was staged that way. Think about it. If you want to kill people and stay under the radar, the best way to do it is to make it look like suicide or misadventure. These men are always found in their homes – hanging, some overdosed, or others with their wrists slit. Different means, but the pattern is the same.'

'It's unusual,' Eve said before smiling. 'Someone's trying to make detective.'

'I feel I'm ready,' Lee said eagerly. 'I've got the instincts for it. I know I do. Despite all those hours of CCTV footage, we still can't understand how The Poet entered the alley the night Paddy was murdered. I went back yesterday. There's a sewer drain in the middle of the alley; I think he could have entered that way?'

'We checked it out already,' Eve said. 'The gap is too narrow for someone to crawl through.'

'Well,' Lee said with a nod, 'what about the emergency exit that connects to the plaza parallel to the alley? Have you looked into that?'

'We checked,' Eve said. 'It's alarmed. If someone came in or out of that door, the alarm would have triggered.'

'Alarms fail,' Lee said. 'Or someone could have tampered with it. Did you check the CCTV footage around the emergency exit?'

'The cameras were down,' Eve explained. 'According to the security guard we interviewed, they were damaged a few days before Paddy's murder.'

'How convenient,' Lee said, rubbing his fingers over his moustache. 'You know what strikes me as odd? Clearwater, the company Paddy co-founded, handles over two hundred billion in assets, yet no one seems to be paying attention to that. I haven't heard one news report lead with Paddy, it's all about The Poet. Paddy was mega-rich, and no one is talking about it. If Jeff Bezos was murdered tomorrow, it would be front-page news in every country. Why is no one talking about Paddy?'

'I've said all this to Mitch,' Eve said. 'He's looking into Clearwater.'

'Let's be real,' Lee said. 'These days, the only thing Mitch is looking into is a glass of bourbon.'

'He's been through a lot,' Eve said.

'I know, but it's your neck on the chopping block if you come up short on this one. You're the rookie, Eve. Mitch is rarely ever in, and you can't do it all on your own.'

'There's not much I can do about it,' Eve said.

'You know I passed my detective exam,' Lee said delicately. 'Let me help you out on The Poet case, and maybe you can recommend me to Chief Cutler if I come through.'

'Deal,' Eve said, a determined glare in her eyes.

'Okay,' Lee said, handing Eve a thick, white folder. 'Here's a list of everyone who works in the office block beside the alley. I've crosschecked all names for anyone with a criminal record, and guess what, the security guard did time for robbery.'

'That's good work.'

'And to sweeten the deal,' Lee added, 'I pulled the CCTV footage of the main entrance for the night Paddy was murdered. I haven't got to go through it, but see what you can find.'

'I think Mitch looked into it already.'

'Best to double check,' Lee said raising his eyebrows.

'Okay,' Eve said. 'You've got good instincts.'

'Just remember who helped you out if you find anything.'

Eve spent the afternoon looking through all the names on the list. Most never had as much as a parking ticket. Eve recognised one company, *Capital Clinic* and her heart skipped a beat when she read the name listed as the owner – Jack Lawson.

That didn't make sense. Jack had said his office was over the other side of the financial district. Why would Jack lie?

Jack probably got the building mixed up. But could he have?

Doubts tickled through Eve's mind as she remembered what Mitch had said about Jack, that his lies would pile up soon enough. She pulled up the suspect sketch provided by Glenda on the night Paddy was murdered. There was a slight resemblance to Jack, especially around the eyes. Eve tried to push the image away, to convince herself that she was just being paranoid.

Am I overthinking this?

That question played on a loop in her head. But then another voice chimed in, colder, more rational. *What if Jack's the killer and I do nothing?*

Eve felt stupid even thinking that, but still, the flames of suspicion burned away inside her thoughts like a dumpster fire. The precinct floor was busy as Eve looked around nervously, drumming her fingers on her desk. She bit her bottom lip, put the thumb drive into her computer and clicked play on the footage. Twenty minutes in, she felt her adrenaline surge again. A man in a black hoody jumped the security turnstiles at 9:33 pm when the security guard had left his desk to do his rounds. She couldn't make out the man's face. He wore his hood over his head and a dark baseball cap was positioned low on his face, but he had a build similar to Jack's.

The room seemed to spin as Eve grappled with the enormity of the situation. She was a detective, trained to follow the evidence, to seek out the truth no matter how painful it might be. But she was also a woman in love, and love had a way of warping things.

What should I do?

Chapter 16

Eve opted to walk rather than take her car. The financial district was less than a fifteen minute walk away. She felt a tinge of anxiety twist in her gut. She tried to ignore Mitch's comments about Jack – how he could be The Poet, snuggling up to her just to get close to the case.

Eve sighed. Mitch had to be crazy, right? He wasn't in his right mind. Perhaps Jack had simply mixed up his office location, or maybe he had recently moved to Berkley Plaza and had forgotten to mention it. But then again, maybe Jack was hiding something.

Eve tried to keep her thoughts light-hearted. *Maybe I'll just show up and surprise him with role-play. I'll put him in handcuffs again. He loved that last time.* But Eve's thoughts had a way of bouncing off in all other directions.

Oh fuck, he's going to think I'm weird showing up like this, but I just want to ask him if he saw anything the day or night Paddy was killed. I want to gauge his reaction. That's fair enough, and we'll get to spend some time together on the city's clock. Fuck, I'm overthinking things again. But the guy in the hoody had a similar build to Jack.

Eve had never been to Jack's office before. His job rarely came up in conversation. In fact, the more Eve thought about it, the more she realised that Jack rarely talked about himself. And where did all of Jack's money come from? Psychologists make a good living, but Jack lived a lavish lifestyle. He drove a Porsche, had a yacht, lived in a fancy penthouse, and had a large watch collection. He always avoided the topic of his past or changed the subject when Eve asked about his family or pried into his childhood. But that wasn't strange, Eve thought, she did stuff like that too. The past can be painful, and some things should just stay locked away.

When Eve arrived at Berkley Plaza, she walked over to the security desk and said she was there to see Jack Lawson.

'What company is Jack with?' The security guard asked.

'Capital Clinic.'

'That's on the seventy-third floor,' the security guard said. 'When you exit the elevator, take a left, and you'll find the office at the end of the hallway.'

Eve glanced at her watch. It was close to 5 pm, and she wondered if Jack would still be there or if she should leave. It was foolish to show up like this, and her cheeks flushed with embarrassment, but some instinct urged her towards the elevator.

You're overthinking things. That could have been anyone jumping the barrier, and Jack wouldn't have needed to anyway, he could have used his access card. Okay, wow. Stop with the premature accusations.

Yet, nagging in those same thoughts, the darkness Eve had seen in Jack gnawed at her, twisting and churning in her stomach, blending with Mitch's comments. She didn't know why she was thinking like that. Maybe she was self-sabotaging their relationship. She'd done things like that before. As soon as things seemed too good to be true, she'd scramble for excuses until everything came crashing down.

The elevator doors opened on the seventy-third floor. Eve noted the corridor's impeccable tidiness, the smell of lavender and pine swarming her scenes. She wondered what she'd say. *Hey babe, why did you lie about your office, and oh yeah, did you jump the barrier here the night Paddy was murdered? Oh my God, that sounds so lame. I'll come off as insecure, and he'll think I'm a weirdo.*

Eve stood frozen as Jack's receptionist opened the glass door and smiled. 'Come in, are you here to see Dr. Lawson?'

'Is he free?'

'He should be,' Jess said. 'I don't recognise you as a client, and I've no appointment scheduled; may I ask why you're here?'

'I'm Detective Eve Salah,' Eve said, lifting her T-shirt to flash her badge.

'Detective?' Jess probed anxiously.

'I'm also Jack's girlfriend. I was in the neighbourhood and thought I'd drop in.'

'Eve,' Jess said, suddenly hugging her. 'It's so lovely to finally meet you. Jack talks about you all the time.'

'He does?' Eve asked.

'All positive,' Jess said, smiling. 'He seems so happy these days, not like...'

'Eve,' Jack said, appearing in reception. 'What are you doing here?'

'Working The Poet case,' Eve said. 'We think he may have used the Berkley Plaza emergency exit to enter the alley where Paddy was murdered. I was running all the names of people who work here and your name popped up.'

'Come into my office,' Jack said, and when he closed the door behind them, he patted Eve's bum.

'Don't,' Eve said, scanning his office.

She felt her legs go weak when Jack pinned her against the wall and began kissing her neck. 'Not now,' Eve said, pushing his head away. 'I need to ask you a few questions first.'

'Yes, detective.'

Eve smiled at the tease before shaking her head more seriously. 'You lied to me, Jack. You never told me you worked here, in this building. You said your office was on the other side of the financial district.'

'Did I?' Jack asked. 'I can't remember it coming up in conversation. Anyway, why does it matter?'

'Some guy jumped the barrier the night Paddy was murdered.'

'And...?'

'He looks like you,' Eve said, her voice trembling slightly. 'I also pulled up the suspect sketch from the night of Paddy's murder and there's a resemblance to you as well.'

'What the hell!' Jack said. 'You really think I could be a serial killer? Do you know how crazy that sounds?'

'Where were you the night Paddy was murdered?'

Jack rolled his eyes and laughed. 'Seriously?'

'Where were you the night Paddy was murdered?'

'Can you hear yourself?' Jack asked, turning to walk away.

'Jack, come back here.'

'If you really want to get into your detective shit, fine,' Jack said, turning around, his eyes as big as saucers. 'I was playing Call of Duty until like 3 am that night. You can pull a record of my log history if it helps. I ordered food around ten. Here,' Jack said, pulling out his phone and clicking into the DoorDash app. 'Look for yourself.'

Eve scrolled through his order history. Most of the recent orders were meals they had shared, and Eve felt strange and foolish, standing there accusing the man she loved of being a serial killer. She scrolled her way to the night Paddy was murdered, and sure enough, at 10:03 pm, Jack had ordered a Pad Thai from a local restaurant.

'Well, do you see the food order?' Jack asked coldly. 'I think it was Thai food or something. I remember the night well. I was waiting in the lobby for another game of Call of Duty when I looked at my phone and was like *Holy Fuck someone was murdered close to where I work.* If you still don't believe me, contact Activision, they'll pull my account history of the night Paddy died.'

It was relief Eve felt at first and then a wave of embarrassment flushing over her cheeks. She wanted the ground to swallow her, staring at her feet, her tummy a little queasy.

'Apophenia,' Jack said as Eve handed him back his phone. 'It's where we detect patterns that aren't really there. You see me in the suspect sketch when initially you didn't. You're overthinking things again or must be having doubts about us.'

Eve felt as though the room closed in around her. She had always prided herself on her ability to read people, to see through their lies. But Jack was impossible to read, to work out, and she wanted to scream with confusion.

'The Forensic Linguist said the killer would try to get close to the case, and we met the night after Paddy was murdered.'

'I met you randomly in a bar. How can you be even thinking this?' Jack asked, shaking his head. 'Mitch put you up to this, didn't he?'

'Why would you say that?'

'He came here a while back,' Jack said, shaking his head. 'He thinks I'm The Poet. I can understand him projecting onto me, but not you. Grief does horrible things to people. They want to tear everything down to their level. He probably looks at you, happy and hopeful of the future, while he drinks himself to death. Or maybe he just wants to screw you and I'm getting in the way of that.'

'Don't be crude, Jack.'

'You said his wife wants a divorce, that he's screwing some witness. Maybe he wants to screw you too.'

'It's not like that,' Eve said.

'Maybe he thinks you're giving off some signal.'

'I'm not.'

'Look,' Jack said, touching Eve's shoulders. 'I've treated patients like Mitch before; it starts out with paranoia, and reality becomes a slippery slope after that. All I'm saying is to be careful of him and don't believe everything he says. The man needs help. You should inform Chief Cutler just in case something bad happens.'

'Like what?'

Jack hugged Eve and kissed her forehead. 'Look into my eyes,' Jack said. 'Ask me what you came here to ask me.'

'I feel stupid now,' Eve said. 'But...I don't know. I have a weird feeling. I've seen your dark side.'

'Ask me,' Jack said. 'Judge for yourself.'

Eve raised her eyes to Jack's intense stare. 'Are you The Poet?'

'No,' Jack said, not blinking. 'I'm not The Poet, and I'm sorry you have doubts. I can't imagine the dissonance you must be feeling right now. You overthink things, and I'm a little hurt that you even have to ask that question, but I know you're not to blame. This is Mitch's doing.'

Eve saw sincerity in Jack's eyes. Sure, he had a dark side, but that didn't mean he was a serial killer. She knew Jack really loved her. He wouldn't hurt her like that. It was all Mitch's fault, prodding her with doubts, charging at her with his scrum of conspiracies. Maybe the guy jumping the barrier didn't look like Jack. Maybe it was all in her head. And suspect sketches are always way off anyway. People sometimes see what they want to see.

'I believe you,' Eve said. 'Oh my God, I feel so stupid.'

Jack held Eve in his arms and lay her head against his chest. 'I don't think you're stupid. But I worry you have doubts about us. That you're making all this up or finding patterns that aren't really there just because you don't feel the same way as I do. I love you to bits, babe. If you truly loved me, you wouldn't have these doubts. You get that, right?'

'I do love you,' Eve said. 'I'm sorry, I shouldn't have let Mitch get into my head.'

'It's okay,' Jack said. 'I'll finish up here and you can make it up to me over dinner.'

'I can think of a better way to make it up to you,' Eve said, biting the bottom of her lip.

'I like the sound of that,' Jack said, walking over and locking his office door.

Chapter 17

Early in his career, Mitch had flown to Boston to attend a seminar on high-functioning criminal psychopathy. The FBI profiler mentioned that those offenders were the toughest to catch. Calm killers who run a thousand iterations, who plan obsessively, calculate every outcome and only leave clues to tease a little danger. They're always in control, until the point where their narcissism usurps their faculties of self-preservation, until their need for mass recognition evolves at a greater velocity than their desire to go undetected.

Soundbites from that seminar occurred to Mitch many times throughout July. Jack was young. He was only getting started. He wouldn't get reckless, not yet. Mitch would have to catch Jack by other means, by bending the rules, by sacrificing everything. People like Lawson didn't accidentally stumble into serial murder, Mitch thought. It was as much a mental journey as it was a physical one. Like all serial killers, Mitch knew, the very seed of evil sprouts between the furrows of a fantasy. The desire to act physically infects every thought until the pressure becomes unbearable. A demon slowly emerges from the chrysalis of a human shell, ready to unleash its hellscape.

But why? But what's the fantasy here? What's the turn-on?

Ever since visiting Jack at his office, Mitch had started keeping close tabs on Jack's social ebb and flow. He knew that by studying the minutiae of Lawson's life, a sideways clue would appear. And so to start, Mitch checked out surveillance equipment from the forensic department and set the spyware up across from the entrance to Lawson's condo. For three days, Mitch watched the live stream on his phone via a weblink until a teenager saw it pinned to the telephone pole and hauled it home. Mitch felt like giving up after that, drinking more than ever and doubling his Oxy use. Emotion didn't really reach him, only impulse, only a slippery intuition that drew him deeper into the dark, shadowy littorals of Lawson's life.

Mitch's obsession saw him withdraw from his family more and more. He no longer cared about his marriage, his children or the ensuing divorce proceedings. And things took a dark turn when Mitch's son ran into their garage after a baseball one morning and found Mitch passed out on the floor amid a sea of violent crime scene photos.

His son's scream almost shook the tiles from the roof.

Judy ran to see what had happened and found their son cowering in the corner of the garage, his eyes shut tightly, tears streaming down his face. Mitch, delirious from drink, crawled along the floor, screaming at his son, thinking that he was Jack. Judy grabbed her son and ran for the kitchen, swiftly locking the door behind her.

'Leave!' Judy roared when Mitch knocked on the door.

'Sorry,' Mitch said, slurring his words. 'I must've been having a nightmare. Who's in there with you, Juds? Is Jack there?'

'Pack your shit up and leave, Mitch. Go live with your whore.'

'Who's in there with you?' Mitch shouted.

'Leave now or I'll call the cops. I'm done with you, Mitch.'

Mitch rented a dank, roach-infested apartment after that. It was furnished with little more than a dusty mattress and the cheap plastic deck chair Mitch had brought from his garage. The faded red carpet was full of tears and stains, and underneath, the rickety floorboards creaked day and night, reminding Mitch of his childhood home and the feeling that ghosts were moving about, watching him from the umbra. The main focal point, spread across the living room wall, was a photo of Jack's face, surrounded by dozens of news clippings, maps, and witness testimonies, all connected by arrows and scribbled notes.

Mitch was trying to build evidence against Jack, something provable that he could take to Chief Cutler. He sat down on his white deck chair and ran an online search for any murder in the past ten years that had a poem left at the crime scene. Apart from the Toronto murders, there was only one other case in Rochester, New York: the brutal slaying of Rachel and Alex Fontaine.

Mitch's eyes widened as he pressed play on the local news report clip on YouTube.

In the quiet hours after midnight, tragedy struck a peaceful Rochester neighbourhood as Rachel and Alex Fontaine were found brutally murdered in their own home, following what was supposed to be a joyful celebration of Rachel Fontaine's 40th birthday. Family and friends were left devastated as they attempted to comprehend the violent events that unfolded at the Fontaine residence. The couple reportedly returned to their home around 1 am, after enjoying a family dinner. However, their night took a sinister turn when an unknown assailant gained entry to their home. Crime scene investigators are meticulously combing through the residence, though the perpetrator left few traces behind. In a particularly harrowing display, Rachel Fontaine was discovered tortured and hanging from the second-floor balustrade. Her husband, Alex, was found in the adjacent kitchen, his body showing the marks of a frenzied attack. Neighbours reported no unusual activity, and a thorough canvas of the area has yielded few clues. There was one chilling piece of evidence left behind by the killer: a cryptic poem pinned to Rachel's chest.

I robbed the harp of its heartbeat,
snatched its soft, silky strings and tied a big ol' noose,
found the brightest flower I could find,
then pinned down that creature so it couldn't wriggle loose.
And when dawn came with its bright sobering light,
hanging there at merry morn,
was the pale rotten sight
of my jealous rotten scorn.
With praying hands,
so tightly bound with grace,
I begged God to forgive me of my sin,
And resurrect the pretty flower,
so I could take its precious life all over again.

'It's him,' Mitch said, lighting a cigarette, inhaling deeply and casually flicking the ash on the carpet. 'Same style of poem. How has this not been connected?'

Mitch lay back in his deck chair, watching rings of smoke rise toward the mouldy ceiling. 'I just need to prove it. I need to get closer. I need evidence.'

After this revelation, Mitch began taking notes, tracking Lawson's every move, going days without sleep or food.

Wednesday, August 8, 6:50pm: Sat in car outside Jack's condo
Jack returns home from work and chats with the concierge man for 12 minutes and 9 seconds. Lots of laughter. Twice, Jack rests his hand on the man's shoulder, showing him something on his phone. What are they talking about? Sports? GET CLOSE TO THE CONCIERGE MAN, HE KNOWS MORE ABOUT LAWSON THAN MOST.

The following day, Mitch brushed his hair and teeth, changed his jeans, and rummaged through a black sack, searching for a clean t-shirt. He looked at himself in the cracked bathroom mirror; his teeth tinged with yellow, his beard ragged as a bird's nest. There were more grey hairs than there used to be. More wrinkles, too. His face looked gaunt, his cheekbones jutting out like tight knuckles, his eyes sunken like impact craters. Mitch rarely ate breakfast anymore; instead, he gobbled down two Oxy tablets and a glass of bourbon before leaving his apartment.

Mitch barely noticed the warm summer air on his skin, walking for half a block to where his rusting Honda Accord was parked on the side street. The previous week, he had purchased the car from Craigslist after drunkenly crashing his last car into a cruiser in the precinct parking lot.

'Give me your badge and gun,' Chief Cutler said afterwards, sighing loudly, looking down on Mitch as a paramedic stitched a gash on his eyebrow.

'No,' Mitch said. 'I'm too close. I know who The Poet is.'

'Can you prove it, Mitch? Is there evidence?'

'Almost, another few days,' Mitch said, slurring.

'No, you don't have another few days. You're a disgrace to the force,' Chief Cutler said, putting out her hand. 'Badge and gun, Mitch.'

'Go to hell,' Mitch said, and when Chief Cutler motioned Detective Ramirez to take Mitch's badge, a fight broke out. Both detectives wrestled on their feet until Mitch punched Ramirez out in front of all the other officers.

Drunk and humiliated, Mitch attempted to run but tripped over an extension cord, hitting his head on the corner of a desk, causing the gash on his eyebrow to burst apart and bleed onto the carpet.

But that was all in the past, Mitch thought as he revved the engine of his rusty Honda. He didn't really care about losing his badge. He still knew how to catch a killer and that's all that mattered. He felt as if his mind was constantly scribbling. Weaving clues like wicker. Threading together theories. His obsession with Jack hardening like grease in a drainpipe.

Twenty minutes later, Mitch parked close to Jack's condo, killed the ignition and lit a cigarette. He stared forward for a moment, keeping a peripheral watch on the sidewalk in case Jack strolled by.

Coast is clear.

Mitch exited his Honda and hurried across the street, looking over his shoulder, practising what he'd say. He took a deep breath and entered the main atrium of Jack's building. It had a minimalistic vibe. The ceiling stretched three stories high, upwardly vast and slightly daunting. Sunlight poured in through the tall glazing, causing Mitch to squint and raise his hand to his eyes.

'Can I help you?' asked Tom – the young man sitting behind the concierge desk.

'Hi,' Mitch said, looking around awkwardly, 'the name's Lance. My wife and I are thinking of moving back to the city. This location is our top pick.'

'Okay,' Tom said in a drawn-out manner.

'My wife's the nervous type. She sent me here to get a feel for the place. Would you mind?'

'Sure, go ahead, buddy. It's a lovely area, close to the Rogers Centre, the CN Tower, and less than a five-minute walk to Marina Quay West if you're the yachty type, but I'll warn you now; these units are pricey. I mean hella pricy. Any condo on the first five floors will set you back five grand a month, the sixth floor is penthouses only, four of them, and they come in at upwards of nine grand a month. These are rental properties only, so if you're looking to purchase, you're in the wrong place, buddy.'

'Okay,' Mitch said. 'The penthouses come recommended by a friend of ours. Jack...'

'Jack Lawson?' Tom probed excitedly. 'I know Jack. He's a great guy. A big Blue Jays fan like me. We plan on going to a game soon, then out on his boat for a few beers. Just sit back and take in the view of the whole city. Sunset, beers, and maybe a few chicks – that's my sorta day.'

'Boat?' Mitch quizzed. 'I didn't realise Jack had one.'

'Well, it's more of a yacht,' Tom said boastfully. 'A Bavaria R55 with a Volvo IPSdrive unit and speeds up to thirty-four knots. Pearl white, sleek lines. Oh man, you should see it.'

'Sounds nice,' Mitch said blankly.

'Nice?' Tom said, laughing. 'It's more than nice, buddy. It's the ultimate chick magnet. F-you money, if you know what I'm saying.'

Mitch nodded, though he didn't know what Tom was saying and didn't really care. 'Where do you keep something like that?'

'Marina Quay West,' Tom said, smiling. 'Jetty thirty-three; Jack's lucky number.'

'I'll have to check it out,' Mitch said, turning to leave. He had a new clue. A new gear to shift his day into at full throttle. He felt the stirring of something alive inside again, the echoes of an old rush, and he would stop at nothing to catch Jack – when the ruination of his life staked the claim of *worth it,* and his obsession returned a small but tangible dividend.

Chapter 18

Marina Quay West was empty as Mitch strolled down the main promenade. Small sailboats bobbed back and forth on the water, while in the distance, mist was forming on the horizon as the hot sun glared down upon the water's surface. Mitch scanned the boats, looking for Jetty 33. He didn't know what a Bavaria R55 looked like but guessed it would be big and bold, just like Jack. His eyes focused on the biggest boat; beside it, a pole was emblazoned with the number 33.

Mitch glanced over his shoulder, checking to see if anyone was around, determined to look inside and rummage around for clues. Walking into the marina, Mitch had noticed several surveillance cameras but reasoned they would only be checked if something was stolen or damaged. This was Mitch's chance. He stubbed out his cigarette, and as he went to climb aboard, his heart quickened and his jaw dropped.

Poetry In Motion was printed in large black letters on the bow.

'Poetry In Motion,' Mitch murmured, shaking his head.

Pushing that thought aside, Mitch glanced over his shoulder again before stepping onto the wooden decking at the stern. Two main doors led into the cabin. Mitch tried to slide them open, but they were locked. He rooted through his pockets, looking for his lockpick kit, which he carried on him as routinely as a flask of bourbon and a pack of smokes. He manoeuvred a small pick and tweezer into the lock, shimmying them from side to side until he heard a click.

The sliding doors opened into a large living area with cream-coloured couches on either side and a low-rise marble table running down the centre aisle. Mitch scanned the room slowly, finding it odd to see a bottle of champagne chilling in a stainless steel bucket with two champagne flutes nearby. He ignored the voice in his head telling him to leave, instead walking towards the end of the cabin, where another door opened into a bedroom. Mitch peeked inside. The room was darker than the living area, with only narrow slits as windows. A bed rose in the centre of the room, propped up by a small base underneath, giving it a floating effect. White wardrobes and storage shelves flanked either side of the room with an ensuite bathroom to the left. Mitch snooped through the wardrobes and drawers, inspecting the white carpet and bed cover for specks of blood. A large painting hung on the wall. It wasn't much to look at, Mitch thought, just splashes of colour on a white canvas.

Slowly, an idea formed, and Mitch lifted the painting off the wall to find a small safe behind it. He ran his finger over the digital keypad, entering 0000. A failure beep sounded, and Mitch tried another combination, 1234. Again, a failure beep echoed around the room, and a message appeared on the digital screen above the keypad: *One attempt remaining.* Mitch pulled at his hair, trying to think, trying to force his mind to uncover some sequence of numbers that might crack the case.

It was too risky to guess again, Mitch reasoned, and as he went to remount the painting, a thought occurred. Tom had said Jack's lucky number was 33. Mitch's palms sweated as he struggled to block out the voice in his head telling him to leave.

'Screw it,' Mitch said, entering 3333 on the keypad.

A double beep sounded, and the safe's mechanism unlocked. Mitch's heart raced as he opened the door and tried to calm his breathing. Inside, there was a small, tattered notepad, dozens of Polaroid photographs, and a vintage, gold Day-Date Rolex watch with 'Clearwater' engraved on the back. Mitch had heard that name before; it was the company Paddy Fitzgerald had co-founded in Dublin.

Most of the Polaroids were slightly corrupted. Mitch rifled through the first few, looking at creepy images of people in Toronto, pictures of black sacks, private planes, a man out running, and a dingy living room. Another one showed two young children that looked like twins eating ice cream. The next showed a man sitting at a desk in a white shirt and navy tie, with a similar-looking Rolex watch on his wrist. Mitch turned his attention to the notepad next. The first page had a list of dates in chronological order moving down the page. Mitch recognised the second last entry. It was the date of Paddy Fitzgerald's murder.

Are all the date entries other victims?

Mitch was taken aback by the number of rows. He flipped through the next few pages, observing eerie drawings of women tied up and couples kneeling on the floor with blood pooled around their heads. He skipped to the last page. It was blank, but when Mitch turned it towards the light, he could vaguely make out an indentation at the bottom of the page, *Dark Finds.*

Mitch gasped, but before he had time to think, he heard Jack's voice on the stern.

'Come on,' Jack said. 'This will be our best trip yet, babe.'

'Just tell me where we're going,' Eve pleaded.

'Anywhere we like.'

Mitch's heart raced as he quickly remounted the painting and surveyed the room.

No, no, no.

He tiptoed into the ensuite, gently shutting the door behind him, trying to calm his breathing.

'Aw babe,' Eve said. 'You have champagne on arrival.'

'I had Pablo arrange it earlier, but he forgot to lock the door.'

'Aw, who cares, it's drink-o'clock.'

'I care,' Jack said sharply. 'One job and he screws it up. This yacht costs a lot, and he just leaves the door unlocked. Check the fridges; did he even stock them?'

Eve opened the fridge door and began listing out the contents.

'So, no bourbon?' Jack said once she'd finished.

'Don't see it, babe.'

'I want bourbon.'

'You're beginning to sound like Mitch.'

'Yikes,' Jack said. 'Don't compare me to him. I don't want to hear that weirdo's name again this weekend.'

'Aw, he's not the worst.'

'Don't make excuses for him. Didn't he crash into a cruiser pissed drunk?'

'Yeah,' Eve said a little sadly. 'But at least he was better than the new guy they have me paired with. Detective Hazzard is the laziest person I've ever met. He's so given up. He just doesn't care anymore.'

'So, I take you still haven't identified the guy jumping the barrier?'

'No,' Eve said. 'He went into the stairwells and wasn't seen after that.'

'Well, as long as I'm not under suspicion.'

'Not one bit,' Eve said. 'I'm never letting Mitch get into my head again, I promise. Anyway, I'll shut up about work. We have five days off and I want to have some fun.'

'There'll be no fun without bourbon. Come on, there's an LCBO around the corner.'

Mitch listened as their voices trailed off into the distance. He waited a few moments before sneaking out of the ensuite, through the living room and back onto the jetty. He kept his head down as he walked briskly along the promenade, heading back toward his rusty Honda, his heartbeat racing in his chest.

Mitch regretted not walking out and showing Eve what he'd found in Jack's safe. Everything had happened so quickly, and Mitch wondered if Eve was covering something up? Who was the guy jumping the barrier? What was all that about? Mitch knew Eve wouldn't listen to him no matter the gravity of evidence, that love corrupts, that even if he produced a photo of Jack rapt in the act of strangulation, Eve would pass it off as a sex game gone awry. Mitch knew he needed hard evidence. Perhaps all the dates in the notepad corresponded to other murders, but Mitch struggled to recall a single one. He wondered how Clearwater and Paddy Fitzgerald were connected. Paddy's murder had meant something to Jack. It was revenge, but for what?

Look into Clearwater, Mitch scribbled in his notepad. *Clearwater will crack this case right open.*

Chapter 19

Jack and Eve spent the weekend sailing around Lake Ontario, filled with wanderlust, moving up along the coastal towns of Oshawa, Port Hope, and Brighton, eventually dropping anchor at Amherst Island to watch a fireworks show at dusk.

'It's magical,' Eve said as Jack held her tightly from behind, watching bursts of colour brighten up the darkening sky.

'I organised it especially for you.'

'Really?' Eve asked.

'I promised you an unforgettable trip.'

'Oh my God,' Eve said, turning to Jack, teary-eyed. 'No one has ever done anything like this for me before.'

'No one has ever made me feel the way you do,' Jack said, kissing her forehead. 'I promise you: you'll have fireworks exploding from your chest every day with me.'

'I love you,' Eve said, feeling her cheeks tighten with happiness.

'I love you too. Every day feels real when I'm with you. You've awakened a side of me that I never knew existed. You're like a lamp in the darkness, and I the moth, outmastered by some ancient instinct I don't understand or know what to do with. I've never had that feeling before.'

'What?' Eve joked. 'Something more than a one-night stand?'

'Connection,' Jack said, smiling. 'The feeling that I can be my true self around you. When I was younger, I flirted with the idea of love. I was reading a lot of Greek mythology, but the more I read, the more I realised that the introduction of love in a Greek story was merely a prelude, a stage for tragedy to strike. It shocked me that people, in all their vast capabilities, chose to squander after love's finality: pain, suffering, and punishment. But you're different. You're not something to be hurt or punished.'

'Something to be cuddled,' Eve said.

'The animal waif finding heat again.'

'What?'

'Fragments reforming back together, a tragedy worth believing in. You had a messed-up childhood, I did too, and yet here we stand, fully capable of love, frost-bound yet kept alive by each other's warmth.'

'Is that the bourbon talking?' Eve asked.

'No. You've awoken something inside me, something pure and freeing and loaded with love.'

'I like hearing this side of Jack Lawson.'

'The violin playing heavy on his heartstrings?'

'I wanna see more of him,' Eve said, turning back to look at the fireworks. 'You're eventually letting me in, babe.'

Silence was scarce that weekend. But standing there watching the fireworks bloom along the skyline, they regarded it as prismatic, allowing each to show off their different colours – the darkening twilight lit up beautifully by a splash of hopeful romance. Suddenly, everything seemed strange and unfamiliar to Eve. Her fifteen-year-old-self could never have dreamed of this life: standing on a luxury yacht at dusk, drinking expensive champagne, sailing to God-knows-where next in the warm embrace of the man she loved. Gone were the anxieties and trepidations that oozed down her brain stem like wax melting down along the sides of a candle, clumping at the bottom in some grotesque shape. Stroke by blissful stroke, Jack was painting a new version of Eve, one she had not foreseen and one that made her giggle all the time for no apparent reason. There were whole days where Eve felt liquefied by love. Where she felt she floated like a bubble along an orgy of decisions that always seemed to make her smile. A great drama was playing out between the chemicals in her brain. The old Eve had fallen like a statue and crashed against the sharp edges of her past. And from the rubble of the old, a new Eve Salah emerged.

They drank late into the night, listening to operatic music. Eve felt shaken to tears as Jack spun her around the stern, exultant and free, like sea birds. It felt good to take a breather and lie down together, gazing up at the stars, ascribing meaning to their shapes. A thick mist formed on the water that night as they cuddled up in bed, the underwater lights shining outward, making the yacht resemble a glowing orb in a sea of black ink.

The next morning, Jack handed Eve a mimosa as she walked out onto the stern, rubbing sleep from her eyes. 'Pancakes will be ready shortly,' Jack said. 'Grab a seat.'

'Thanks, babe. Where are we off to next?'

'It's a surprise,' Jack said, swatting the air with his spatula (or, as Eve liked to call it, his spatchy-spatch).

'Give me a little clue.'

'It's a secret island. We'll have to drop anchor and swim to get there.'

Eve beamed with excitement. 'Last night was fun,' she said. 'It was nice to hear you open up. You never speak of your past, and I know nothing about your family.'

'Not much to tell,' Jack said, carrying the plate of pancakes to the table.

'Really?'

'I told you before my family died in a car crash when I was little. I was shipped over to Toronto afterwards to live with my aunt. The rest is history.'

'But you lived in Ireland, right?'

'I really can't remember it; I was too little.'

'Not one memory?'

'My mind erased them all,' Jack said distantly. 'The hurt was too heavy to hold on to, I guess.'

'I want to know more.'

'You never talk about work,' Jack said. 'A beautiful young woman around all those middle-aged men.'

'Are you jealous, babe?'

'Curious.'

'You have nothing to worry about. I don't even know if I want to stay in homicide anymore. PI work pays better and has fewer hours.'

'When did all this come on?' Jack asked. 'I thought you loved your job.'

'Things just ain't the same anymore with Mitch gone, and I don't think he'll be coming back either. The guys at the station reckon Mitch has completely lost it. It hurts to hear them laughing about him. The names they call him are horrible. They never liked Mitch, but they respected him at least. Now they just think of him as some drunk bum. Chief Cutler will never let him back.'

'Really?'

'No way,' Eve said mournfully. 'She's furious. Before Mitch got suspended, he checked out some really expensive surveillance equipment and never returned it. Supposedly, it got stolen, but who knows? The guys think he sold it for Oxy. They found like ten empty bottles when they cleared out his locker.'

'Ah, enough about Mitch and his drama,' Jack said, sitting in beside Eve. 'Time to dig into these pancakes.'

~~~

Jack and Eve spent the morning sailing toward a small island on the US side of Lake Ontario. Eve sat beside Jack in a large, leather bucket seat, drinking mimosas and checking the navigation equipment from time to time. The water felt smooth as glass as Jack motored on at full throttle. He seemed slightly aloof. His mind was elsewhere, back in Toronto, wondering if Mitch had captured anything on the surveillance equipment. Jack's memory was meticulous, almost photographic. He retraced his movements over the prior few weeks, wondering how he could have missed Mitch lurking close by.

An unsettling thought began gnawing when Jack remembered that the door of the yacht had been left unlocked the morning prior. 'Can you steer for a few minutes?' he asked Eve. 'I need to make a quick call.'

'I don't really know how,' Eve said as Jack hurried to the bedroom to check the safe. The contents weren't the way Jack had left them, and the Polaroids were in the wrong order. Jack sat on the bed and rang Pablo.

'Hello, Mr. Lawson,' Pablo answered.

'Hi Pablo. Did you leave the boat unlocked yesterday morning?'

'No, no, Mr. Lawson. I locked it up, I'm sure.'

'Did you see anyone hanging around yesterday morning?'

'No, but I can check the cameras.'

'Okay, call me back if you find anything.'

'Yes, Mr. Lawson.'

Chapter 20

The weather was hot and humid when they dropped anchor less than half a mile from a small island with a sandy shoreline. Eve changed into a red bikini and tied her hair with a bobbin tie. 'Okay, we're here,' Eve said, her caramel skin glistening in the sunlight. 'What's the plan, babe?'

'Diving,' Jack said, smiling back at her.

Eve looked nervous. She'd never dived before and felt alarmed by all the equipment Jack had strewn across the stern.

'You okay?' Jack asked.

'What if something happens to us?' Eve said, her arms wrapped around her tummy.

'Like what?'

'Like I get tangled up, lose you, or come up too quickly and get the bends.'

'Sounds exciting, right?'

'I'm serious, Jack. How many times have you done this before?'

'Never, but I've watched lots of YouTube videos. I know what I'm doing.'

Eve laughed nervously. 'Why the hell are we going diving in the middle of nowhere when neither of us has ever done it before? Don't we need an instructor or something?'

'I thought it would be exciting.'

'Or deadly.'

They settled for snorkelling instead, with their feet clad in long flippers and their faces covered with an Aqua Lung Smart Snorkel. The water felt cold at first. Eve threaded the gentle chop waiting for Jack to join her. She plunged her head below the surface and looked around for fish. Just a vast darkening abyss lay beneath. She remembered how her father had taken her swimming when she was a girl, a frightening experience which seemed to consume her now. Flashbacks of Hanlan's Point Beach on Centre Island flooded her mind. How her father had pushed her down into the water, yelling at her to sink or swim. She remembered trying to pull herself up but instead sinking further and inhaling gulps of water. 'Sink or swim!' her father had shouted. 'Adapt. Life will devour you if you don't, girl.'

She remembered everything going black after that, waking up sometime later as her father performed chest compressions and blew air into her mouth. 'I won't always be here to save you,' he shouted as her eyes flickered open. 'No one will, you hear me? No one.'

The noise of Jack jumping into the water broke Eve's reverie. 'We'll swim towards the island,' Jack said. 'Just follow me. There's supposed to be a shipwreck off the coast.'

'I don't do well in water, Jack. Stay close.'

'I will,' Jack said, pulling down his aqua mask and swimming ahead.

Eve's limbs felt heavy at first, trying to keep her tummy tight, using all the power in her legs to move her large flippers forward. She controlled her breathing, trying to offset some impending panic, trying to rid her mind of Hanlan's Point Beach.

She could see the trailing bubbles of Jack's flippers up ahead.

Stay present. Keep calm. Be in the moment.

Sunlight flickered through the water. Little bubbles sparkled like diamonds on the choppy surface. Eve drew calming breaths, feeling the soft undulations of water move between her fingers.

She flinched as a fish brushed by, tickling her leg, causing her whole body to shudder. A school of rainbow trout paced alongside her in unison. All of a sudden, Eve felt free, ascending, awestruck. The world had a wildness to it, a naturalness Toronto had hidden from her with its patchwork of monotony and obligation. Life in the big city just always seemed like one long-ass, monotonous day, repeating with only small variations. But Jack had changed all that, Eve thought. He made her feel alive in a way she had never felt before.

When Eve looked forward again, she noticed Jack had stopped and was pointing down towards the rising shore. As she got closer, she saw what he was pointing at: a sunken shipwreck around five meters down on the lake floor. Taking a deep breath, Eve followed Jack, exploring the wreck for nearly half an hour, only surfacing to take deep breaths before submerging again, rubbing their fingers along the barnacles and algae that covered the hull. Half-crushed beer cans were littered around the wreck, a short shovel had been planted upright, and a faded American flag collapsed along a pole, shuddering in the gentle current. Coloured fish drifted by, trailing tiny bubbles, and as though some miracle had been performed, Eve no longer felt afraid of water. She felt born of it. Cast anew by something gentle and warm, at times, brutal and crushing.

Emerging from the water, they flopped down on the sandy beach, smiling and panting heavily. There were no other people around, just white sand, tall trees, and birds circling overhead. Nothing had ever given Eve the rush she felt now, lying back against the sand, looking up at the clouds gathering in the sky. The weather was changing quickly: white clouds turning dark, a grey mist and downpour moving along the lake towards the shore. And then Eve felt it, hot drops of rain gently landing on her face, mixing with the hot tears rolling down her cheekbones. Eve felt she belonged in the moment, a part of a world far larger than her past.

Toronto, the Toronto that stirred with so many echoes of her childhood, seemed faded, washed away, sinking towards the lake bed like some huge wreck of past trauma.

'What should we call it?' Jack asked.

'What?' Eve asked breathlessly.

'This island. It's ours, there's no one else around.'

'Paradise,' Eve said, sitting up, closing her eyes, and feeling the hot rain tickle her arms and legs. 'We should keep sailing until we reach Sydney and start a new life there. There's nothing left for me in Toronto, Jack, only bad memories. Everything's so messed up; I don't want to go back.'

'I feel the same.'

'Really?'

'You're all that matters,' Jack said. 'Wherever you go, I go.'

'Then let's go to Australia,' Eve said excitedly. 'It's always been my dream, ever since I was a girl. To live down under, in an opposite world, in an alternate reality.'

'I like the sound of that.'

'We sell everything and jump on a plane,' Eve said. 'I wouldn't even bring a bag, just the clothes on my back. I could work as a PI, and you could set up a new practice there.'

'It might take a few weeks to get everything in order,' Jack said, toying with the idea.

'Just imagine,' Eve exclaimed, jumping atop Jack, 'us walking down Bondi Beach, hand in hand, without a care in the world. No, in a new world.'

'A fresh start,' Jack said, curling his body upwards to kiss her.

'Where the past will never find us,' Eve said between kisses.

They spent the latter part of that afternoon exploring the island, moving inward, over foothills, ducking beneath branches and picking wild berries. Nature bloomed in abundance. Cicadas squealed from leafy branches. An orchestra of animal and insect noises drummed eerily. All forms of life seemed to be summoned to watch their every footstep. They felt like the last people on the planet, moving through a new realm of psychology, a secret history where suffering did not exist. Nothing mattered, only their next step, their island, and the heat of each other's proximity.

Finally, the scrub grew sparse, and the trees parted as they reached the other side of the island. The view was much the same. A vast expanse of water with no signs of human life. They moved further along the coast, around small cliffs and rocky shorelines.

'Look over there,' Jack said, pointing to a large cove carved into a cliff.

Eve's eyes widened as she looked up at the large limestone archway. 'Oh my God. It looks unreal.'

The rain had worsened. Thunder boomed all around them as blue veins of lightning flashed across the lake.

'Let's find some shelter until this storm blows over,' Jack suggested.

Twenty meters in, the water gave way to sand, and smooth limestone slabs rose in all directions. Daylight faded back towards the entrance as they paused to rest. Jack took two beers out of his backpack and twisted off the caps.

'To us,' he said, toasting Eve.

'To Bondi, our new beginning.'

The idea of Bondi grew larger every time Eve said the word aloud, as though some childhood storybook was becoming real. She had always felt like a spectator, a girl watching life from the sidelines, shackled there, unable to move any closer. Eve wished she'd known her mother, that she hadn't died in childbirth, that she could see her daughter now, in the echoey twilight of a cave, a woman moved breathlessly by love.

'I've got another surprise,' Jack said with a boyish smirk. 'Close your eyes.'

'Okay,' Eve said suspiciously. 'But don't scare me.'

She could hear Jack rummaging in his backpack as she stood stiffly, with her arms hanging awkwardly by her sides.

'I've been waiting to find the right spot,' Jack said. 'Open your eyes.'

Silhouetted in silvery light, Eve saw Jack kneeling on one knee with a ring clamped between his thumb and index finger. 'We only get one life, and I want to spend mine with you. You're like a bright light making all the darkness inside me disappear. I never want to spend a day apart from you. Marry me, babe.'

Eve's lips moved, but no words came out. Every fibre of her being felt shaken out of orbit by a few words, by a gesture, and Eve collapsed to her knees, touching Jack's face with her hands. 'Yes,' she muttered breathlessly and then again a little louder. 'Yes, yes, babe. Oh my God, yes!'

In the twilight of the cave, the world seemed to tilt right off its axis. They made love against a stone slab, with seawater rustling at their ankles and the whoosh of waves echoing all around them. Jack hoisted Eve into the air and splashed her down upon him. She felt the sweet current of emotion running through them, biting the bottom of her lip with the wildness of an animal in ecstasy. And in the silence afterwards, as they lay together, the truth of the moment would live on, inexorably, like myth.

Chapter 21

Eve lay on the bed, staring at the ceiling, with her sandy legs dangling over the side.

What the hell have I just done?

She loved Jack but knew so little about him, the real him, the man beneath the charm. The sides Jack chose to show Eve sometimes scared her in the same way her father had, the intensity in their eyes, the darkness brooding under every action, the question mark stamped across their souls.

Eve shook her head.

Stop overthinking things. You're happy. This is what you've always wanted. Jack loves you. Let yourself be happy for once.

Jack smiled at her when he emerged from the ensuite bathroom, a puff of steam spreading through the room like a cloud. 'Go get your shower, I know a place where we can celebrate.'

It was nightfall when they motored into Sodus Point marina, a small coastal town on the US side of Lake Ontario. Jack slowed the vessel to a few knots as he edged closer to the slip. The marina consisted mainly of small sailboats and old fishing trawlers. Locals watched from the bars along Greig Street, surprised to see such a large vessel manoeuvre through the basin.

'We just got engaged!' Eve whooped, stepping onto the decking, stirring a few cheers from the locals who raised their beers.

'She's beautiful,' one man said, his eyes fixated on the yacht's sleek lines. 'What is she? Sixteen meters? Bigger?'

'Five foot five,' Jack responded, smiling at Eve, who looked stunning that night: her bronze skin glowing in the soft lamplight, her slender body dressed in a pink denim mini skirt, a bone-white crop top, and white high heels. 'Where's good to grab a drink?' Jack asked one of the locals.

'Captain Pete's,' said the man. 'Best beer in town.'

'Is it far?'

'Around a two-minute walk that way,' the man said, pointing down Greig Street.

'I can't believe we just got engaged,' Eve said excitedly.

'This feels like the best day ever,' Jack added before his phone began ringing in his pocket. 'I need to take this,' Jack said, walking away, his mood changing instantly.

'Hello Mr. Lawson,' Pablo said on the other end of the phone.

'What have you got for me?'

'Someone was on your boat. It's crazy, I think he picked the lock.'

'What did he look like?' Jack asked, his voice calm but chilling.

'Sending you some screenshots now.'

Jack instantly recognised Mitch in the pictures. His thoughts raced. Mitch had been on his yacht, rummaging through his safe, collecting evidence. 'Call me if you ever see that man hanging around again.'

'Yes, Mr. Lawson.'

'Thanks,' Jack said, ending the call.

'Everything okay?' Eve asked, noticing how dark Jack's eyes had grown.

'Yep,' Jack said, forcing a wide smile, taking Eve's hand again and walking towards Captain Pete's.

~~~

Captain Pete's was packed that night. Over a dozen Harley-Davidson motorcycles were parked outside, while inside, burly bikers paced about, chugging beers and jamming out to the rock music booming from a nearby jukebox. Other locals watched askance: hipsters in woolly caps, fishermen dressed in lumberjack plaid, jocks in leather football jackets.

Eve looked at Jack and laughed. 'Well, it ain't the Ritz, babe.'

'You wanna go someplace else?'

'Nah, let's get one here first. Their finest champagne for me.'

'Okay, try to grab a table,' Jack said, moving around all the lively bodies, making his way to the bar where a neon Coors Light sign flickered. Cigarette smoke filled the dimly lit bar. All types of animal heads hung on the walls: bear, moose, deer, and wolf. A small rowboat hung upside down from the ceiling, and nearby, a large statue of a pirate had a biker jacket draped across its back.

'Posh boy,' Jack heard one of the bikers sneer. He wasn't one for regrets, but standing there in cream chino shorts, a crisp white shirt, navy deck shoes, and a white Ralph Lauren jumper wrapped around his shoulders, he felt like an oddity amidst a sea of patchy leather and sweat-stained lumberjack shirts. Pushing the remark aside, Jack motioned to order drinks, but the barman ignored him each time and served the locals instead.

'Hey,' Jack eventually shouted. 'I've been waiting five minutes. Can I get a drink or what?'

The barman glanced at him blankly, eager to move on to the next customer, but Jack held his stare eerily. 'Fine,' the barman said, 'what do you want?'

'A pint of Coors and a bottle of your best champagne. Oh, and two flutes.'

The barman burst out laughing. 'Yo, yo,' he teased, putting on a show for the bikers standing around the bar. 'Posh boy wants a flute.'

A familiar rage formed in the pit of Lawson's stomach. A disorienting slope that normally tilted him towards some cruel act of violence. He stared intensely into the barman's eyes, smirking slightly, his knuckles turning white with anger.

'Give him a tampon instead,' a bloated biker mocked.

'Go back to the city,' another teased. 'You don't belong around here, kid.'

Unnerved by Lawson's sustained, penetrating stare, the barman tried to loosen the mood. 'Ain't got champagne, but we have white wine if that'll do? I'm told it tastes just as good, and I can throw in some tonic water to give it the bubbles.'

Lawson never spoke, only nodded, his face pale with rage, his eyes like saucers. The barman's hands held a slight tremor as he poured the wine. When he glanced at Jack again, it looked like his face had changed completely, distorted by some feral attention.

'That'll be nine bucks sixty,' the barman said, swallowing deeply.

Lawson held out a twenty, and when the barman went to take the note, Lawson tugged it back forcefully, causing the barman to startle.

'Take it,' Jack said snarling.

'Everything okay?' one of the bikers asked, stepping up to Jack.

Like the flick of a switch, Jack unpinned his stare and smirked at the barman. 'We're all good,' Jack said, placing the note on the counter. He tried to calm himself, walking back to Eve, imagining lifeless figures slumped over chairs, their necks slashed open. Bikers strewn across the floor, their skulls burst apart, bits of brain matter squidging underneath his deck shoes – best of all, the barman flayed and skinned and worn across his shoulders like a pelt.

'What took you so long?' Eve asked.

'The barman had to check the storeroom for champagne,' Jack said, trying to regain his composure. 'We had to settle for white wine and tonic water in a pint glass.'

Eve snorted. 'I've had worse.'

Jack tried to force a smile.

'Are you okay?' Eve asked. 'Your eyes look all weird.'

'I'm fine. This is the best day of my life.'

'Aww,' Eve said, curling out her bottom lip. 'This is the best day of my life, too.'

'To us,' Jack said, raising a toast.

They clinked glasses, and Eve grimaced at the first sip. 'It tastes like vinegar, but you're all the sweetness I need.'

Jack smiled at her remark.

'Okay,' Eve said, her eyes simmering with questions. 'So, when you were at the bar, I got thinking. Since I'm going to be your wife and all, I have to ask; where does all the money come from?'

Jack smiled again. 'I invested in Bitcoin early on and made a killing. All my clients are investment types. They tell me all sorts of insider knowledge – upcoming merges, IPOs, new product launches. I use our therapy sessions to game the market, not entirely legal either, but I squirrel everything away in offshore accounts so nothing will ever lead back to us.'

'How much are we talking about?' Eve asked nervously.

Jack's face tightened in thought. 'Roughly about twelve million liquid and another ten to fifteen in assets.'

Eve spat out her drink in shock. 'What the hell, babe!'

Jack felt confused by her reaction. 'What?'

'That's a lot of money.'

'I guess so.'

'Oh my God, we could travel the world a hundred times over on that, have a beachfront house in Bondi or a villa in Bali. We wouldn't even have to work. You get that, right? We could live off that money for the rest of our lives.'

'I never really thought about it, but yeah.'

'Why didn't you say anything about it before?'

Jack took a gulp of beer. 'It didn't seem to really matter. It's just money. It comes and goes. I was poor most of my life, and money didn't change much, not on the inside anyway.'

Eve appeared baffled by Jack's response, by the proverbial shrugging of his shoulders. The music had grown louder, and the locals a little rowdier. Jack tried to look calm, but the intensity in his eyes, and the crazed way he glared at the bikers, gave it all away.

'Are you okay?' Eve asked. 'Are you mad I asked about the money? I'm sorry. I was just curious. It's your money. You can do what you want with it. I just thought it would be exciting to disappear into some whirlwind adventure.'

Jack softened his stare and looked at Eve, smiling. 'It's our money, and we can do whatever the hell we please with it. I haven't travelled much and there are so many places I want to see with you.'

'Yay!' Eve exclaimed. 'Come on, let's get out of here before lasers shoot from your eyes.'

'Those fucking bikers,' Jack said sharply.

'You know how these small towns are. They don't like strangers, especially my big, sexy man outshining them all. Come on, we'll go.'

'I need to use the washroom first,' Jack said, standing up and chugging his beer. As he moved through the crowd, he heard one of the bikers jeer. 'I bet posh boy sits to piss.'

'Leaving that pretty girl alone,' sneered another.

As Jack stopped to glare, a drunk teenager stumbled forward, spilling a pint of beer down Jack's shirt. A few of the bikers cheered from the bar as Jack walked towards the restrooms, agitated and feral, prowling like a large, wounded cat. He felt humiliated in a way he'd almost forgotten, feeling bare and exposed, turning more nuclear with each passing frame. He headbutted the cubicle door and punched the walls before sitting down on the toilet, breathing heavily. He buried his fists deep into his pockets and screamed, resisting the urge to tear his shorts to shreds. There was graffiti all across the cubicle walls, biker musings, smiley faces with Xs for eyes, love hearts pierced by an arrow. He spotted a marker on the floor and picked it up, searching for a bit of white space to scribble on.

Dark Finds
August 2019
Body Count, 19
Lots more to come. On a break for a while, will start back soon.

Writing those words, Jack relived each murder in his head. They were his possessions now, like spent pieces of a board game, like change rattling in his pocket. He felt the urge to kill again, to trade his anger in for another's terror. He clawed at his face and bit down hard on his fist causing blood to ooze from his knuckles. He sucked the blood from the cut and spat it on the walls. Even when his eyes closed he could see his rage throbbing like a strobe light. His mask was crumbling, slipping from his grasp like an oyster off a spoon. The features of his face looked bleached with anger, his tongue flapping out his mouth trying to redirect the current of his thoughts. He just wanted everything to end, to take the earth in his hand and crush it like an egg.

When he walked back into the bar, two bikers were sitting beside Eve, harassing her as she shouted at them to 'go away.'

'Smell the dead men off that,' said a heavily tattooed biker, lifting his fist to Eve's nose.

Jack knew what happened next. His body calmed and his heartbeat slowed. He cracked his neck from side to side, and moved ritualistically, like a satanic priest about to summon a demon. Without hesitation, Jack picked up an empty pint glass and shattered it against the corner of the table. Swiftly, he stabbed the glass shards into a biker's eye socket and twisted until blood poured down the biker's face. Shocked onlookers cheered as Jack launched for the biker standing next to Eve, cracking his fist against the biker's nose, causing a fine red mist to splash Eve's bone-white crop top. The other bikers pounced on Jack as he lifted his hands to protect his face. They bruised up his flank with heavy punches and wild kicks. Jack had practised martial arts from an early age. He could handle himself, maybe take two or three, but not eight. He swung his fist and cracked the largest biker between the eyes. Yet the mob grew more frenzied as he struggled for an opening. From the corner of his eye, he saw Eve smash her pint glass over a biker's head. 'Back the fuck off,' she screamed.

There was a momentary lull when Lawson lunged for the broken pint glass and began slashing faces, swinging for jugulars and trying to take a few more eyes. The escalation in violence slowed the biker's flurry. They stood back nervously. Four of them slashed across the face, another unconscious on the floor.

'Come on,' Eve cried, grabbing Jack by the arm and moving for the exit.

Jack smiled and bowed to the bar, saying, 'A pleasure.'

Most of the locals would remember that night for the rest of their lives. But it wouldn't be the blood or gore they'd remember, but Jack Lawson's eyes, how his face seemed to morph into something they could only describe as demonic. The bikers refused to call the cops. They stomped about the bar, scared and bloodied, whooping and hollering, boasting about how they would find the *posh boy*, tie him to the back of their Harleys and drag him back to the city.

Chapter 22

Back on board the yacht, Eve remembered Jack moving with the swiftness of a rabid animal. She was still coming to terms with what had happened. Everything seemed so blurry. As though the border between a nightmare and reality had folded over, and events were trampling through without a screen of sanity. Eve sat beside Jack on the bridge, trying to catch her breath. When she licked her lips she tasted blood. When she put her hand to her chest to feel her heartbeat, it didn't feel like her own. It was only when they had left the marina that Eve spoke. 'My God, what the hell is wrong with your eyes?' Eve said cutting through the awkward silence. 'Your face looks weird, not like the Jack I know.'

'Happens from time to time,' Jack said, grinning at her with a black eye and busted lip. There was so much blood on his clothes he looked like he'd just come off the set of a horror movie.

'What the hell was that about, Jack? And don't smirk at me. I'm being serious.'

'Just restoring a little balance to the universe is all.'

'Enough with the smart remarks.'

'They were bullies,' Jack snarled. His eyes growing larger. 'And bullies need a beatdown. You, of all people, should understand that. You're going to be my wife. I need to protect you. When I came back from the washroom and saw those vermin sniffing around you, I lost it.'

'I didn't need protection,' Eve said hoarsely. 'I've dealt with ten times worse than them. You were just looking for an excuse to unleash whatever darkness was brewing up within you. I know you have a dark side, but that shit can't happen again, Jack. I don't want you getting carried away and killing someone. I'm only looking out for you.'

'I have tendencies,' Jack said, pushing the throttle to full speed.

'I know what you are,' Eve said nervously.

'What am I?'

'I'm a homicide detective, Jack. I've been around psychopaths before. It doesn't scare me, but that crazy violence does.'

'I've never felt anything my entire life,' Jack confessed in a slow, seductive tone. 'It's like my mind can't grasp emotion. My soul feels numb. My eyes feel flooded with darkness. I latch onto people and use them as fuel, like a flame leaping from one tragedy to the next, desperate for some instinct to drown me out.' Jack paused and looked at Eve. 'But you've changed all that,' he added in a softer tone. 'You've changed everything.'

'How?' Eve asked. Tears forming in her eyes.

'I don't know how to express it with words. It's like the shadow inside of me is disappearing. I love you. I want to spend the rest of my life with you.'

'I'm scared you can't feel love, Jack.'

'I can. I do, for you.'

Eve wiped tears from her eyes.

'Do you still want to be with me?' Jack asked. 'With someone like me? And be honest, Eve, if we're going to spend the rest of our lives together you can't have doubts about me, about us.'

'I should take the loss and run,' Eve said, breathing sorely. 'Falling in love with you is like bleeding into a shark's mouth, and I can't help myself. Life would be so dull without you, almost unbearable, and I don't know which fate is worse.'

'If we end it here,' Jack warned, 'we'll shatter into a million pieces and spend the rest of our lives trying to piece ourselves back together with bad decisions. Everything will feel like an imitation. Fuck that,' Jack said, his smile offered up as an olive branch. 'I love you, and I'll prove it to you every day in every possible way.'

'Do you really mean that?' Eve asked, her mind mauled with doubts. 'Don't just say what I want to hear. Will you really try to change, or I don't know, be more normal?'

'Absolutely.'

Eve softened and cuddled close to Jack. She just wanted the arguing to be over. She wanted to believe that love could conquer all. She hoped psychopaths were a little like mistreated dogs, that love and care could overwrite the instinct that made them want to snarl and bite.

'I want to be in love with someone I can trust,' Eve said. 'You don't have to go around trying to impress me or charm me. Just prove to me that I can trust you. Be honest with me, open up, let me in, Jack. Sometimes, I feel I don't know who you really are.'

'It's hard to open up and let people in,' Jack said, bowing his head, 'when life has taken all the good things people normally look for in their other half. My past is a torture chamber; I keep that door sealed up, but sometimes, I can still hear the screams on the other side, I can feel the darkness seeping through the hinges trying to coax me back. That's not something you share; you bury that as deep as you can and hope no one will ever know.'

'What happened to you?' Eve asked. 'You can tell me, babe?'

'I saw what evil looked like as a child, and I don't know, my brain told me to befriend it or spend my life being afraid of it.'

'But what happened?'

'Don't make me go back there,' Jack said. 'I will, someday. I'll open that door and slay what's on the other side, but not tonight.'

'We can do it together,' Eve said. 'Your hurt is my hurt now.'

134

Jack felt warmed by Eve's words, wrapped in the sweetness of her gesture. He had once read that psychopaths were incapable of emotion, that the areas responsible for affect aren't fully developed, the reactors powered down, the structures damaged by some early childhood trauma. Jack wondered about his feelings for Eve. What were they? Thoughts? Cold cognition? Flowers without petals? A sitcom without the audience's laughter chiming in? Why was he feeling like this, he wondered. Like something had changed, a threshold crossed, a new state breached. In the same way traumatic events can switch off emotion in a psychopath's brain, Jack wondered if a counter-event could switch it back on. Could meeting Eve have rewired the circuits of the past? Was her love lofty enough to open the door of his past, hold his frightened four-year-old-self and whisper into his ear that everything will be okay someday, that's it's safe to come out into the world again?

They spent another three days sailing around Lake Ontario, laughing and smiling, kissing like newlyweds. Eve called Chief Cutler to share the news of her engagement and hand in her resignation. She said her head wasn't in the job anymore and that she planned to leave for Australia in a few weeks. When Chief Cutler flipped out, Eve said. 'I'm not coming back, deal with it,' and she ended the call, feeling free and fortified, dreaming of all the places she wished to visit with her fiancé.

Jack felt excited about their future, too. Their escape to Australia. A new adventure. A new identity. Toronto felt like dumpster overflowing with body parts. Misadventures. Mayhem. Murders strewed across the GTA like offcuts in a butcher's bin. He knew he would eventually have to leave. Kill Mitch, then leave. Change. Become something new. Stop killing. Live a normal life and settle into middle age. Maybe Eve could change him wholly.

Maybe he could transform like one of those insects that sacrifice fangs for feathers.

Or maybe not…

Chapter 23

When the needle hit the floor, Mitch's eyes opened, red and raw, like peeled grapefruits. Was it all a dream? Some nightmare? Had he really scored heroin from a street dealer in the projects?

Everything had changed like a hurricane had swept through during a few hours of slumber. This was the moment Mitch was dreading, his high wearing off, the dry, cotton mouth, itchy eyes, panicked breath and the feeling that his blood had been replaced with bleach. He looked around the dim, airless room. His mattress felt damp with sweat, ash stains smudged in black smears, a pool of vomit crusted on his pillow. Mitch searched the floor, picking up empty bottles of bourbon, looking for the last dribble. There were pages of writing everywhere, scattered across the floor, pinned to the walls, more spilling out of garbage sacks, one even rolled up inside an empty bottle of bourbon.

Mitch picked up one of the notes and scanned the text.

Look into Clearwater. It's all connected to Paddy's murder. Call back Detective *McGuire in Ireland. He worked the Clearwater case, he knows what happened, he can crack The Poet case.*

The word *Clearwater* was scribbled all over the walls in red marker, across the broken bathroom mirror, even on the fridge door. Mitch didn't know how to even imagine what had happened.

The last few days had been a blur, mental quicksand, not a trace of memory left, only sheets of paper. Jack had left Toronto, and with nothing to obsess over, Mitch had descended into the depths of a drink-fuelled frenzy before crashing out on dope.

He found a half bottle of bourbon under his deck chair and necked it raw. What did it all mean, Mitch wondered. How was Clearwater connected to Paddy's murder? He took out his phone, and it opened in Facebook Messenger. There was a DM chain with Alan McGuire.

Mitch: Hi Detective McGuire, this is Detective Bauer in Toronto. I read your article in The Sunday World Online, the interview you did on what happened at Clearwater in 1996. Would you be free for a call?

Alan McGuire: Missed call yesterday.

Alan McGuire: Missed call yesterday.

Alan McGuire: Missed call yesterday.

Alan McGuire: Incoming. Answered.

McGuire: Thanks for reaching out, Mitch. It was great to chat to you. As I said over the phone, something sinister happened at Clearwater all those years ago, and my hunch is it connects to Paddy's murder. But be careful, the current CEO, Jennifer Sullivan, will sue you for even asking questions. She destroyed my career and I'd hate to see the same happen to you. I couldn't really hear you on the phone so I'll call you back tomorrow.

My career is already fucked. What happened at Clearwater? Who's Jennifer Sullivan?

Mitch scrolled through his text messages next. There was one from Glenda asking if he wanted to meet up soon. Mitch ignored it before clicking into his most recent message.

Mitch: Hi James, this is Detective Bauer. I need you to look at a suspect photo related to the Carmady murders. Where can I find you?

James (Spadina Store Manager): Hi Detective Bauer. I'm a bit spooked someone was able to track me down. After I provided u with that suspect sketch a few years back, my wife got scared and we moved out of Toronto. You can call me, but I'm not telling u where u can meet me just in case it's not really u.

Mitch: Outgoing call. Answered. 5 minutes.

James (Spadina Store Manager): Thanks for confirming it's really u, Mitch. Sending u the location of the store I'm working at in Kingston.

Mitch couldn't remember sending that message, or his call with James or where he'd even got James' number from. But that didn't matter. Mitch's heart raced with excitement. James could crack the case wide open. He'd seen the Carmady suspect, and Mitch would bet his life it was Jack. He unpinned Jack's headshot from the wall, slipped it into his pocket, and set off for Union Station.

Mitch walked in weird movements. His lips continually blew on the bristles of his moustache. He appeared sloppy drunk, walking in diagonal movements, spooky sidesteps, trying to translate sensations into thoughts – sharp drops in blood pressure and panicked inhalations. The face of every stranger looked like Jack, smirking back, daring him to pull out his pistol and squeeze the trigger.

Mitch boarded the train bound for Kingston. He sat into an empty seat and drank from his flask of bourbon, occasionally peering down the centre aisle suspiciously. The train was warm but Mitch shivered in his seat. His eyes felt heavy and he drifted off to sleep, twitching at times and waking up in a panic.

It was after midday when Mitch arrived in Kingston. He stepped off the train and asked around for directions to the Metro Store on Brock Street.

Please, please, please let James confirm Jack as the mystery man hanging around the Carmadys.

'Where's James?' Mitch asked an employee mopping the floor near the entrance of the Metro Store.

The employee scrunched her nose at Mitch. 'Probably in the back office,' she said, leaning on the mop's handle. 'Why?'

'Tell him Detective Bauer's here to see him.'

'You sure as hell don't look like a detective. Where's your badge?'

'Screw you,' Mitch said, brushing by her, determined to find the back office, walking to the far end of the store, trying to shake off his stupor.

'Detective Bauer?' James called from a doorway near the cereal aisle.

'James?' Mitch said excitedly.

'That's me,' James said, opening the door. 'Are you okay?'

'I just need you to look at the photo,' Mitch said, unfolding Lawson's picture. 'Is this the man you saw hanging around with Roger and Emma?'

James looked around awkwardly. 'Let's take this to the back office.'

'Just look at this photo. Is it him?'

James swallowed deeply, taking the photo in his hands, glancing at it briefly before looking away and closing his eyes.

'Well?' Mitch asked. 'Is it him?'

'I don't know. Maybe. The eyes look similar, but the man hanging around Roger and Emma was clean shaven and had longer hair.'

'But is it him?' Mitch asked. 'Would you go on record?'

'Wow,' James said, handing Mitch back the photo of Jack. 'I agreed to look at the photo, but I never agreed to make a statement. I've a family, and I don't want to be looking over my shoulder all the time wondering if this monster is coming after me next.'

'Is it him?' Mitch asked more gently.

'Maybe,' James said. 'I'm about seventy per cent sure.'

'You don't have to make a statement now,' Mitch said, putting his hand on James' shoulder. 'But please think about it. You could save a lot of lives. You'll be protected, I promise.'

The world felt bittersweet as Mitch left the Metro Store. James had all but confirmed it was Lawson, but it wasn't evidence unless he went on the record. There still wasn't enough to bring to Chief Cutler, and the knot in Mitch's stomach made it feel like Jack had won again.

Mitch sat on a bench in Skelton Park, taking sips from his flask of bourbon. His head rolled back, his eyes staring upwards into the sky, searching for answers. Hours passed. Everything became a blur again. People seemed to move by at supersonic speed. Clouds raced by overhead. The sun falling on the city at an angle. Mitch reflected on how things had changed. Everything seemed so broken these days. He felt a tinge of sadness at the thoughts of Judy and the kids, like far-off stars in another galaxy, their love replaced by the needle in his pocket, like a wizard's wand, casting enchanting spells that felt more like curses. And then there was Betty. He hadn't thought about her in a while. Where had all the grief gone?

It was close to dusk when Mitch felt his phone vibrating in his pocket. Detective McGuire was calling through Facebook Messenger.

'Hello,' Mitch answered.

'Hey Mitch, Detective McGuire here. You sound much better than the last time we spoke. If you're free, I'll bring you through my theory on what happened at Clearwater.'

'I'm free,' Mitch said. 'Fire away.'

Part Three

Chapter 24

Dublin, decades earlier

Jack Lawson inherited his father's charm and psychopathic traits, though Anthony Murphy wasn't murderous or sadistic.

Like many Catholics born in Dublin during the 1960s, Anthony started life with very little, growing up in the north inner-city tenements. But Anthony's ambition refused to be blunted by poverty. He began stealing at the age of seven, ran a thriving gambling racket at twelve, and by seventeen, he had saved enough money to move out of the tenements and attend college. He studied business and economics at University College Dublin during the 1970s, where he became known across the campus as Mr. Impeccable. Anthony was renowned for his popularity and deft ability to fit into almost any group. In any situation, he could wield a cinematic concoction of charm so sweet and endearing that people felt glazed in a sugary glow.

It was Anthony's charm that caught the eye of Jennifer Sullivan. Her peers regarded her as a real oddball, wandering through life aloof, only ever speaking to contradict or insult. Her privileged upbringing cast a snobbish air of entitlement that grated against the free-spirited vibes of college life. In her first year of university, she only had one acquaintance, a neighbour from a similar background: a skinny, red-haired chap named

Paddy Fitzgerald. Their fathers were partners at Dublin's largest law firm, and while Jennifer didn't enjoy Paddy's company, at least he was from *similar stock*.

Jenny had little interest in men up until that point. Men were too confusing, she reasoned, their attention too deciduous. However, meeting Anthony Murphy changed all that. After taking her first drag of a joint, her eyes seemed to glaze over, and all Jenny could focus on was Anthony's smile between wisps of smoke. She kissed him and laughed. A real laugh, using certain muscles in her face for the first time. The kiss wasn't sexual; it felt more like rebellion, and afterwards, as Anthony took back the joint, he inhaled deeply, saying, 'To friendship, Jenny.'

'To friendship,' Jenny repeated, but the moment felt more like possession, as though Anthony Murphy was something to be owned and worn like a necklace or a diamond ring. Even though Anthony came from the northside slums, Jenny saw beyond it for a short time, saw the person and not the place.

Throughout their college years, Jenny, Anthony, and Paddy became friends, if only superficially, if only ever in a thawing form. Anthony always took centre stage, captivating his audience with his charisma, leaving them wide-eyed and eager to hear more. Jenny was the only one who grew immune, nagged by a growing jealousy that saw her recede to the periphery once again, believing that Anthony did not deserve the admiration of his peers.

'He's a con man,' Jenny told Paddy over lunch. 'All charm and no substance. He only tells people what they want to hear.'

'He's nice to me,' Paddy said, 'and not many people are, Jenny.'

The trio kept in touch after graduation. Casual phone calls, a letter sometimes landing in the post, lamenting the boredom of their professional lives. Paddy and Jenny choose clerkships in two of Dublin's largest banks, while Anthony, burning with ambition, moved to London to become a stock trader for a prestigious

Square Mile firm. His talent was spotted early on, and he was hailed as an oracle among his peers, a machine that could crunch more data than the whole trading floor combined. Anthony profited the firm over three million pounds in his third year, but a sickening blow was delivered when his promised promotion was offered to a poor-performing Oxford grad. Most of the money Anthony earned went back into the company's coffers rather than his own. After a few years in London, lonely and disillusioned, Anthony handed in his notice and flew back to Dublin with the dream of establishing his own firm.

Dublin was grim in the 1980s. The economic boom felt across so many other countries failed to make landfall on Irish shores. But where so many saw destitution and economic collapse, Anthony saw boundless opportunity. He bundled all his savings together, applied for his trading license, and rented a small office in the city's commercial centre. A small sign over the door read, **Clearwater Capital**.

For months, Anthony phoned prospective clients, pitching percentage rates and expected earnings. His opening gambit always being, 'Would you like to retire as a millionaire?' But Anthony's charm was less convincing over the phone, and his reputation as a financial oracle had not travelled home with him from London. With his savings dwindling and his dream fading, he considered travelling back to London to figure out his next move. It was then, on an arbitrary Tuesday morning, Jennifer Sullivan called by his office, keen to catch up over lunch. In a smoke-filled bar off O'Connell Street, Anthony said, between sips of whiskey, 'It's not as easy as I thought it would be, Jenny. I'll be broke in a month. London made me too optimistic.'

'Maybe I can help,' Jenny said. 'Daddy was made president at his firm. They're looking for a new pension fund and I recommended you.'

'Jaysus Jenny!'

'There's a catch,' Jenny said, holding Anthony's stare. 'Daddy said you have to make Paddy and I co-founders in Clearwater. Paddy's Dad was the deciding vote that convinced the board to take a chance on you. Don't get me wrong, they did their research. They saw what you were capable of in London.' Her voice hushed a little as she leaned in. 'But a few were hesitant to hand over their capital to someone from the tenements. You know what those highbrow types are like; they'd be surprised people like you can even read.'

Two weeks later, on Friday the thirteenth, the ownership of Clearwater Capital was amended. Anthony Murphy would retain a fifty per cent stake, Paddy and Jenny a twenty per cent stake respectively, with ten per cent going to Donald Foy, the son of a dodgy politician who could *open doors.*

Clearwater Capital boomed throughout the 1980s and early '90s. Capital flowed in from all directions, earnings soared, and the staff count grew from three employees to over three thousand. Clearwater was seen as a triumph on the global financial scene, often considered *a sure bet.* Anthony travelled to London and New York, opening more offices and expanding operations in larger markets. He felt at the zenith of existence, marrying a beautiful Galway girl named Maire McElhanney in 1987, their first son, Brian, born in 88, Ashley, two years later, and then twins Sean (Jack Lawson) and Mellissa in '92. Despite Anthony's ruthlessness in business, he was a loving father, doting and proud, though he struggled throughout his life to form any meaningful emotional connection.

Most nights, Anthony stayed up late drinking whiskey in his study, candlelight flickering, classical music playing in the background, his ears attentive to the crackle of the vinyl, the rattle of ice cubes in his glass. There were dark forces at play within Clearwater: whispers of a coup, attempted takeovers, and rumours of insider trading. The heights of success cast a hollowness in Anthony, like a witch's spell, a medieval hex, so base not even his children's laughter could fill the emptiness he felt within. For a familiar spectre had begun to stalk the halls of Clearwater as an even greater jealousy burned within Jennifer Sullivan. She considered herself more capable than Anthony, but her role within Clearwater was barely known outside the office. People didn't hail Clearwater as a great success. It was Anthony Murphy that received their adulation. He was bigger than Clearwater, and all those years in his shadows fed a darkness Jenny wanted to unleash.

In January 1996, she began sharing her thoughts with Paddy Fitzgerald and Don Foy. *Anthony Murphy did not deserve to be CEO. Clearwater wouldn't exist if it wasn't for her, Don and Paddy. They were the rightful owners. Not Anthony Murphy. It was a crime that he had taken all the credit, a crime that deserved to be punished.*

The trio became like medieval warlords, gazing into the fires of divination. They tried a hostile takeover in March that year but when the board shot them down, they switched tactics, feeding insider information to the head of trading, forcing him to place big plays in obvious patterns. Murphy survived the scandal that summer, but his reputation was marred in the process, with some of Clearwater's biggest investors moving their capital to another firm.

Over drinks in Keogh's Bar on a rainy Thursday evening, Jenny surprised Paddy with a question. 'You have an uncle in the IRA, right?'

Paddy rolled his eyes. 'The IRA threw him out. He's a rogue.'

'Where is he now?' Jenny asked.

'Locked up in Portlaoise Prison. Why?'

'You know why,' Jenny said. 'He knows people.'

Don Foy looked confused. 'What do you mean, Jenny? What sort of people?'

Jenny looked at Don coldly, toying with a cross pendant around her neck. 'People who are used to getting their hands dirty.'

Paddy shook his head. 'I don't know what you mean, Jenny.'

'Where's this going?' Don asked curiously.

'You want me to spell it out? Fine. Anthony has to go, one way or another. We need someone that will make him go away, permanently.'

Paddy stood up, his face noticeably paler. 'Jesus Christ, Jenny! You've bloody lost the plot.'

'Sit down,' Don said, relaxing back in his seat. 'Jenny has a point. We've tried everything, and Anthony's still taking all the credit for something we built. We secured the funding at the start, and if we hadn't, Anthony would still be a journeyman in London.'

Paddy opened the top button of his shirt, pulling at his necktie, trying to get more air into his lungs. 'I don't like where this conversation is going, and I don't want any more to do with it.'

'Set up a visit to Portlaoise Prison,' Jenny instructed as Paddy walked out of the bar, disoriented, but not from drink.

Over the following months, Jenny and Don absorbed Paddy further into their plans. Every day, Jenny unleashed her diatribe against Anthony, with Don chiming in, startling Paddy with their rage and rancour. Paddy knew his back was against the wall, and under coercive pressure, he rang Portlaoise Prison to arrange a visit to his Uncle Mick.

Chapter 25

Dublin, 1996

Paddy's uncle, Mick Devine, was a rogue republican from the Louth and Armagh border. He was arrested in Wicklow in '88 when the van he was driving pulled up to a Garda checkpoint with a shipment of drugs in the trunk. The IRA expelled Mick after the incident, labelling him a rogue without a cause. After his court case, Mick was sentenced to ten years in Portlaoise Prison and was ostracised by the other paramilitary members.

'I need you to put me in contact with someone,' Paddy said nervously, his voice hushed, sitting in the visitor's room of Portlaoise Prison, taking in every detail, the desks filled with graffiti, the hard plastic chairs, the other prisoners pausing their conversations to glare at him.

Mick hadn't seen his nephew in over eight years and gave him a sidelong glance as he spoke sarcastically. 'How are you getting on Uncle Mick? How has prison been? Are they looking after you okay in here? Jaysus, you look great.'

'Sorry, Mick. I'm a bit nervous. How are you getting on?'

'What did you bring me?' Mick asked, shooting him a look. 'A few books? A nice pair of trainers? A few cartons of cigarettes?'

Paddy swallowed deeply, a red hue blushing his cheeks. 'Sorry, Mick, I forgot.'

'Jaysus boy, you've a neck like a jockey's bollox! Turning up here empty-handed, looking for a favour, no doubt.'

Paddy looked down at the linoleum floor, cussing to himself with his arms tightly crossed. 'I'll come back next week with lots of fags and a few pound for ya.'

Mick scoffed and raised his eyes. 'What do you want?'

Paddy leaned in a little closer.

'What! Are you going to kiss me now?' Mick sneered, causing Paddy to back up and roll his eyes.

'I need a favour,' Paddy whispered.

'Oh, I got that much,' Mick said, rubbing his thumb and index fingers along his thick, black moustache.

'I got a problem,' Paddy said, looking around, 'that needs permanent removal.'

'Did you catch something riding a whore,' Mick laughed mockingly. 'Best go see the doctor for that, boy. I can't help ya.'

Growing more frustrated, Paddy leaned in again. 'I need someone murdered.'

'Is that so?'

'I'm serious, Mick.'

'And why did you come to me?'

'Figured you'd know people. Someone that's used to getting their hands dirty.'

'You've got the wrong guy.'

'Please, Mick. We'll pay whatever it costs.'

'We?' Mick probed. 'So, there's more than just you involved.'

'Can you arrange it or not?'

'I'll tell you what: the best thing you can do is feck off and don't come back unless you have more than just shite talk.'

Paddy arrived home that evening after dark. His wife was in the kitchen cooking dinner while their two boys wrestled on the couch in the sitting room, jumping off the coffee table and shouting in deep, threatening voices, 'Everybody's got a price.'

Paddy kissed his wife on the cheek and gawked around the kitchen, his features drained, his eyes on the verge of tears. He feared his wife knew what was going on, where he had been, the internal ooze of shame bubbling up inside of him like a breached ulcer.

'How was your day, hunny?'

Paddy never heard his wife. His eyes were fixated on the cold bottle of stout in the fridge, his thoughts elsewhere, foggy and suspicious. Mrs. Fitzgerald was about to ask him again when the phone rang loudly, causing Paddy to startle.

'Hi Jenny, how are you?' Mrs. Fitzgerald asked with the receiver to her ear. She listened for a moment, taking a long drag on her cigarette. 'Paddy is just home. I'll put him on to ya now.'

'I'll take it in my office,' Paddy said sorely. This was the moment he'd been dreading. Reporting back to Jenny and listening to her reproach. Deep down, Paddy was happy with his failure. Anthony didn't deserve to die. He was a friend with a family just like him, who had earned his success and helped him, Jenny and Don amass their fortunes.

Paddy threw his briefcase on his desk, slumped into his leather chair, and braced himself. 'Hi, Jenny.'

'Why do you sound limp?' Jenny asked sharply.

'What?'

'It sounds like you didn't do what you were supposed to fucking do, Paddy!'

'Sorry, Jenny. Uncle Mick told me to piss off. Maybe we should just leave all this business behind. Why don't the three of us set up a meeting with Anthony and talk things through? Maybe we can buy him out or set up our own company. I even thought of a name on the drive home. Oystercatcher Capital. Think about it: the way you catch oysters is by...'

151

'Shut up,' Jenny screamed down the phone. 'Get back down to Portlaoise Prison tomorrow morning and convince your uncle to help us or you'll be the one in the body bag.'

Paddy never slept that night, the pillow too hard and lumpy, his feet cold and frigid, his forehead hot and fevered. Every time he closed his eyes, he felt close to panic, his thoughts searching for an exit, feeling around for an off switch.

The following day, Paddy returned to Portlaoise Prison with three cartons of Major cigarettes and a new pair of Reebok trainers. Mick smiled when he saw Paddy, but he didn't sit down. 'Have one hundred thousand in cash ready by Sunday,' Mick said, picking up his loot and turning to leave.

'For who?' Paddy shouted after him. 'Where will I meet them?'

'They know where to find you,' Mick shouted before disappearing through the heavy steel doors.

Afterwards, Paddy rang Jenny from a payphone in Portlaoise town. The rain fell in sheets as people scurried to eject umbrellas or hurry in through doorways.

'I think it's done,' Paddy said.

'You think, or you know, Paddy. Use your words.'

'He said we need a hundred thousand in cash before Sunday morning. Someone will meet me.'

'Where?'

'I don't know. He said they'll find me.'

'Can you do anything right?' Jenny reproached. 'You're a fucking imbecile, Paddy.'

'That's all he said,' Paddy pleaded. 'There were prison guards around. I couldn't run after him asking for more information.'

'What?' Jenny mocked. 'So, someone will meet you somewhere? Great.'

Paddy shook his head. 'How can I get the cash without it being traced back to us? I've already compromised myself by visiting Mick.'

'Relax,' Jenny said. 'There's plenty of cash in the safety deposit box on Moore Street. Take it out of that and tell your uncle to make Anthony's death look like an accident.'

'An accident?'

Jenny slammed down the phone while Paddy stood in the phone box for a time, staring at the rain.

All weekend, Paddy felt as though he was being followed. He tried not to think of what would happen to Anthony. However, the more Paddy tried not to think of it, the more his mind fixated on that scene, his thoughts strangled by some unwanted intruder. Then, on Sunday morning, as he left Donnybrook Church after mass, a pair of headlights flashed in the car park. A man in a monkey hat smiled at Paddy, motioning him toward the passenger seat. Paddy hoped his wife hadn't seen. He handed her his car keys, saying, 'Head home with the kids, hunny. I just remembered I have a squash match at twelve.'

When his wife was out of sight, Paddy walked over to the car, his heartbeat thumping loudly. He sat in the passenger seat and began studying his fingernails.

'You're Mick's nephew, right?' the driver said, who went by the name Trevor; a strong-looking man in his mid-thirties with broad shoulders, large hands and a thick black beard. Much like Mick, Trevor had been ostracised by the IRA for caring more about criminal gain than fighting for Irish freedom.

Paddy nodded.

'I hear you have a bit of business that needs sorting out?'

'I do,' Paddy said, looking at Trevor for the first time, noticing a small ghost tattoo on the inside of his wrist. 'Can you make it look like an accident? And please don't make him suffer.'

'Accidents are the trickiest to pull off,' Trevor said, in a thick Northern Irish accent, 'especially if there's a family in the house. Who is this guy anyway?'

153

'A friend,' Paddy said, his voice trailing off. 'Someone... I don't even know anymore. But I'll say he's a bad man if it will make it any easy for you.'

Trevor laughed, gazing off distantly. 'I don't give a fuck if the sun shines out of his arse. This is all just business to me. So, I'll ask again. Who is this guy? I don't want to know your relationship to him, just who he is, what he works at, the routes he takes, where he drinks, who he fucks.'

'You'll find everything you need to know in the duffel bag,' Paddy said. 'It's tucked away at the squash courts around the corner.'

'And my payment?'

'That's there too. Just please get this over with as quickly as possible. Locker 23, the combination is 1118.'

Trevor pulled off soon after, leaving a smell of burning rubber in the air. Paddy spent the next few hours wandering around Donnybrook, stalked by the ghost of regret, some fingernails almost bit to the bone. It was close to 3 pm when he walked into Fintan's pub, perching himself on a bar stool and placing two fingers in the air. 'A double whiskey, please.'

The pub was loud as Paddy sighed into his hands. The man sat next to him sucked on a tobacco pipe, smiling through the smoke. Paddy wondered if he'd ever be able to genuinely smile again – to smile and actually feel it. Paddy, a year before, or even six months ago, would have detected the disturbance in the air, in himself, in Jennifer Sullivan when she causally said the words. 'Maybe we should kill the whole family.'

The following day, Jenny phoned Portlaoise Prison from a payphone on the corner of Leeson Street. 'I need to speak to Mick Devine,' Jenny said.

'Who's calling?' the prison guard asked.

'His wife,' she replied. 'My father has passed away. I'd like to tell Mick myself. They were very close.'

'Okay, give me a few moments.'

Jenny was put on hold, and when Mick picked up the phone a few minutes later, he blared, 'I've no wife. Who the fuck's this?'

'Shut up and listen,' Jenny said calmly. 'Do the whole family. Make it look like the father did it all, then himself. There's an extra two hundred thousand pound waiting in locker 33 at Sutton Tennis Club; the combination is 1312. If this call is being recorded or monitored, use some of the money to pay off the guards and have it erased. Do you understand?'

'Who is this?'

'Do you understand?' Jenny repeated.

'I think you have the wrong guy.'

'Are you sure about that?' Jenny asked. 'There's a lot of money on the line.'

Mick didn't speak for a moment. 'I suppose there is.'

'There'll also be a retirement package for you when you get released.'

'Make it three hundred thousand.'

'Done,' Jenny said. 'Locker 33 at Sutton Tennis Club, the combination to the lock is 1312. This needs to be done as soon as possible, and your nephew can't know about this. Do you understand?'

'I do.'

After that call ended, things fell into place. The money was collected, Anthony Murphy was tracked for a week, and a list of scenarios was drawn up like the commercial forecast of a standard business order. Paddy toiled over the gravity of such an invoice, the receipt of which would see a brilliant man laid to rest, his energy spent, sealed away like a glob of nuclear waste.

Paddy barely slept throughout those days, the wait excruciating, the forced facade of normality eating away at him like a cancer. What frightened Paddy most was Jenny's unsettling calmness – her and Don's renewed friendship with Anthony, the mawkish adoration she publicly exuded, and the friendly lunch dates he refused to attend. He couldn't go along with the charade, avoiding people at all costs, bunkering down in his home office as though an atomic bomb had exploded on the other side of the door, some post-human world where only his shame had survived.

Chapter 26

Dublin, Halloween day 1996

Anthony Murphy's residence was prominently positioned at the top of Howth Hill, offering a spectacular view of Dublin Bay. The 523m^2 Victorian villa consisted of three connected buildings, and was hidden from the road by a expertly manicured ten-foot-high cherry laurel hedge.

On Halloween day 1996, Trevor knocked on Anthony's front door, dressed in a black suit, with a backpack strung around his shoulders, holding a clipboard against his chest.

'Hello,' Maire Murphy said, answering the door. 'Can I help you?'

'I'm here for a census follow-up,' Trevor said, smiling. 'I just need to do a few checks. Is the family home?'

'That's odd,' Maire said. 'The census was back in April.'

'Just a few discrepancies to clear up,' Trevor said, stepping into the hall unexpectedly. 'It happens from time to time. Gather the family in the living room, and don't worry, I'm not here about your taxes.'

'Okay,' Maire said, laughing. 'As long as you're not the taxman.'

Marie called her husband and children downstairs as Trevor sat calmly on the couches in the living room, scanning its dimensions, entry and exit points, obstacles, the position of the windows and the width of the doorframe. His gaze swept through the room mechanically, noting the large family portrait over the mantelpiece, the navy and gold patterned wallpaper, and the children's fingerprints smeared on the coffee table.

A few moments later, Anthony appeared with Ashley and Brian by his side. 'What's this about?' Anthony asked suspiciously.

'The census,' Trevor said. 'I've been sent out to follow up with you. Are all the family here? There's six of you, right?'

'Can I see some credentials?' Anthony asked, holding his children close by his side.

'Sure,' Trevor said, working through contingencies. Two of the children were absent, but he'd made entry, and if he aborted now, he might not get another chance. He bent down, unzipped his backpack, took out a Beretta M9 and aimed it at Anthony. Maire Murphy screamed. Brian and Ashley looked up at Anthony, unsure of what was happening.

'Quiet now,' Trevor said, motioning the family to gather on the couch beside him. 'I'm only here to rob you. Stay calm, don't get brave and no one gets hurt. Nod if you understand.'

'You'll pay for this,' Anthony said, hugging his family close. 'I might live in this posh house, but I was raised far from this. I know people worse than you, and they'll mess you up in ways you can't imagine.'

'No speaking,' Trevor said, taking zip-tie handcuffs from his backpack.

'If you leave now,' Anthony said calmly, 'we'll forget about all this. The neighbours have just as much as us and they'll be far more passive. I'll fight to the death for my family.'

'No speaking,' Trevor said again. 'Last warning.'

In the moments that followed, Trevor ordered Maire to zip-tie Anthony's hands behind his back, followed by the children. She sobbed throughout the ordeal, muttering prayers, afraid to look at Trevor's face. Once finished, Trevor tied her hands, guided her into the downstairs bathroom, and locked the door. When Trevor returned to the living room, Anthony was trying to calm his children. Trevor ordered Anthony to stand, and when he refused, Trevor delivered a heavy blow to his liver, causing Anthony to fold over, heaving on the floor. He marched the children into the hallway and told them he wanted to play a game of hide and seek. 'This is what grown-ups do at Halloween,' Trevor said, smiling. 'Now run along and hide.'

Ashley smiled contently, scurrying up the stairs, moving awkwardly, her hands flapping behind her back. Brian appeared more sceptical, trying to scratch his cheek against his shoulder. 'Are you sure you won't hurt us, mister?'

'I promise, it's only a game,' Trevor said, watching the children ascend the stairs. They wouldn't be hidden long. Trevor knew what happened next. It was hard to tell if it bothered him. He showed no signs of qualm. No last-minute doubts. No thawing of his stare.

Anthony was still breathing heavily on the carpet when Trevor entered the living. 'Don't hurt my family,' Anthony said, wriggling around. 'I'll pay you whatever you want, just name a price.'

'It's too late for that,' Trevor said. 'I have my orders.'

'From who?'

Trevor never answered him. He took a plastic bag from his backpack and stood over Anthony, shaking out the creases.

'From who?' Anthony shouted. 'What's the orders?'

'Give a guess,' Trevor said.

Anthony thrashed around on the floor, trying to prop himself up on the couch and get to his feet. But Trevor stuck him down, placing the plastic bag over Anthony's head and fastening the zip tie around his neckline. Trevor sat on the couch afterwards and pressed the chronometer function on his watch. It would only take three minutes or maybe less with the energy Anthony was expending trying to get to his feet. Anthony fought hard, thrashing violently from side to side, stabbing his tongue against the plastic bag, trying to punch a hole. Nothing seemed to work, and frustrated, he made gasping, retching noises. Trevor had heard those sounds many times before, the variceal gurgling and high-pitched gasps of someone fighting for their life. He watched Anthony smash his head against the carpet, desperately trying to create a tear in the plastic bag. But soon the room was quiet again, and Trevor stood up calmly and walked toward the bathroom. He opened the door and nodded at Marie Murphy to follow him. She had heard the noises coming from the living room but reasoned it must have been birds in the chimney again. That's all. Those damned birds making their nests for the winter months. Trevor led her to the kitchen before walking over to the cutlery drawer and scanning the knives for the sharpest one.

'What do you want over there? Our valuables are upstairs. Please don't hurt us,' Marie pleaded.

Trevor never answered her. He picked up the largest carving knife and ambled towards her, stabbing her swiftly in the chest, piercing her heart and lungs. He watched her bleed out on the floor before stabbing her another twenty times in the torso. It would have to look like a frenzied attack.

Trevor walked upstairs next and finished off the children in the same fashion as Marie. He spent the next forty minutes covering his tracks, hoovering the floors, cutting off the zip ties, and securing a noose around the second-floor balustrade. The noose was looped around Anthony's neck before he was thrown over the railing. The knife was dabbed with Anthony's fingerprints. The family's blood was gathered on separate spoons and finely splashed on Anthony's clothes and hands.

That'll do, Trevor thought, *that'll do.*

Chapter 27

The bodies were found two hours later when the next-door neighbour dropped home Sean and Mel from their Halloween party. Unable to get an answer at the front door, she circled around the back of the house. Upon peering through the kitchen window and seeing Marie on the floor in a pool of blood, she fainted from the shock. When she came around a few minutes later, she found Sean and Mel sitting in their mother's blood, peeling back her eyelids, trying to wake her up.

The news made headlines all around the world. Big shot CEO murders family then kills himself on Halloween. Jenny was out for dinner when the news broke. Onlookers would remember how she fell off her chair in fits of tears. 'No...why? It can't be.'

Afterwards, she phoned Don from a nearby phone box. 'It's Jenny.'

'There's only one woman who can deliver Christmas on Halloween.'

'Are you trying to flatter me, Don?'

'You've outdone yourself, Jen. Now, go and lead this company with that same determination. And don't you worry; the lawyers have been taken care of. Anthony's last testament and will sees all his shares redistributed back amongst the shareholders.'

'As was his wish,' Jenny said mockingly.

'If that's what we're calling it,' Don said, laughing. 'I've bribed the head of legal. He's backdated Anthony's will to 1992. There'll be no suspicion, Jen. Just a man who put the company first and his family second.'

'You're a real shyster,' Jenny beamed. 'I'll have to keep a close eye on you, Don.'

Don's next phone call with Jenny was less amiable when it was reported that two of the children were still alive.

'What the fuck, Jenny!'

'Calm yourself,' Jenny warned. 'It's a shock to me as well. We just need to get on with things. The children won't have any claim to the company. That's sorted with the will.'

'It's messy,' Don snarled.

'Murder is messy, Don. What the fuck did you expect?'

Paddy Fitzgerald lost a significant amount of weight in the weeks that followed. He just sat in his home office, drinking whiskey and smoking cigarettes. He struggled to comprehend the tragedy, unable to fathom how Anthony's wife and eldest children had also been murdered. He began to think that maybe it was true, that Anthony had killed his family and then hung himself. That made more sense. *Surely.*

When the funeral was set for two weeks later, Paddy didn't attend. Neither did Don or Jenny, which Detective McGuire noted as very strange. Sean and Mel became wards of the state as most of Anthony's family had died or were locked up in prison. Marie Murphy was an only child; her mother was dead, and her father was in a nursing home in Galway with Alzheimer's disease. Social services approached Jenny, inquiring if she could temporarily care for the children until a permanent solution was arranged. But Jenny refused, saying she had to manage the company; *livelihoods were at stake.*

Anthony Murphy had an estranged sister living in Toronto, an Old Testament religious type with a morbid drug addiction. In late November, Sean and Mel were sent to live with her in a dank hovel in the heart of Parkdale. It was worlds apart from the life the twins had known in Dublin. Filth lined the floors. The bathroom hadn't been cleaned in years and the smell stung their eyes. It was easier not to shower, to avoid the bathroom altogether, to urinate in bowls and pour their soil down the kitchen sink. Cardboard had been taped against the windows instead of curtains, so fresh air rarely breathed in. Some nights, the twins awoke to find strangers walking down the halls, stumbling into their bedroom, moaning, and breathing heavily like zombies. There was no heating during the winter months, and twice the twins awoke to find dead bodies in the living room – one an overdose, the other suffocated under a swathe of strangers piled on top of each other seeking heat.

The proceeding years warped the twins in unimaginable ways. They had escaped the horrors of Halloween, but the hellscape they survived into was far crueller than any death. Suffering became a way of life, their nature kneaded by neglect, trauma scrubbing their emotions bare. They prayed most nights, kneeling at the end of their bed, hands joined tightly, begging God to save them. But God never showed up, so they started begging Satan instead. The seed of horror sprouted in them as they sat in school listening to their classmates talk excitedly about their weekend plans, hearing them reflect on family time and all the sentimental stirrings of a happy childhood.

By the time adolescence rolled around, they had already begun to fantasise about murder, staying up late most nights talking about all the serial killers they admired. Other nights, they wandered downtown, with Jack detailing how he'd like to kill the people who walked by, while Mel joined in, listing out the clever ways she would cover up the murders. It wasn't that the twins didn't know right from wrong. They just couldn't feel the difference anymore – they couldn't feel anything at all.

Part Four

Chapter 28

After speaking on the phone with Mitch for almost half an hour, Detective McGuire said. 'I'm convinced that Jenny orchestrated the murder of the Murphy family, co-conspiring with Don Foy and Paddy Fitzgerald. I was so close to proving it, Mitch. They ordered a hitman through Paddy's uncle, Mick Divine. I obtained records from Portlaoise Prison, and Paddy visited his uncle twice before the murders. Mick was connected to bad men, this sort of thing was right up his alley.'

'Did you talk to Mick?'

'He wouldn't talk,' McGuire said. 'However, about a year after the murders, a lawyer from Clearwater approached me, revealing that Don had bribed the Head of Legal to backdate and alter Anthony Murphy's will.'

'But let me guess,' Mitch said. 'They wouldn't go on the record.'

'It breaks my heart,' McGuire said painfully. 'To be so close. The lawyer even said Paddy Fitz had a breakdown after the murders, came in steaming drunk one day to a board meeting and confessed what they'd done. But Jenny shooed him out, saying that Paddy had lost his mind with grief.'

'Did you ever talk to Paddy?'

'Aye, I did,' McGuire said. 'But I was too late. Paddy did a long stint in some special rehab centre in Scotland, sent there by Jenny, of course, and afterwards, he came out different. I don't know what they did to him, but he wouldn't talk; he just stared at me blankly, like nothing was going on behind his eyes. I heard they wiped him with that electroconvulsive shock thing.'

'Paddy's murder sounds like revenge to me,' Mitch said, 'and the poem left at the scene almost confirms it.'

'The Murphy twins survived, Mitch. I contacted social services here in Ireland, and they confirmed that the twins were sent to live with their aunt in Toronto.'

'I believe Sean Murphy is living under a new alias here,' Mitch said, almost sobered by Detective McGuire's story. 'Look up The Poet murders in Toronto.'

'I already have,' McGuire said. 'You mentioned it the last time we spoke. If it is Sean, it all makes sense. He's trying to destroy the love and happiness that was taken from him. He's recreating his mother and father's death; a wealthy couple, in the prime of their lives, mercilessly murdered.'

'But why the poem?' Mitch inquired. 'What does it signify?'

'What I'm about to say was never in the papers,' McGuire said, 'and understandably so. When the neighbour was on the phone with the Gardaí, she watched Mel nurse Jack in her arms as he recited an old Irish poem that children often recite on Halloween. I can't remember the words but the poem is all about bringing people back to life. Maybe he's killing these couples as surrogates for his parents, leaving a poem, trying to resurrect them in a weird, ritualistic way. It might sound far-fetched, but that's the best I can come up with.'

'That theory makes sense,' Mitch said. 'I'm certain Jack is The Poet. All the murders connect in a warped way.'

'But can you prove any of it, Mitch?'

'Not yet, but I will.'

'Take it from me,' McGuire advised, 'it's best to move on and forget about it. I lost everything chasing an idea I couldn't prove. Jennifer Sullivan and her merry band of lawyers made a fool of me. I almost drank myself to death. All these people are cursed,

Mitch. Stay away from them. Forget about this case. Hand over what you have and let someone else destroy themselves chasing ghosts.'

'I can't do that,' Mitch said. 'Let me know if you find anything else about the twins.'

'You're opening a door to a world where people like you and I don't belong, Mitch. Mind yourself and stay safe. They'll come for you next. That's who these people are.'

Mitch lay awake that night, his thoughts chewing through him, his eyes raw and itchy from looking at his phone screen, searching for information on *Clearwater, Jennifer Sullivan, Mel Murphy* and news articles on Detective McGuire's downfall. Mitch tried to ignore McGuire's warnings. He felt he'd nothing left to lose anyway. He was already trapped between the crosshairs of a curse, tumbling through the avalanche, hope shot through the darkness like a flare. If he stopped now, he'd never be able to mentally move on. Every time he'd close his eyes, he would see Jack smirking back at him, kicking over candles, setting Mitch's mind on fire.

A little after 8 pm the next day, Mitch arrived at Lawson's condo, crossing the road and concealing himself on a bench behind two cars. He could just about see the entrance through the car windows. A woman was sitting on the steps outside the main doors. Mitch was struck by her attractiveness. She had one of those unforgettable faces. Plump arching lips, high cheekbones, a slender nose, bright emerald eyes that seemed to sparkle lightly. There was a playful air of promiscuity about her. The way she pursed out her lips when someone walked by, the quick sultry glance she gave them, revealing a portion of her neck, like a woman fully aware of her sexual prowess. Her hair tumbled down her shoulders in wavy auburn coils. Mitch imagined how her hair would smell, a fruity scent exploding in his nostrils, the bubbly lather of attraction, like those Herbal Essence advertisements he always enjoyed some years ago.

Mitch watched the woman through his cigarette smoke. She was dressed in tight blue jeans and a white blouse. He took a quick swig of bourbon when a cold chill washed over him, so sudden and intense that the cigarette shook between his fingers. As Jack Lawson arrived home and stood beside the woman, Mitch sensed a familial recognition between them.

Mel Murphy.

Chapter 29

'Hey, Seany baby,' Mel Murphy called out, standing up from the steps outside Jack's condo.

Jack stiffened when he saw her. 'Not here,' Jack said, flashing Mel an alarmed look. 'I've got heat on me.'

'Oh, sounds sexy,' Mel said in a playful tone, throwing her arms around Jack and placing an awkward kiss on his lips. 'Why do you always look so sad to see me lately?' Mel asked, holding Jack's face in her hands.

Jack shrugged her off and entered through the main doors. Mel followed, and always one to make an entrance, she threw her hands into the air and shouted. 'Tom, darling.'

Tom, the concierge man, beamed from behind the desk. 'Mel, great to see you again.'

'My brother doesn't care about me anymore,' Mel said, sighing.

Tom hoisted himself straighter in his chair, peacocking hard but trying to look relaxed. Everything felt more exciting when Mel was around. She had a way of fortifying men, making them feel powerful and noticed, like a flashy car or some expensive watch.

'Did you hear Jack's big news?' Tom asked.

'What news?' Is Seany keeping secrets from me?'

'That's not my name,' Jack reproached. 'Come on.'

'Tom, look at you,' Mel said, ignoring Jack. 'You've got so lean and strong looking. Your skin is glowing. What's your secret? Green shakes? Turmeric shots, the cold pressed ones with ginger?

No,' Mel said teasingly. 'You've been working out. What, two, three times a day?'

Tom chuckled. 'More like three times a week, but thanks, I didn't realise the pump was showing so quick.'

'Show us the guns,' Mel insisted.

Tom lifted his arms and hit a front double bicep pose.

'Stop the lights,' Mel whopped. 'Man of steel.'

Tom swatted the air contently, the muscles in his face tight from smiling.

'Come on,' Jack said, grabbing Mel by the arm and pulling her towards the elevator.

'He knows I like it rough,' Mel joked, flashing a wink at Tom.

'What!' Tom said, laughing. 'Aren't you guys like twins?'

'Never let anything get in the way of a good time,' Mel called out from the elevator.

'Girl, you're crazy,' Tom said as the elevator doors closed.

'He's nice,' Mel remarked.

Jack didn't respond.

'He's nice,' Mel remarked again, slightly shouting, the soft, flirtatious look vanishing from her face. 'Why won't you answer me?'

'You shouldn't have come here, Mel. I told you, I'm being watched. The last thing I need is some pesky detective figuring out who you are. Mitch has pinned me as The Poet.'

'Oh, boring,' Mel scoffed. 'Just kill him already. Do the family, too. Who cares?'

'I intend to, but it's complicated, and I need more time. Nothing can tie back to me on this one, and you showing up like this messes things up.'

They entered Jack's condo on the top floor. Mel sank into the comfy L-shaped couch and turned on the TV. 'I wonder if it's still on the news,' Mel mused, scrolling through the news channels.

'What?' Jack asked.

'Where have you been all weekend? It's all over the news and social media.'

'What has?' Jack asked, squatting down, reaching out to pet his tabby cat, Ohana, as she sniffed his hand and rubbed her teeth and gums along his finger.

Mel smirked and glanced at Jack menacingly, enacting a spooky voice. 'The mysterious happenings in a Mississauga HomeStay.' Her voice deepened as she went on. 'I better get a Dateline episode for this one. It's my best work, Seany, but the detectives in this city are so incompetent they'll probably blame it on carbon monoxide poisoning.'

On the spectrum of God's light, Mel Murphy was the pixel at the darkest point, only ever feeling the worst of humanity like a sewer or septic tank. When she spoke, she had a way of draining out a person's thoughts, leaving only the remnants of intrigue, awe, and a rapid intensification to know more about her. She was like a beautiful cake without sugar, an alluring gift that, when opened, is found to be bottomless and empty.

Years later, after a battery of psychometric testing, renowned psychiatrist Professor Penry Wasserstein would confess that the DSM-8 lacked sufficient sophistication to define her. 'She's a sort of fringe creature,' the professor would recount at a press conference. 'There is no comparison, so few commonalities with anything we have ever seen before or will likely see again. My profession is averse to using the word evil to describe the actions of the human psyche, but being in Mellissa Murphy's presence, one gets the sense of something demonic. Something wholly removed from the normative realms of human nature. Something that looks like us, but is simply not.'

There was almost some fatal percolation in Mel's eyes, and those who had stared into them lustfully for long enough felt some unreadable thrill right before their death, a sense of being swept along amusingly, then crushed with brutal force. She preyed on people's lust, their fascination with her beauty as she passed them in a bar or at a party, how she would approach them first, all smiles, injecting her venom of self-confidence in the ego of her prey. Her body count was higher than Jack's. Her MO was to charm wealthy, misogynistic men, bring them back to expensive penthouses where privacy was ensured and then murder them in a manner that looked like suicide or misadventure. But lately, Jack had lost interest in hearing Mel regale him with the clever ways she'd killed her latest victims. He worried she'd become too reckless, especially after she murdered a famous Toronto rapper the previous year.

Presently, Mel felt thrilled by the details of another murder. Months prior, she had procured a new identity, signed up to the HomeStay app, and began booking lodgings all over Mississauga and Toronto. She scouted for the perfect scene, the perfect place, for the perfect murder. Then, she found it. A large suburban house named Sunnyside situated close to Jack Darling Memorial Park in Mississauga. It boasted six bedrooms, four bathrooms, a home theatre, and a sprawling backyard with a small wood to the side.

Mel set up a small spy camera in an artificial plant in the corner of the dining room before searching through the pantry. The house came fully stocked with condiments, a large spice rack, various types of infused oil, and more basics such as flour and baking soda. Mel unscrewed the top of the salt grinder and emptied the contents down the sink. She took a bag of concentrated potassium cyanide crystals from her handbag and poured the deadly poison into the grinder. As Mel put the grinder back on the rack, she wondered if it could really be that easy. She'd researched the effects of cyanide, even in tiny doses, it was an instant killer.

Afterwards, Mel sat out on a deck chair by the swimming pool, staring up at the stars. Everything felt more beautiful in the darkness, all the sounds more intriguing, the shadows more alluring: a state, Mel imagined, where death could enter buildings and take a host of its pleasing. To Mel, the world was a small lamblike creature, malleable and tender, as soft clay. The night was a sort of balm to the banality of it all. It was the only time Mel didn't feel out of place or lonely. She rarely slept, only ever crashing out for short naps around midday. Instead, she prowled the streets of Toronto most nights, trying to feel something, trying to ward off the intense bouts of boredom that only made her feel more murderous. On other nights, she entered chat rooms on the dark web trying to find someone else like her, someone just as bored and just as murderous at 4 am.

Mel left Sunnyside before dawn, walking down to Lake Ontario, whistling the theme tune to Baywatch. The water looked black and inky, waves lapping over rocks, the smell of algae in the air, the sun about to sprout. Mel hugged her arms around her shoulders and looked out across the water, smiling at the little piece of suffering she had sown in Sunnyside.

For weeks, Mel watched the live feed on her phone. Families came and went. Frat parties raged every Thursday. Swingers parties wet the sheets on weekends.

Someone just use the fucking salt.

Then, on the same weekend that Jack dropped down on one knee, the Roberts family arrived at Sunnyside early on Friday morning. At dinnertime, as was tradition, the Roberts family held hands before their meal, taking turns saying grace. Little Benny thanked God for his family, while Popa Jim ended grace with the words, 'Thank God, now let's eat.'

Unaware of the danger, they all seasoned their meal with Mel's *special salt*. Little Benny was the first to feel weird. He had trouble seeing his bowl of chowder, and his lungs felt tight as he tried to catch his breath. 'I don't feel so well, Popa.'

'Neither do I,' Popa Jim said. 'My head's all dizzy and sorts.'

Popa Jim's face collapsed into his bowl of chowder, sending cream and fish juice splashing across the table. Benny ran for his mommy but collapsed before he reached her arms. Mrs. Roberts stood up, heaving, falling back into her chair and tipping over. The eldest daughter was found with her face in the downstairs toilet bowl. Little Nora wasn't hungry and had opted instead for orange juice. She was seen on Saturday morning, walking around Jack Darling Memorial Park pointing toward Sunnyside, saying, 'Momma wont wake up.'

'And that's why I always say,' Mel said, finishing her story. 'Never use the condiments in a HomeStay.'

'We agreed no children,' Jack said. 'You're out of control, Mel.'

'The toddler survived,' Mel said casually, 'and she'll be like us, Seany, saved from her family's reaping. Born of the narrow human mould and now set free from the psychic destruction of normalcy.' Mel paused, deep in thought. 'Do you ever wish we hadn't survived?'

'No.'

'I do. At least then I wouldn't feel so bored all the time, so hungry and never fed. It's like the darkness inside of me is yawning all the time and I can't seem to please it.'

Mel rose from the couch lazily, walked over to a shelf and picked up a small figurine of Freud. 'You're the head guy,' Mel continued, 'what's wrong with me, Seany? Why do I feel so bored?'

'The world stopped spinning for us long ago,' Jack said, trying to catch his sister's eye. 'We never had a chance. How could we, finding Mam like that?'

'I still remember trying to pry her eyes open,' Mel said, looking back at her brother as though it explained everything. 'Sometimes, I can still feel her blood on my hands, webbing my fingers together. We never left the kitchen floor, did we?'

'It doesn't have to be like that forever.'

Mel glanced at Jack with hopeful curiosity. 'It doesn't?'

'We're stuck in the past. We can't change what happened to us, but maybe we can move on, settle down, and try to live a normal life.'

'You know I can't,' Mel said, putting down the Freud figurine, 'and don't you be thinking that way either.' Then, changing the subject as deftly as she could, Mel skirted to Jack excitedly. 'Do you want to see the video?'

'What video?'

'Sunnyside, I have the live recording.'

'Jesus Christ!' Jack said, putting his palms to his face. 'Delete it, Mel. It's evidence.'

'I thought you'd be impressed,' Mel said, bending down and picking up Ohana.

'You need to cool off. You'll get busted, and killing children, what the fuck is going on with you?'

Mel Murphy screamed, causing Ohana to jump out of her arms. 'BORING! You're boring me, Seany. Everything about you is so boring these days.'

'Lower your voice,' Jack said, their eyes locked, neither one blinking.

'Frog,' Mel muttered before bursting into laughter. 'You've become so civilised. You're like a toilet bowl. People will shit all over you. *Seany the Stain*. That's what I'm going to call you.'

'Are you done?'

'No,' Mel said, falling back onto the couch, feigning exhaustion.

'I don't want to see you for a while,' Jack said, walking over to the window and peering down into the street. 'There's too much going on. I can't have you messing things up.'

'We spent our entire life thinking that our father murdered our family, and it wasn't until you found that article online where Detective McGuire claimed that Jenny, Don, and Paddy were involved that it dawned on us what really happened. Killing

Paddy Fitzgerald doesn't change anything,' Mel said, kicking her feet. 'They all need to die, Seany. You said Paddy confirmed everything before you killed him. Jenny is the new target. She was the ringleader. You need to get to Dublin like you promised, and end her and dear old, Don Foy. Or do you not care about what happened to us? Do you not care what happened to mam and dad, Brian and Ashley? Do you not care that we lived out entire lives thinking that our father butchered our fucking family?'

'I have other priorities.'

'Like what?'

'I got engaged,' Jack said blankly, 'and I'm moving to Australia to start a new life.'

Mel's face changed in an instant. Her facial bones appeared more prominent, and her emerald eyes appeared black and wide. She couldn't comprehend what Jack was saying. She imagined them together always, as partners, and partners didn't marry other people, run away to other countries and start a new life.

'Who?'

'It doesn't matter,' Jack said, pouring himself a whiskey.

Mel stormed over to him. 'Is that where you were all weekend? With some slut? Who the fuck is she, Sean?'

Jack downed his whiskey, the fiery taste tingling down his throat, the woody notes settling on his tastebuds like needles.

'Eve,' Jack said at last.

'The detective?' Mel shouted, edging up to her brother.

'She understands me,' Jack said. 'She knows what I am, and she accepts me.'

The odd glare in her brother's eyes confused Mel. There was something in them, some intrusion into their lives, into the way things were and had always been.

'I understand you,' Mel shouted. 'I accept you, not like her. She only sees a part of you. I see it all. Accept it all. Why do you need someone other than me?'

'I love her,' Jack said. 'You should be happy for me.'

Love wasn't something Mel quite understood, like some algebraic equation, emotions multiplying into a form of meaning she would never grasp.

'End her, or I will.'

'Touch her, and I'll end you,' Jack warned.

'You don't want to play this game, Seany. I've nothing to lose or live for, but it seems you do.'

Chapter 30

Mel stormed out of Jack's condo, ignoring Tom's pitch for a date, his petting words, his attempt to leave the concierge desk and follow her. He'd outlived his usefulness, tossed aside like an old board game, swept away like crumbs.

Jack's comments lit up inside Mel's mind like fireworks, her anger exploding out in all directions. Jack didn't really mean what he'd said. Eve was only a fling. A plaything. He'd forget all about her in a week or so. Nothing would really change. They would travel to Ireland together and butcher the whole Clearwater board. Jack had promised her they would, and people don't break promises.

Mel couldn't fight the jab of old memories punching away inside her head, visions of herself carried away like those unwanted goldfish people haul home from funfairs in clear plastic bags. She tried to act like nothing strange had happened, nodding at people passing by, smiling at them, like a pig smiling in a slaughterhouse. She felt bound by a dark fantasy, imagining how she'd tie her brother up, slit Eve's throat, then make him drink her blood. The thought made Mel smile. She didn't know if her fixation with Jack was romantic or murderous. They had been very close as children. They only had each other, but over the previous year, they had grown distant, their meetups less frequent, less engaged, their conversations only hinging on the talk of murder. Kill counts tallied up, like some adult game of Xs and Os where people died in gruesome ways.

Mel boarded a streetcar at Spadina & Bremner, feeling bored again, rolling her eyes, and drifting between thoughts. A group of girls took selfies in the centre carriage. They talked loudly, giddy drunk, finding everything hilarious. Mel wondered what their lives must be like. To have friends, to laugh, to feel excited about a night out on the town. They were college girls, no doubt. They would probably go on to be doctors or dentists, marry attractive men and have perfect little families.

Mel slapped her palms against her face as though to block out her thoughts, as though to peel the flesh from her cheekbones and use it as a cloth to wipe away her anger. The girls were smiling and posing when Mel looked over. Some were twerking to RnB music that played from a pocket-sized speaker while others touched up their make-up and sang wisps of lyrics. No one else seemed to care. Only Mel. Labouring hard not to say something cruel or do something violent. The youngest girl put a quart of vodka to her lips. 'Girls, take a picture of this,' she said, pushing out her bum and pouting hard.

'You're such a babe,' her friend said, barely looking up from her phone.

'Work it,' whooped another, trying to join in, bending over to twerk. 'Bad bitches coming through.'

Those girls were like a scene from a world where Mel did not exist, some other dimension, a familiar confusing situation. She felt like a reptile sat before a movie, expected to understand the plotline, to be moved by the arc. A look passed between the girls when they noticed Mel glaring at them, her eyes glossed with hatred.

'What's your problem?' the oldest girl asked, laughing a little before glancing at the other girls.

Mel never spoke. She just glared back at them.

179

'What the hell!'

'PCP trance,' said the youngest.

Like a statue suddenly coming to life, Mel moved toward the youngest girl, grabbing her by the hair and smashing her head against the vertical hand railing of the streetcar. Mel angled the girl's head back a few inches and smashed it again, multiple times, making sure her nose went forward first. Blood gushed as the other girls stilled with shock. No one spoke. The only sound in the usually noisy streetcar was the music from the pocket speaker rolling eerily down the centre carriage. Other passengers pretended not to notice what had happened, looking at their phones, some sitting motionless like mannequins.

Mel exited the streetcar at Spadina and Dundas West, disappearing down a dark side street on her way downtown. She felt transported back to the land of the living. It had been nearly a week since she had felt like that. Wooed by some internal valentine, her dried-up parts drenched again, the fog of boredom lifted. She felt no worries or regrets. Those girls meant nothing to her – little wax figurines who made noises with their mouths, whose eyes sometimes ran with tears. Mel breathed in the night air and listened to the sounds of the city grumble. She had a love/hate relationship with the city. When she first arrived in Toronto, it felt strange and foreign, like a toy she didn't know what to do with. The people who visited her aunt's apartment weren't like any other people she had ever met before; their faces smeared with scabs, the nasty smells that clung to their clothes, and the strange places they would touch her during the middle of the night. It was only when Mel got older that she realised what they had done to her. Those memories moved around in the shadows of her mind, tethered to her thoughts, like a kite blowing in a storm.

Mel didn't look over her shoulder that night. She didn't see the man stalking her less than fifty yards away.

Chapter 31

It was after 10 pm when Mel arrived at Klub Kava, a strip club close to University Avenue, nestled between an after-hours club and an all-night coffee shop.

Mel winked at the bouncer on the door. 'Hey, Big Marc.'

'Hey Mel, doing a show tonight?'

'Maybe,' Mel said.

She often did a show on nights when she felt more bored than usual. She didn't need the money. After the Carmady murders, Jack shared some of the profits with her, which Mel used to set up a multi-level-marketing supplement company, profiting over three hundred thousand dollars in her first year.

The strip club was located underground in a vast basement, while upstairs was a well-known swingers club. Music played loudly as Mel entered through the main doors. The club owners were standing behind the bar, chatting quietly amongst themselves. Mel waved over and blew them a kiss. 'Hey, Gio. Hey Runner. I'm back.'

'Hey Mel,' Gio said in a deep voice. 'What's up?'

He swallowed deeply after that. Mel often made him feel uneasy. Gio was six-foot-four, heavily tattooed and built like a bodybuilder; not much made him nervous, but Mel was different. He and Runner called her *Saucers* because her eyes were always dark and dilated, not like eyes at all, just empty objects with nothing going on behind them. But deep down, they had a soft affection for Mel. Most of the girls working the club were hauling around some childhood baggage, fucked over somewhere along the road, and had turned to drugs and other bad choices for some escape. But Mel was cast of a different constitution, more spectral, as mysterious as dark matter. She rarely drank or did drugs and never got all tangled up in her feelings like the other girls, bawling in the locker room, regretting bad decisions. Mel offered cold pragmatism, and Gio and Runner respected her for that: a successful businesswoman who chose to dance for the fun of it all. They looked at her as liberated, a real radical type, circuitry and steel in place of blood and guts, an empty chair where a soul might sit.

'Not much,' Mel said, leaning on the counter, 'I was in the neighbourhood and figured I'd call in and see the girls.'

Eighty or so men were sitting around circular tables, some in groups of three and four, but most sat alone with their stares fixated on the dancer moving slowly around the pole on centre stage. Three smaller stages were scattered around the club, circular platforms with a pole reaching into the ceiling. A large curtain had been drawn across the back of the club, where ten small rooms were nestled away for private dances.

'It's free entry before twelve,' Runner said, knocking on the bar counter. 'We're expecting a big crowd tonight. Some high rollers too.'

'It better not be full of college students again,' Mel said. 'I ain't taking loose change tonight.'

'Nah,' Gio said. 'We don't let them in anymore. They cause too much trouble. One broke a bottle off Runner last time.'

'Take a look,' Runner said, turning his head to reveal a scar running down his face.

Mel tutted. 'I always miss the fun nights.'

'You've a strange idea of fun,' Gio said, tucking his hands into his armpits.

'And behave yourself tonight,' Runner warned. 'If there's trouble, come get us or Big Marc. Don't go taking on these guys by yourself. Capish?'

'Got it,' Mel said, strutting off.

Ten large vanity mirrors covered the back wall of the locker room with bright lightbulbs running around each frame. A few of the girls were sitting in front of the mirrors, applying make-up and drinking hard liquor.

'Hey Mel,' the girls said in unison, catching sight of her.

Mel smiled contently. 'Hey, ladies. Ready to wash rocks tonight?'

Three of the girls ran to hug Mel, their glittered skin rubbing off onto Mel's white blouse, making her shoulders sparkle in the warm light.

'Where have you been?' Amber asked. 'We've missed you.'

'Life's been hectic,' Mel said. 'You know, with the company and all. If any of you girls want a side hustle, just hit me up. We be booming.'

'I don't wake up until midday,' Barbie said, knocking back a rum and coke, 'and I usually start drinking then.'

Mel laughed softly. 'A real employee of the month type.'

Barbie stood up from the mirror and began showing off her slender body. 'Rum and coke,' she whooped, flexing her biceps. 'Breakfast of champions, baby. How do you think I keep this body like a temple?'

'Sit your ass down,' Brandy shouted as she applied false eyelashes, 'jumping around like some anaemic-looking prawn.'

All the girls giggled. Some clinked glasses. Others shook their heads with an excited flurry. Mel had forgotten how much she missed these moments, to feel some presence of connection. She would kill again a few days later, but at that moment, her darkness felt fluoresced, her anger furnished with a soft, comfy ease.

'I'd kill for your cheekbones,' Ginger said, breaking the laughter, admiring Mel's face with her hands. 'I swear you get hotter every time I see you. You're such a bitch.'

'It's the red hair that does it for me,' Amber said, giggling. 'Cherish dressed up like you last week. She wore a wavy auburn wig, and we contoured her cheekbones like yours. The men went wild for it. They probably thought she was you.'

'Made a bomb that night,' Cherish said in a husky voice. 'It's hard for an old hag like me to wash rocks these days. I've tried every outfit, all the fantasy shit and all I got was five and ten dollars. But as soon as I put on that dang wig and pretended to be Miss Wish over there, I hit four digits.'

'Aw, I miss you girls,' Mel said, looking around the room.

These girls were the closest Mel would ever get to friends. A sisterhood formed in the crucible of hardship, their steely wit hardened by trauma, their laughter filling the air like some brief amnesiac. They shared a common bond that wasn't easily explained through words. Mel was known as *The Mechanic* among the sisterhood. She was always pottering around trying to fix them, prying into parts of their lives, offering them a job, suggesting self-improvement books, and doling out advice on how to treat men who had mistreated them.

The next thirty minutes passed cordially, punctuated by howls of laughter and crude comments. Mel slipped into a pink neon thong with a matching see-through bra. Afterwards, she scanned the club floor, moving from table to table, chatting up the patrons, making sure she'd have their full attention when she greased the pole.

'Miss Wish is like an orchid,' the club MC announced as Mel hit centre stage. 'That flower only blooms a few nights of the year. Everyone, get out your wallet. Make it rain on that flower. Don't be shy now.'

Mel finished her set twenty minutes later, and a frenzy broke out as men scrambled to bring her for a private dance. She was walking backstage declining offers when a dude lurched in, saying, 'Your eyes are beautiful, like *clear water*. Can I get a private dance?'

Mel felt startled by the comment. The man's face had a mild familiarity, but it was so dark, Mel couldn't tell from where. Intrigued, she took his hand and led him back towards the private rooms. She was thinking of her father as she drew across the curtains. Flashbacks of the early days. Her dad's impeccable appearance – how, on Sundays, he would wear bright white socks with slippers and they would watch a movie, snuggled up on the couch together. She remembered the smell of fresh popcorn wafting through the air, the warmth of her father's body as she snuggled in, like freshly baked bread hot out of the oven. Happy days, Mel thought, that seemed so foreign now.

The ambient light cast sensual shadows on the wall as Mel danced in sultry motions. She thought it was weird that the dude's eagerness had ebbed. He looked disinterested, and things grew even weirder when he stopped Mel from sitting on his lap.

'What's your deal?' Mel asked.

'It's something else I want,' the man said as he grabbed Mel by the hand. 'Let me introduce myself. I'm Detective Mitch Bauer. I've been following your brother's work for years, and you might just be the domino that brings down the whole house.'

'Oh no,' Mel mocked. 'You have me shaking in my little thong, detective.'

'I was on your brother's boat,' Mitch said, unfazed. 'I found the notepad where he writes his poems, and I've a store manager who can identify him as the mystery man hanging around the Carmadys before they were murdered. That's hard evidence. Witness testimony. Your brother is The Poet, and I can prove it.'

'That proves nothing.'

'I've also been in contact with Detective McGuire back in Dublin, and he laid out his theory on what happened on Halloween 1996. You remember that day, don't you?'

'Can't say I do,' Mel said.

'Think a little harder,' Mitch urged. 'Detective McGuire confirmed that the Murphy twins were sent to Toronto. The same city where Paddy Fitzgerald was murdered, and a poem about revenge was left at the scene. The same Paddy Fitzgerald who was involved in your family's murder. I've enough to get a warrant and to reveal your brother's identity as Sean Murphy.'

The veneer of Mel's boredom had drained away. 'No one will believe a washed-up bum like you.'

'They'll believe the evidence,' Mitch said, deadpan. 'I don't want the glory. I never cared for it, but the other detectives ain't like me. They only care about the glory, the headlines, and seeing their face on TV. And they'll do just about anything for it.'

A wry smile curled on the corner of Mitch's mouth. 'The cops are already on their way for you. I told them what happened on the streetcar and where to find you.' Mitch checked his watch. 'I called it in when you were on stage. They should be here any minute. You won't get away with what you did to that girl on the streetcar, and once they have you for that crime, they'll start looking into you and your brother's past.'

Mel grabbed Mitch by the neck, staring into his eyes, her hand contorting around his arteries like a vice. 'Some bum cop ain't going to stop me and Seany killing. We have Satan on our side, see.'

'And I've got evidence on mine,' Mitch muttered through bated breath. 'And now your confession.'

'You're like an insect,' Mel went on, 'crawling through the undergrowth so unaware of the foot about to stamp you out. I've killed more men than you've had dinners. Men, just like you, who make big threats and try to act all though around women. Most

186

were dead before they knew what was even happening, but you, detective, you'll be a hammer and knife job. I'll take my time with you.'

Mel released her grip and grinned before smashing her face against the wall half a dozen times. Blood poured from her nose as Mitch watched on, emotionless. 'Enjoy what's coming your way,' Mel said before screaming loudly and running out of the private room, holding her face and begging Gio and Runner to help her. 'That sicko attacked,' Mel screamed.

The other patrons began looking around at the commotion. Runner wrapped a silk robe around Mel and held her tightly in his arms. Crocodile tears dribbled from her eyes as her mind scrambled for a plan. Gio radioed Big Marc on the walkie-talkie, and they rushed to the private room, hyped up like line-backers about to lay a beat down in the fourth quarter. Mitch was still sitting on the couch in the private room when Gio and Big Marc burst in. He knew what happened next, the punches and kicks hurdling towards him like a Jack-knifed truck. But Mitch didn't care as he sat preening under the satisfaction of Mel's revelation.

Mitch stumbled home a while later with two black eyes and a busted nose. Mel sneaked out of the club's back entrance and ran for over thirty minutes, trying to collect her thoughts. She didn't realise that no cops had turned up to arrest her, that the officers who received Mitch's call had simply laughed, saying, 'Mitch really needs to lay off the booze, eh.'

Chapter 32

Eve woke to hear her phone vibrating on the bedside locker. Her eyes opened slowly, squinting at the harsh screen light on her cell phone. Mitch was calling her, and she wondered what he wanted, what web of delusions his mind was spinning like a spider in the dead of night. She saw he'd called her eight times and sent a message.

'What the hell?' Eve said, rubbing the sleep from her eyes before clicking into Mitch's message.

Mitch: If ur with Jack get out now. Hes dangerous. Him and his sister have killed loads. Answer ur fone.

Eve sat up to re-read the message before switching on the bedside lamp. The master bedroom of Jack's condo had two large suitcases strewn across the floor, half packed with clothes and toiletries. Denim jeans, white shirts, short skits, bikini bottoms, a t-shirt that had the slogan *Stay Alive* printed on the front. Jack and Eve had started packing early. In a little over a week, they planned to leave Toronto, bound for Australia.

Jack woke a few moments later, his eyes squinting against the bright light. 'What time is it?'

'Crazy time,' Eve said, glancing over at him. 'You wanna see the message I got from Mitch?'

'Yeah,' Jack said, rubbing Eve's upper back in slow, supporting motions.

Jack read the message slowly. 'You're kidding,' he said. 'Mitch sent you that? He's still going on about this?'

'Yeah,' Eve said. 'Do you even have a sister?'

'No,' Jack said. 'But he already thinks I'm The Poet, so why not add more madness into the mix. Honestly, what's this guy's problem?'

'I don't know,' Eve said.

'I think he has psychosis,' Jack continued. 'When I worked in the mental health centre in Parkdale, I treated a few patients like that. The wires in their head were all jumbled up. Everything was a conspiracy.'

'That sounds awful,' Eve said, shaking her head sadly.

'A few of those patients went on to kill people. Friends, spouses, even their own children. That day Mitch came to see me at my office, I knew something wasn't right. His paranoia walked him on a leash. I should've done more to help him.'

'Don't beat yourself up, babe. He was beyond help, even then. No one could get through to him. It was like a switch had gone off in his head.'

'I don't want you seeing him in this state,' Jack cautioned. 'He's unpredictable.'

'I can't leave without saying goodbye, Jack.'

'We can phone him together when we get to Australia.'

'He doesn't even know I'm leaving.'

'And telling him now could be a trigger,' Jack said, drawing back the duvet and getting out of bed. 'I mean it, don't meet up with him. Not like this. He already fancies you or something, and if you tell him you're leaving with me, he could flip completely.'

Jack's mind felt dizzy. He knew Mitch's message wasn't psychotic rambling. Mitch had figured something out, but what Jack wondered. What frayed thread had Mitch's obsession unravelled like a cat clawing at a ball of wool? And how did he know about Mel?

He must have been staking out my condo. Why the hell did Mel have to show up? Mitch needs to go, and soon.

Jack showered sometime later, massaging his scalp with a lather of shampoo, thinking of probabilities, possibilities, scenarios sluicing through his thoughts like pounds of paydirt. He debated changing their flights and leaving Toronto sooner, running away to Ecuador or Thailand, some village in the Himalayas, a winter cabin in the Klondike where they could light fires in the morning and drink hot cocoa by candlelight in the evening. Maybe he could convince Eve of an adventure wholly off the grid, and just disappear like water down the drainpipe. But that could arouse suspicion. He didn't want Eve scrambling to fill in the blanks, to mull over a sudden change of plans or pick at the sutures of an old life that had grown septic overnight.

Things had changed. Jack loved Eve. She was a part of his life now, as vital as an organ, a part he could not just discard like dross, like all the ones before. Jack couldn't remember ever feeling like that, visible and cherished in the warm glow of a woman who had accepted all the sides he'd shown; to feel loved, if such a state was possible in a mind that could not feel embarrassment. He never imagined his life as having stages, different parts, different gears that shifted things beyond his own desires. He wondered what would happen now. Run away with Eve, tie a rock around his rage and dump it out at sea, or change his flights completely and book one-way tickets to Dublin for him and Mel to finish off Jenny and Don.

Jack dried himself in the master bedroom before making his bed, meticulously running his palms across the duvet, erasing all the creases and ensuring that the pillows were arranged in perfect symmetrical alignment. His need to reinstate order over things felt stronger than ever that morning. He had banked on people not believing Mitch. But what if only one person believed him, scratched deeper, looked beyond the obvious and found the remnants of him and Mel burning in the crater of Mitch's madness?

Eve was in the kitchen making breakfast, whisking scrambled eggs in a pan, her eyes staring forward, lost in thought. 'Is it bad I want to drink before nine?' she asked when Jack appeared in the living room. 'I'm not like you, Jack. I can't just put things to the back of my mind. I feel sick with worry.'

There was such purity to Eve's empathy. Jack loved that about her, a living testimony to something he could never feel, the trophy of a game he wasn't permitted to play. 'You should call his wife,' Jack said, trying to assimilate support. 'Maybe she can help pull him back towards reality.'

'Maybe,' Eve said.

'Where did this all start?' Jack asked, sitting down at the kitchen table.

'When Betty died,' Eve said, turning off the heat on the induction hob. 'He hasn't been the same since. It makes me so mad. He could've talked to me. I would've understood. I could've helped him through the grief.'

'Time to move on,' Jack said coldly. 'We'll be gone in a few days and Mitch won't matter anymore.'

'I'm not like you mister-fucking-robotic. Why can't you understand these things?'

'What things?'

'Things,' Eve yelled. 'Human things. Emotional things. Normal fucking things. Not every problem has a cookie-cutter solution. Most people can't just shut off their feelings like you. They actually care about people. They mean something, Jack. You sit there like I'm one of your patients, barking out ways to move on.

I don't want to move on. I want to try help one of my friends. I want to be there for him. You do this all the time, and I can't fucking stand it. Can you just listen and understand me for once?'

The scrambled egg stayed in the pan that morning, giving an uncommon disorder to a usually pristine kitchen. Eve stormed away in tears, afraid that she was in the wrong. Jack had never seen her rant so decidedly raw, and he wasn't sure how to play it or what to say next. He stood up, confused. 'I'll talk to you later,' he said, walking toward the front door, shaking his head, checking his pockets for his phone and wallet, and grabbing his car keys from the counter.

In a world where everything felt like Daddy's fault, both Eve and Jack ran from their problems, like a cop yelling freeze, bundling off in different directions: Jack growing suspicious of Eve's loyalty, Eve later regarding Jack's outburst as jealousy.

Chapter 33

Jack usually remembered his drive to work, alive and in the moment, exuberantly aware, moving as freely as electricity along a copper wire. But that morning, Jack arrived at his office wondering how he had got there.

It was a gloomy morning, grey hues leaking through the windows, his thoughts concealed like some ugly scar. Jack cancelled his only appointment that day – a goodbye session really with his longest serving client. His fingers fleeced through his hair before picking at the label of a water bottle, piling up the scrapes on his desk, imagining he was tearing strips off Mitch. What was happening? This wasn't him. Why could Jack suddenly feel the movement of his jaws? The tectonic tension, enamel moving from east to west then back again. He opened YouTube and cracked up the volume. This was his release, listening to Drill music, the lyrics rearranging things, revenge the theme of almost every song. Jack could relate to the words, finding himself alive between the bars. A scene where killers rose to the top like cream. The scum rising too. No regard for human life. Death as a game, a tallying up of the scores, tit for tat, and tat. Jack cranked up the music to max volume and began rapping bars in his head. He freestyled with his fists clenched, reliving all the murders he had committed, describing the look in his victim's eyes, their last moments alive again in the form of lyrics.

There were blotches of awareness Jack tried to ignore. He debated the choices he'd made. He didn't have a Netflix documentary regaling his crimes with psychologists and detectives obsessing over his motivations and murderous machinations. He wasn't a trap star spitting bars, making bank, boasting of body counts and the mental ease of watching lives expire. He saw himself, sitting there alone, some out-of-body perspective that mocked itself from every angle. A different version of Jack Lawson appeared in that airy office; his arrogance seen retreating, on the back foot, reality throwing combos, knockout punches bringing bad memories into focus. He considered going out to reception and killing Jess, taking a ballpoint pen to her face and prying out her eyes. He imagined her turning mute, going dark, all her energy flatlining as he stood over her, unflinching, dreaming up lyrics to a drill song. Jack hadn't looked at his phone that morning. He hadn't seen the missed calls from Mel. The message typed in bold.

Mel: MITCH KNOWS. ANSWER YOUR PHONE. PLEASE.

Jack was startled when Mel stormed through his office door. 'You're not talking to me anymore?' Mel screamed. 'This is serious.'

Jack looked confused. 'What?'

'Mitch knows,' Mel said. 'He followed me to Klub Kava last night, brought me for a private dance and laid out our worst nightmare.'

'Be precise, Mel. What does he know?'

'Everything. What happened to our family. Your motive for killing Paddy. He even has some store manager who can place you around the Carmadys.'

'We always knew this was a possibility,' Jack said, leaning back in his chair.

'This is your fault,' Mel shouted. 'Killing wasn't enough. You had to go and play with the detectives, snuggling up to that slut.'

194

'Careful,' Jack warned, his teeth stripped like a rottweiler.

'Mitch nearly had me arrested last night,' Mel shouted. 'I'm on the run. I won't do prison. Screw that, Seany.'

'Relax,' Jack said. 'The cops would have already nabbed us if Mitch's threats were real. They probably don't believe him. No one will, and anyway, we have contingencies.'

'You have,' Mel said coldly. 'You're just going to run away with your new plaything and abandon me like everyone always does. You act like nothing's changed between us, like we were never close. The shit we've seen, Sean, and the only way I got through it all was knowing I had you by my side. You were my hero, always so calm and unbothered by the pounds of shit thrown our way. But I mean nothing to you, and I probably never have. You just take what you want from people then move on to the next.'

Mel looked up to the ceiling before burying her face in her palms. 'I'm your twin sister. I love you and I need you to be here for me now.'

Jack's face remained expressionless. 'Come here,' Jack said, holding Mel in his arms, and kissing the top of her head. 'Don't worry, I have a plan. All this will be over in a few days and Mitch won't be a problem anymore.'

'Really?'

'Yes,' Jack said. 'I care for you, Mel, but I also care for Eve. Maybe you can come stay with us when we get settled in Australia. We'll make it like old time's again, I promise.'

'I'd like that,' Mel said. 'Yeah, maybe.'

Later that night, Jack apologised to Eve, presenting her with a bunch of yellow roses in his living room. As soon as the harshness in her eyes softened, he pounced on her, pinning her down on the couch and kissing every inch of her face. 'I love you. I love you. I love you.'

Jack used his smile like a swab of sulfuric acid, dissolving Eve's anger; all the arguments in her head bubbling up, fizzing out, and disappearing.

'I love you too,' Eve said, and love, Jack thought, was something he could manufacture with flowers and fleshy kisses. They were both victims of their own chemistry, inciting performative gestures, an ancient mixing of molecules, controlling them in every way, like the moon meddling with the tides, ebbing and flowing, revealing and concealing glimpses of what lay beneath, shrouded by disguise.

Chapter 34

M itch woke in a fit of panic, emerging into reality like meat forced through the narrow holes of a mincer. His hands and feet felt numb, the bed was drenched in sweat, the pillows lacquered with snot and drool, his face pockmarked from scratching in his sleep. He'd been sober for a few days, ever since he left Klub Kava. Was it morning or evening, he wondered, Wednesday, Thursday, or even Friday? He felt like he'd woken into a nightmare, remembering the words he told himself when he woke in hospital after overdosing at seventeen.

Sucks to be alive again.

Those words didn't ring true all these years later. Things were different. More complicated. The drowsy memory of his wife and children would not let his thoughts drift towards suicide again. Mitch wished the pain would end, that the numbness in his hands and feet would make its way to his brain and dull his migraine.

That was it, Mitch reasoned, *last time, never again*. He'd go clean for good. Sober up, reconcile with his wife and children, expose Jack and dust the cobwebs off his career. He searched the room for his clothes, determined now, desperately wanting to move forward with his life, but the seesawing of his eyes sent him stumbling. He hit his head off the doorframe and crawled along the floor trying to summon up the strength to stand.

'Judy,' Mitch shouted, begging her to appear, to somehow help.

It had been ages since Mitch felt this humiliated. His shame as raw as sunburn. The pain of regret twisting through him like a corkscrew. His legs felt slack as he stood again, waddling like a toddler learning to walk. Mitch pressed on, feeling his way forward with his hands, slow, unsteady steps. He eventually got to the front door, stumbled down the busy sidewalk, and boarded a streetcar sometime later. He shut his eyes to starve his shame, to block out the people sneering at his clothes, holding their noses and wincing at the smell. Could things ever be right again, Mitch wondered. Where had he been all these months? Every memory felt unreliable, blurred out, like words smudged on a page.

It was after 10 am when Mitch stood at the front door of his home, willing himself to press the doorbell. Judy was surprised to see him standing there. 'What do you want?' Judy asked, shaking her head, a little frightened at the sight of Mitch's black eyes, bruised face, and scabby skin.

'Please,' Mitch said. 'Let me come in. I want to explain everything.'

'You can't just show up like this,' Judy said, shaking her head. 'Did your whore toss you to the curb, Mitch? Is that why you're crawling back to me?'

'Let me explain, please.'

'Five minutes,' Judy said, opening the door. 'I can just about understand the cheating, things had been distant between us, but all the prescriptions and drinking, what the hell is going on with you, Mitch. Chief Cutler rang me; they found drugs in your locker?'

'I wasn't dealing with Betty's death.'

Judy looked much younger than Mitch remembered her. He hadn't seen her in nearly two months. She dressed differently now, her clothes looked a little tighter, her body leaner, wearing black Lulu Lemon yoga pants with a matching t-shirt, and pink Nike runners. Mitch thought it was strange to see her wearing a full face of makeup so early in the morning. He wondered what the neighbours thought. What gossip had been served up with a side of slaw at weekend BBQs? What image of him they'd held in their hands before tossing over a flame to roast?

'Why are you here?' Judy asked. 'Why now, Mitch? You look like death. I barely even recognise you.'

'It's a long story,' Mitch said.

'You better make it quick,' Judy replied, toying with her wedding ring. 'I've a spin class in thirty minutes.'

'Don't be so cold,' Mitch said in staggered breaths. 'I'm sorry. I'll explain everything but it's gonna hurt to hear.'

Judy would miss her spin class that morning. Over cups of coffee, Mitch explained everything, starting with his childhood, a secret he'd kept locked away from his wife like a loaded gun. His father was a brute who died in a freak construction accident when Mitch was ten. He was fixing the track on an excavator when the hydridic jack failed and crushed him to death. His mother began popping pills soon after – breakfast consisting of vodka mixed with lumpy orange juice, a handful of barbiturates, watching morning chat shows on the TV with a slip of drool leaking down her chin as though a slug had crawled out the corner of her mouth. She took her own life when Mitch was thirteen. He found her hanging from the rafters in the garage. Her body looked so cold and grey, so thin and frail, Mitch could see the outline of her bones jutting through her skin. Kneecaps like the butt of teacups. Her collarbones spread across her chest like the handlebars of a bike.

Mitch had sat down on the garage floor, puzzling over the colour of her lips, the shape of her face and the matted clumps of hair stuck to the side of her cheekbones. He didn't feel anything at that moment. It was difficult to detect any daily change, any improvement or dis-improvement in things, no weakening or strengthening of circumstance. It was just his mother, hanging

199

there in a different pose, like a familiar string of oddly skinny shapes.

People thought it was strange that Mitch never cried at his mother's funeral. He just stood there in the church, a flat affect on his face, like a bus driver coursing the same route day in and day out. It was hard to trace the outline of Mitch's emotions. He locked himself away from the world, dressing up the limbs of reality, like a child dressing up a doll.

Mitch's strangeness snowballed soon after, careening down the slope at such velocity he rarely found himself between the crosshairs of normality. However, reality wrangled him like a rancher when he was sent to live with relatives after his mother's funeral. They quickly became chilled by Mitch's strangeness, the way he'd sit on the stairs peeping through the bannisters as they watched TV in the living room. The way he'd stare into his cousins eyes as they asked questions, not responding. How he'd steal his aunt's clothes and cut them up with a scissors after she reproached him.

Mitch ran away after a few months, living on the streets of Toronto, sleeping on subway grates during the winter months trying to keep warm from the steam evaporating from the underground. Drugs kept him from ending his own life. He started out with weed at first, living with vagrants in an abandoned building on the outskirts of Cabbage Town before moving underground, living with tweakers out in Parkdale. Everything changed when Mitch first tried heroin: his body, like a bundle of hacked meat, felt stitched back together in the shape of a swan.

Judy cried into her palms as Mitch opened up about his childhood. It was hard for her to hear the details of Mitch's blunted emotional development, the drug use, the enigmatic forces of right and wrong quacking inside him like a lame duck. She didn't know where to place these other sides of Mitch, the details fanning out across her memory, like a warlord conquering whole swathes of their history together – the various vicissitudes Mitch played like a violin – its theme was revelatory, its tune steeped in sadness.

'Why did you never tell me this before, Mitch? This isn't something you keep from your wife?'

'I thought you'd look at me differently, like I'm trash. And maybe I am, but I didn't want you to think of me like that. I wanted you to think of me as someone else, but I guess that's always been my problem, eh?'

'If you had told me all this before, I could have helped you.'

'No one could have,' Mitch said tearfully. 'Everything just fell apart again when Betty died.'

'Don't,' Judy said, tearfully.

'You never want to talk about her,' Mitch cried. 'No one does. It's like everyone just wants to forget she ever existed.'

'No, we don't, Mitch. Everyone has their own way of dealing with grief.'

Mitch burst out crying, and Judy held him in her arms, wiping the sweat from his brow, trying to soothe the shivers vibrating through his body. In college, Judy had trained as a nurse. She knew alcoholics could die if they suddenly stopped drinking. The feeling overwhelmed her. Mitch wasn't target practice anymore. He'd morphed into her husband again, open and honest, warts and all. Judy ran to the pantry and fetched a bottle of Scotch they'd been given as a wedding present. She took two glasses from the cupboards and poured them to the brim.

'What are you doing?' Mitch asked sharply. 'I'm sworn off it, Juds. I want to change.'

'You need to wean off slowly,' Judy replied.

Mitch downed his Scotch and poured another. He knew Judy was right. On the streetcar, he'd felt his consciousness fade like the end of a firework. His breathing grew shallow and the numbness in his hands and feet crept further up his arms and legs.

'We'll get you signed into somewhere,' Judy said, knocking back her Scotch, wincing halfway through and spitting it back into the glass. 'I can't understand but I don't need to. There's a place in Montreal. Their twelve-week programme has a seventy-five per cent success rate. They could be here this evening.'

'No,' Mitch protested.

'Don't worry about the money,' Judy said, trying to calm him again. 'I'll call Pop, he'll be happy to help out. He's worried about you. Everyone is.'

'It's not the money,' Mitch said, pouring another glass and downing it. 'It's the case I've been working on, Juds. If I give up now, they'll vanish, and the last few months will be for nothing.'

'Who?' Judy exclaimed. 'What case? Chief Cutler told me you were fired.'

Mitch excavated his theory like an archaeologist, slowly exhuming facts and esoteric detail, claiming that Jack was The Poet and that Mel was responsible for multiple murders across the city.

Judy's empathy wavered throughout her husband's monologue. She didn't know what was real or drink-induced, especially when Mitch claimed that Jack had been stalking him since the Carmady murders. 'I think he's the one who ran down Betty,' Mitch said. 'That's what he does, Juds. He's a tightrope act, thrilled by everyone else's fear, so sure of his own footing.'

'That's grief talking, Mitch.'

'No,' Mitch said. 'He killed Betty knowing my life would spiral out of control. He wanted me to fall apart. It's all a game to him.'

Judy shook her head. 'That's on you, Mitch. You need to understand that. You chose to relapse. You chose to turn your back on your family, and you need to admit that if we're to move on from this.'

'Okay,' Mitch said before going on to tell Judy about his call with Detective McGuire, and how the Spadina store manager recognised Jack's photo.

'These sound like dangerous people,' Judy said nervously. 'Are we in danger, Mitch?'

'No,' Mitch said, 'but make sure you keep the doors locked.'

Mitch was on his fifth glass of Scotch when his phone vibrated. Judy was in the toilet, wiping the tears from her eyes, gazing into the mirror numbed with shock. Mitch unlocked his phone and felt a jolt of panic when he saw the message.

Glenda: We need to talk. How quick can you be here?

Mitch: Leaving now, be there in 30 minutes.

Mitch would keep the message a secret. Things were still too raw. He'd rolled over his wife like a Mack truck and he wasn't sure how much else she could take.

'I've gotta go,' Mitch said when Judy reappeared. 'Last loose end, I promise.'

'I don't like you leaving in this state.'

'I'm fine,' Mitch reassured. 'I'll be back soon.'

'Be honest, Mitch. Where are you going? We can only move forward if you tell the truth.'

'Let me talk to Chief Cutler,' Mitch pleaded. 'After that, I'll go anywhere you want, dry out and be back for Christmas.'

'Okay,' Judy said. 'Let's meet later, but not here. I don't want the kids to see you like this. I told them you were gone catching bad guys in BC. I'll meet you off Queen Street. Text me.'

Mitch kissed his wife on her forehead and held her in his arms. 'I love you,' he said, sweeping back Judy's hair and staring into her eyes. 'But I never told you enough. I won't make that mistake again. Things will be different, Juds.'

'I love you too,' Judy said. 'Keep in contact with me, Mitch.'

They were themselves again, though different, like survivors of some calamity, happy to be alive, viewing each other from different heights, some morphed perspective that saw them smile at their own genesis again.

Chapter 35

Glenda seldom worked on Thursdays. She usually bought a coffee from her local café, where she would sit, reading romance novels and gazing at the other patrons, infinitely curious about their lives. Her loneliness was hard to ignore, a deep sadness sunken into the hollow of her eyes, the way she stirred her coffee, looking around the café, smiling, hoping to catch someone smiling back at her. After leaving the café, Glenda usually did her laundry at the nearby laundromat. Jack often watched her sorting through her clothes, separating her garments into different washes, dark colours spun in one machine, light colours in another. Jack dreamed up a little poem one morning, sipping coffee, watching her from a café across the street.

Swish swash, swish swash,
Its laundry day
And I've clothes to wash.
The machine spins off,
And memories toss,
So clothes come clean
Out of the wash.
Clean for now
But at a cost,
The grime has gone

But the memories lost!
To the dull, drumming groan
Of swish swash, swish swash.

With her laundry done, Glenda often stood in her living room, painting oils on canvas, with a large glass of chardonnay in hand. Jack reasoned Thursday at lunchtime was his best chance to strike. He ate lunch in Castor's Bar, ordering a Caesar salad and a pint of IPA, sitting at a window booth with a clear view of Glenda's apartment. Like clockwork, she appeared in her living room after lunchtime, wine in hand, twirling around the room in a lemon-coloured sundress.

Jack left Castor's Bar, dressed in black gym attire, calmly walking to the back of Glenda's building, entering through the emergency stairwell and ascending the steps to the third floor. Jack had practised this route many times. Ever since Eve mentioned that Glenda had provided a suspect sketch, Jack had added her to his list of *things to bludgeon*. There were no cameras in the hallways of her building, back entrance, or stairwells. Most of Glenda's neighbours had left for work before 10 am and delivery men had usually passed through before midday.

Jack knocked on Glenda's front door, smiling into the peephole. She opened the door slowly and peeped out. 'Do I know you from somewhere?' Glenda asked. 'Your face looks familiar.'

'I don't think so,' Jack said, shaking his head and looking to the floor. 'I'm here with troubling news. It's about Mitch.'

'Mitch Bauer!' Glenda exclaimed. 'Is he okay? What's happened?'

'You're going to want to be sitting down for this,' Jack said, pausing to sniffle softly. 'May I come in?'

'Sure. Sure,' Glenda said. 'Oh, Jeez. Please tell me he's okay. Such a nice guy. Jeez. Mitch. Really. Is he in trouble? I hope nothing bad happened. Did something bad happen?'

'You're under suspicion,' Jack said, a coldness settling in his voice, walking towards the living room, scanning for exit and entry points. 'We know about your affair with Mitch. I guess you weren't aware he had a wife and children.'

'What do you mean? Suspicion for what?'

The living room was spacious, with an open-plan design connected to the kitchen. Jack pointed to the leather couches. 'You're gonna want to sit for this.'

'For what?' Glenda asked, toying with her pigtails. 'I've done nothing wrong. You're creeping me out. I don't like this. Can you please leave?'

'This is serious,' Jack warned, his eyes dark and empty. 'When did you last meet with Mitch?'

Glenda threw her hands in the air. 'I haven't seen Mitch in weeks. Can you just tell me what's going on? What has happened to Mitch? And who are you? Are you a cop or something?'

'I'll get you a glass of water first,' Jack said, walking towards the kitchen, slipping on a pair of leather gloves and taking a large meat knife out of its block.

'I don't want a glass of water,' Glenda protested. 'I want to know what's wrong with Mitch. I told you, I haven't seen him in a while. Jeez,' she shouted. 'What's going on? Can you please answer me?'

'Sure,' Jack said calmly, walking back towards her with his hands behind his back. 'Mitch is going to be in serious trouble real soon.'

'What?' Glenda exclaimed. 'I don't understand. Can you please leave now? This is weird.'

'No,' Jack said, 'you stupid bitch,' lunging forward, pinning the knife to her neck and breathing onto her face. Glenda screamed, but Jack subdued her, pressing the blade against her Carotid artery. 'Make another sound, and I'll slit your fucking throat. Nod if you understand.'

207

Glenda screamed, and when she went to flee, Jack tripped her legs, sending her tumbling over the coffee table. Glenda crawled along the floor, scratching at the large, cream-coloured rug.

'Relax,' Jack said, standing over her. 'It's Mitch I want. I just need to send a text message from your phone.'

Jack bound Glenda's hands with zip-ties, tied a gag around her mouth and left her on the floor like a strung-up piece of lemon curd. He retrieved her phone from the coffee table and unlocked it with her thumbprint. The mood was calm and relaxed. Glenda found that odd; it confused her more, like some weird sex game she had read about once in an erotic romance novel. She half expected Mitch to appear through the door, that this was some hero fantasy of his, where he would save her from some faux pas killer and they would have a threesome in her living room.

Jack knew otherwise. He clicked into Glenda's messages with Mitch and started typing.

Glenda: We need to talk. How quick can you be here?

A minute later, Mitch responded, dissolving Jack's doubts about his plan.

'Mitch will be here soon,' Jack said. 'Now relax. You'll live, it's Mitch I want.'

Classical music played from a nearby speaker. Jack scrolled through Glenda's Spotify account and smiled when he saw Leonard Cohen's *You Want It Darker* in her recently played songs. Jack pressed play and began shuffling his shoulders, his feet dancing to the rhythm. It was a sort of ecstasy Jack experienced. His eyes closed in rapture, so many tingles racing up and down his spine, like little sparks hissing from a fuse and fizzling down into a powder keg of pleasure. Glenda struggled on the floor at first but settled into her predicament, a strange form of hope and obedience settling in her limbs. She loved that song too. It brought her some semblance of comfort. The ritual of it all, the song playing on repeat, Jack dancing and breathing heavily, joining in the chorus each time. Glenda even muttered the chorus to herself. If this was a fantasy, Mitch had hired a very convincing actor, Glenda thought. She rolled her head to the side and peeped behind her shoulder to watch Jack dance, noting the reptilian coldness in his eyes when he looked at her before his stare bounced off again, somewhere distant. He was like a far-off figure from another world. Glenda wondered how God could permit such people entry into existence. People with no internal jury shaping their feelings, no conscience scrubbing over their actions, their morality melted down and wrought into a weapon. She wished she could ask Jack some questions. To understand what he was like as a boy. Had he ever felt love or fear? Regret? Were other people merely meat in his refrigerated world?

The song had been playing on repeat for over thirty minutes when Jack walked over to the window and looked down the street, glancing in each direction, scanning for Mitch. A few moments later, Jack caught sight of Mitch turning a corner around three hundred yards away. Jack guessed he would have around five minutes to complete the job. He gripped the knife in his hand, forced Glenda to her feet and cut the gag from around her mouth.

He didn't expect Glenda to scream so loudly, and when she kicked him in the groin, he fell to his knees in pain. Glenda saw her chance and ran for the front door, screaming, 'Help. Help' She turned her back to the door handle and tried pressing it downwards with her bound hands. 'Someone help me. I'm being attacked. Help.'

Jack struggled to his feet eventually. 'I'm not going to hurt you,' he shouted after Glenda. 'I just want to talk to Mitch. I'll let you go once he arrives.'

'You were going to hurt me,' Glenda screamed, jumping up and down, trying to push down the door handle. When she looked up, Jack was standing in the living room doorframe, his eyes black as ink, the features of his face weirdly distorted. 'Come here.'

'No way,' Glenda screamed. 'Help, someone help me.'

Jack never spoke as he walked towards her calmly. He grabbed her by the hair and dragged her back into the living room as she screamed and struggled in his grip.

He cut off the zip-ties. 'Look,' Jack said, 'I'm letting you go.'

'Really?' Glenda asked, tears streaming down her face.

'No, you dumb bitch.'

Jack slashed her arms when she raised them. There was no hesitation in his eyes, no comfort of emotion, or flicker of humanity. She was just a thing, like a boxing bag he jabbed at with his knife. Her head began to roll and twitch as he stabbed her a few times in the torso. But a cold front of panic washed over him when he heard the police sirens wailing in the distance.

'Fuck,' Jack shouted. 'Someone must've heard you screaming.'

He buried the knife in Glenda's chest and left her condo swiftly. He jogged down the stairs as Mitch called the elevator on the ground floor, stumbling inside, thinking of what he would say to Glenda. Neither man caught sight of the other. Perhaps some other version of reality would see their roles reversed, their instinct swapped during childhood, stoked and fed, given strength and mirth by the mauling of the mob within. Jack believed it was possible, that there were other versions of himself, infinite realities, a multitude of universes where he was the victim of this crime, the woman bleeding out on the floor or the unbeknownst man ascending in the elevator. But not today, Jack mused. He was the fruit of this life. A dark stain on reality's conscience, gazing at itself in a broken mirror, wearing the crown of creation on his head, carrying the scythe of death in his hand. Jack, by vigorous contrast, made the distinction between soldiering and sadism. The attack on Glenda was an act of soldiering, an instinctual obligation towards self-preservation.

Jack's motorbike was parked close to Glenda's condo. He walked through the backstreets, the hood of his jacket wrapped around his head, his face lowered to the pavement, wiping the blood splatter from his neck with his sleeve. He could hear police sirens wailing, the shrill of an ambulance getting closer, car horns honking erratically. Things hadn't gone to plan. He hadn't managed to kill Mitch and he worried that Glenda might just survive.

Chapter 36

The streetcar CCTV cameras captured Mitch in a maniacal state, walking up and down the centre carriage, talking to himself; the Queen Street sidewalk trailing away in the distance like a film reel. Mitch found himself in the lavatory of inebriation again, his mind flushed with alcohol, his sobriety breaking apart like a stool.

When he arrived at Glenda's apartment, he found the door slightly ajar. The hallway was quiet, and he detected a faint metallic smell. 'Glenda?' Mitch called out, stepping through. 'Are you at home? I'm glad you messaged me. I've been meaning to reach out.'

Mitch could hear an eerie, heaving noise coming from the living room. He moved slowly through the hallway, and a cold chill washed over him when he found Glenda lying on the living room floor. Blood was pooling around her body and a large kitchen knife was sticking upright from her chest. Everything seemed surreal, some cinematic haze, and Mitch closed his eyes, unable to contemplate what he saw.

'This isn't happening. This isn't happening. This isn't happening,' Mitch repeated, like a spell of sorts, trying to summon up a different scene where Glenda was alive and happy to forget their time together. When Mitch opened his eyes again, he screamed before falling to his knees and crawling over to Glenda's body. She was barely alive. Her eyes were wide, but her breathing was laboured and blood gurgled in her throat. Mitch shook her shoulders and gazed into her frightened eyes. Police sirens wailed outside the window, car doors slammed shut, and staticky voices came in and out over police radios.

'What have you done?' Mitch shouted, not realising the unlikelihood of Glenda stabbing herself or that he was contaminating a potential crime scene and her blood was smeared all over his hands and clothes. All of Mitch's academy training evaporated, pulling the knife out of Glenda's chest and attempting to perform CPR. Mitch drunkenly believed he could bring her back, breathing through her mouth, performing chest compressions, and saying prayers in his head.

Two young cops were first on the scene. A neighbour close to the elevator peeped out from behind her front door and directed the cops towards Glenda's apartment. With their guns drawn, the cops entered through Glenda's front door and paced slowly through her hallway. The sound of blood gurgling in Glenda's throat drew them closer to the living room. The younger cop, Officer Brady, was fresh to the force. He hadn't seen much action; he barely looked twenty-one, but darkness came early that day. The proceeding image would haunt him for the rest of his life. The sight of Mitch, drenched in blood, down on his hands and knees, bent over Glenda's body, trying to eat her face. It didn't occur to Officer Brady that Mitch was trying to perform CPR.

Mitch was startled when the cops appeared.

'Hands where I can see them,' the older cop shouted. 'Move away from the body.'

'Help,' Mitch cried back, his hands raised, his clothes drenched in Glenda's blood. 'Please help her.'

'Lie face down,' Officer Brady shouted. 'Hands behind your back.'

'This wasn't me,' Mitch cried.

'Hands behind your back,' Officer Brady shouted again.

When Mitch lunged forward, Officer Brady squeezed the trigger. There was a muzzle flash, a loud bang, and then another. Two bullets pierced Mitch's chest, and he collapsed to his knees before slumping over onto Glenda.

Through panicked breath, Officer Brady announced over the radio. 'Shots fired. Suspect down. Requesting backup. He was eating her fucking face. Send medical.'

~~~

When Jack arrived back at his condo, he stood before his bedroom mirror looking at all the specks of blood dotted around his face. He relived the murder, scene by scene, remembering the expression in Glenda's eyes: something more adjacent to awe than fear. Her power of feeling was much beyond his own, as fine as gauze, alone and helpless, trapped in a war she would not survive. But what if she had, Jack wondered. What if he left evidence at the scene? What if Mitch had revived Glenda and was hailed as a hero instead of being pinned for the murder/suicide Jack had planned to stage?

Jack showered a while later, scrubbing his hands and face with a thick lather of body wash, turning up the heat, causing the room to fill with steam. He dressed sometime later, opened his phone and messaged Mel.

Jack: Things got messy. We need to talk.

He lay on the bed staring at the ceiling. It was mainly hunger Jack felt now. The yearning for a steak, a glass of red wine, a side of beef dripping fries and thick pepper sauce with a subtle hint of vinegar. He was dreaming of food when his phone vibrated on his bedside locker. Mel was calling.

'Hey,' Jack answered. 'You got my message?'

'What happened?'

'Things didn't go as planned,' Jack said distantly. 'A neighbour must have heard her screaming or something. I don't know. The cops showed up before I could take care of Mitch and call it in.'

'Shit,' Mel said. 'We needed him dead and discredited. That's the only way any of this works.'

'I know,' Jack said. 'This is bad.'

'I did the wife as well,' Mel blurted excitedly. 'I followed him to her house this morning and saw them crying in the kitchen together. He told her about us, so I made it look like he killed her.'

'Knife?'

'Yeah,' Mel said. 'Real messy. There could be a silver lining here, Seany. It might look like Mitch killed them both. Unhinged former Toronto detective kills his ex-wife and then his girlfriend.'

'I'm not sure Glenda died,' Jack said. 'This could backfire on us big time, Mel.'

'Aw, screw it.'

'Best to lie low,' Jack said, with a strange tension in his voice, 'and if we get cornered, let's go out in a blaze of bullets. Do something that will have them writing books about us for the next thousand years.'

'Sounds exciting,' Mel said. 'Can we just do that anyway, Seany? I feel so bored all the time. Killing is the only time I feel alive. Maybe I should just kill myself. Would you miss me?'

'Sure, Mel, I'd miss you like a hole in the head.'

'Asshole,' Mel said, laughing.

'Were the children there?' Jack asked.

'No,' Mel said. 'I only did the wife. She was a fighter, Seany. I think we could have been friends; she had an animal inside of her.'

'You don't have friends,' Jack said. 'Anyway, I'm out of here in a few days. I'll ring you when I get to Australia. That's if I make it there at all.'

215

Chapter 37

'Good morning, Toronto,' the female CTV News anchor announced the following morning. 'A forty-year-old man is in custody facing multiple murder charges after one woman was found stabbed to death at her condo near St Lawrence Market, while another woman, alleged to be the suspect's wife, was found dead at her house in the Forrest Grove area. The suspect is in critical condition after receiving two gunshot wounds to his chest. In a warning, some viewers might find the rest of this report disturbing.'

The news segment went on to report how a disgraced, former Toronto homicide detective was suspected of stabbing his wife in the family kitchen. Judy Bauer received over thirty stab wounds to her torso. Her throat was slit so deep she was almost left decapitated. CTV News played the CCTV footage of Mitch, appearing crazed and frenzied, talking to himself on a streetcar after leaving the family home in Forrest Grove.

'This is former detective Mitch Bauer,' the female news anchor said, 'a once decorated homicide detective who helped catch murderers but is now suspected of committing two. The question on everyone's lips this morning is, how can this happen?'

The news report then switched to Forrest Grove, where a reporter stood outside the family home interviewing a neighbour. 'Mitch always looked at me oddly,' the neighbour said nervously into the camera. 'He had frisky eyes. This doesn't come as a shock to me. I just feel so bad for the children, little Rachel finding her mother like that.'

'And the rumoured drug use?' the reporter probed.

'Mitch was an addict,' the neighbour went on. 'Heroin, booze, prescriptions, even the stuff that makes you hallucinate. Judy told me herself. We were very close,' the neighbour said, shedding a few tears, as the reporter put his arm around her for comfort. 'Judy threw Mitch out of the house months ago. She was afraid of him around the kids. I knew something like this would happen. I tried to warn Judy, but she wouldn't listen to me. I should have done more, but Mitch was a cop, and they wouldn't have listened to me either. He was one of their own. You know how these things go; cops cover for each other.'

'Well, this story just keeps getting stranger,' the reporter said. 'How will the Toronto Police Service explain this one? Was Detective Bauer on drugs while on the job? Did he use his position of power to cover up other murders? Could convictions related to the cases he worked on be overturned? Back to you in studio, Joanne.'

At a press conference that morning, Chief Cutler resigned after news leaked that she had allowed Mitch to work under the influence of booze and Oxy. In her resignation speech, she reassured her fellow Torontonians that one bad apple does not muddy the batch, that they must maintain faith in the brave men and women who put their lives on the line to keep the city safe. A scrum of journalists rushed with questions, but jaded by it all, Chief Cutler walked off stage, her head downed by defeat.

The mayor of Toronto appeared on CTV News next, promising an independent investigation into the integrity of the Toronto Police Service. One reporter shouted from the back of the press conference, 'Violent crime is soaring in Toronto. The homicide rate is the highest in the country. Is Toronto a safe city anymore?'

'Thank you. Thank you very much for that,' Mayor Adams said, toying with her pearl earring. 'Let me reassure everyone. Toronto is a safe city, and I won't stop working until every person in the city feels safe.'

'There were over twenty murders last month alone,' another reporter hurled, 'and most are still unsolved. Toronto doesn't feel like a safe city.'

Over the next twenty minutes, Mayor Adams felt the full force of public outcry, concluding each answer with the words. 'This is a safe city.'

CTV News replayed grainy CCTV footage of Mitch on the streetcar throughout the morning news cycle. Other news channels reported that one of the victims had half of her face eaten, and by 11:30 am, Mitch had become nationally known as 'The Cannibal Crackhead.' But Mitch was unaware of his new found notoriety as he lay in the ICU at Toronto General Hospital, handcuffed to the bed after undergoing major surgery to remove two bullets from his chest. The doctors had put Mitch in an induced coma. Still, his vitals were improving, and the detectives working the case, his former colleagues, were overly insistent that Mitch needed to be woken to answer questions.

Chapter 38

'I can't believe Mitch would do this,' Eve said, sipping coffee in Jack's living room. 'Addiction is one thing, but murder. He loved his wife.'

'You seen the police report,' Jack said, walking his fingers over Eve's head as a gesture of comfort. 'When the cops showed up, he was eating a woman's face.'

'We don't know that for sure,' Eve said nervously, 'but you know how the media is, they'll do anything for ratings.'

'I told you Mitch was dangerous,' Jack said, leaning back into the couch. 'He was operating outside the bounds of reality. People like that do crazy things.'

'I know,' Eve said. 'I guess, I didn't want to believe you. I still don't. Mitch is a good man. He's not a murderer, Jack.'

'You would have said he wasn't a smackhead either,' Jack remarked, switching between the news channels. 'You said once that Mitch was the straightest arrow in the sleeve. That remark didn't age well, babe. Don't go around talking about how good of a man Mitch is. Look what's happening, Chief Cutler has had to resign, and I bet the other detectives aren't happy about Mayor Adam's investigation poking around in their private lives.'

The stress made Eve's eyes look larger, more intense, that morning radiant. She stayed silent for a time, revolving the mystery in her head, awaiting some suggestion that Mitch was innocent. At times, he had been like a father figure, and she couldn't understand how all that had suddenly changed.

'In a few days, we'll be out of here,' Jack said, glancing at his watch. 'Another world awaits, and we can leave all the crazy stuff behind us.'

'I've never flown on a private plane,' Eve said distantly. 'Are those planes safe? They look small. It makes me nervous.'

'Everything makes you nervous,' Jack said. 'It's cute.'

Eve's face assumed a cartoonish sadness, her eyes large, her lips pursed out like a child's. 'I mean it,' Eve said. 'New things freak me out sometimes. I've never flown to another country and Oz has all those creepy crawlies. What if I get bitten by a spider or a snake eats me? They have snakes that big, you know? The scrub python can grow up to eight meters long. I only weigh a buck twenty; I'd be like a little snack.'

'You're lucky you have me to protect you so.'

'Where's my passport?' Eve exclaimed, withdrawing from Jack's embrace. 'I haven't seen it today.'

'It's in the travel bag, where you put it three days ago.'

Eve scampered down the hall. 'I know I overthink these things but let me check.'

~~~

The large safe in Jack's bedroom was locked but empty. The walk-in wardrobes barren, the bedroom drawers cleaned out and neatly packed away in storage boxes. Jack planned to ship his belongings over to Oz once he and Eve got settled. Jack's yacht and Porsche had been sold; his motorbike was gifted to Mel later that evening when they met up in secret at Castor's Bar, toasting drinks, and laughing in a corner booth.

Neither suffered any qualms of conscience. There was an all-tidings atmosphere, swallowing tequila shots as though the new year had arrived early. How tolerable the world felt, problems extinguished like candles, their grins as savoury as gravy. Their gloating couldn't wait; they had to meet up sooner, a dark subconscious instinct forcing them together like magnets.

Mel giggled into her hands. 'The Cannibal Crackhead. I had to laugh when I read that headline, Seany. The cops must've burst in as he was attempting CPR. How lucky are we?'

'Maybe Dad was looking down on us.'

'Do you think he'd be proud of us?'

'I don't know,' Jack said, licking tequila from his drunken lips. 'It's not like we got to know the guy. I just hate how we grew up hating him all our lives.'

'If only we had known the truth sooner; we might have turned out differently.'

'Nah,' Jack said. 'The truth wouldn't have mattered – we were doomed from the moment we touched down in Toronto. We lived through hell, and that sort of hell gets into the marrow of your bones – it plants itself deep in your brain stem and slithers around your thoughts, looking for something soft to sink its teeth into.'

'Maybe revenge will cure us,' Mel said, shooting another tequila. 'After Paddy confessed, you promised to take care of Jenny and Don, but instead, you'd rather run away with your piece of skin.'

Jack raised his hands in defeat. 'I'm in love.'

'No, you're not,' Mel said, laughing. 'If Eve ever found out what you really are, you'd kill her in a heartbeat. You just like the game and the rush of it all. People like me and you can't fall in love, Seany. We have dinosaur brains; we look at people like they're food.'

'You have a nose like one of those big dinosaurs,' Jack mocked.

'Rah, rah,' Mel said, reaching over the table, trying to slap him. 'Go bleed out somewhere else. You know, when I get caught, whenever that is, I think I'll write a book about all this – about the dinosaur who wears pretty lipstick so the world doesn't notice how big and sharp her teeth are.'

'What would you call the book?' Jack asked.

'Dino Girl,' Mel said excitedly. 'No. Miss Wish.'

'I like Miss Wish.'

'Me too,' Mel said, giggling. 'What would you call yours?'

Jack grinned, thinking of the possibilities. 'Dark Finds.'

'Remember when you used to call yourself that? You said your superpower was the ability to find darkness in everything and everyone. Now, look at you, Toronto's most active serial killer.'

'Keep your voice down.'

'Aw, screw them,' Mel said. 'You know, you still haven't told me why you leave the poem.'

'Maybe I want everyone talking about me and not the victim.'

'I never understood that side of you,' Mel said, shaking her head. 'Why do you want to bring that sort of attention on yourself? That's when everything falls to shit. My way is much better; I fly under the radar, the cops haven't linked my murders together. I'm like a ghost prowling the city.'

'But no one will remember you.'

'Maybe I'll go on a spree, a real hamburger and cheese job. Mel's recipes on how to boil, broil, and pan fry a man's little brisket. They'll remember me then.'

'Nice,' Jack said, downing another tequila.

'I mean it,' Mel said. 'I'm so hungry for death, I fear I'll eat myself.'

'Shush now. We've survived worse than a bored mood.'

'Screw it,' Mel shouted, causing some of the other patrons to look in her direction. 'One more for old time's sake.'

'I can't drink any more tequila,' Jack said, his hands raised.

'No,' Mel said chillingly. 'Let's go kill something else.'

Chapter 39

It was one of those dark evenings in Toronto where the sun seemed to set earlier, darkness swallowing daylight, the clouds hiding stars, mist skirting across Lake Ontario, giving the city a spectral feel along its edges. And while Jack and Mel drank secretly in Castor's Bar, Eve set out on her own secret escapade. At 7 pm, she got a call from Officer Lee informing her that Mitch had woken and wouldn't speak to anyone except her. Eve mused over her decision – overthinking outcomes, but compelled by curiosity and some semblance of friendship, she put on her coat and caught a cab to Toronto General.

Eve walked through the sliding glass doors of the hospital. The smell of antiseptics mingled with the scent of hospital food wafting from the nearby cafeteria. Eve held her breath for a moment as nurses and doctors rushed by her on their way to the ICU. Amidst the usual hospital stirrings, a tense atmosphere had settled, heightened by the uniformed police officers stationed at strategic points throughout the halls. Eve felt sick with nerves, walking down the main corridor, panged by the heightened police presence, some of whom she knew, instigating chitchat, some offering commiserations – *whatever the hell that was about.*

Eve felt a heaviness in her chest, a knot of anticipation and resentment that had lodged there from the moment she had received the call about Mitch. She wondered what Jack would say if he knew where she was. He had warned her not to visit Mitch.

And why was she here anyway? She didn't owe Mitch anything, not after what he had done. Part of her wished Mitch had died, saving her the shame of walking down these halls with everyone looking at her as Mitch's partner, as though she was somehow complicit.

As Eve reached the guarded entrance to the ICU, she noticed Officer Lee, dressed in a suit and tie, talking to some beat cops. He'd been promoted to detective after Mitch's suspension and he had a green look about him.

'Hey Eve,' Detective Lee said.

'You got promoted,' Eve said, smiling. 'Congrats.'

'Thanks. I've never wanted anything so much. It's always been my dream, you know. It just feels weird that my first real case is one of our own.'

'I still can't get my head around it,' Eve said. 'How is Mitch?'

'I don't know,' Lee said, pausing. 'It's hard to know what to believe anymore. We used to joke that Mitch was the sort of cop who would arrest his wife if he caught her speeding. This doesn't make any sense. Mitch was by the book. As honest as they come. Yeah, he fell off the wagon after his daughter died; I was critical of his behaviour, but booze and prescriptions don't turn someone into a killer. At least, I don't want to believe they do.'

'I don't want to believe it either?'

'We're the only ones,' Lee said, staring off distantly. 'The department is fuming. Fassnidge told the surgeons to let Mitch die in surgery or else he'd make their lives a living hell. They want Mitch dead one way or another. You should have seen the uproar when they heard he'd survived.'

'I can understand their frustration,' Eve said. 'But if Mitch really did these murders, he needs to be brought to justice. Letting him die on a gurney won't give us any answers.'

'I agree,' Lee said, 'everyone is just worried about how it'll look, how the media will spin it. Imagine what the trial will be like.'

'A damn circus,' Eve added.

'When people lose faith in the force, the city falls. Things are bad enough as it is. The unsolved rate is through the roof, and we have at least one if not two active serial killers on the loose. Anyway,' Lee said, looking at Eve again, 'it's not your problem anymore. I heard you handed in your badge.'

'Getting out of dodge at the right time, eh?'

'Where are you off to?'

'Australia.'

'Doesn't look at all suspicious,' Lee said. 'When do you leave?'

'In three days.'

'You might have to cancel that for now,' Lee said more seriously. 'You'll have lots of questions to answer, being Mitch's partner and all.'

'Ex-partner,' Eve said, feeling the knot in her chest tighten even more.

'You know how these things go. Take it from a friend; stick around a little longer.'

Officer Lee then nodded to the private room behind him. 'Mitch is in there. See what you can get out of him.'

Eve nodded before stepping into Mitch's darkened room.

'You always loved a good headline,' Eve said as Mitch raised slightly in the bed. 'But I never thought you'd inspire one. The Cannibal Crackhead. What the hell, Mitch?'

'That's not me,' Mitch muttered through bated breath. 'You're the only one left who understands that.'

'Was,' Eve corrected, folding her arms. 'The evidence tells a different story.'

'Look closer to home.'

'What does that mean?'

'Jack,' Mitch snarled. 'This is his doing. Him and his twin sister, Mel. I thought I could catch them, but they are soulless, like trying to catch smoke in your hand; they disappear the closer you get to them.'

'How much morphine have they got you on?'

'I bet you didn't even know he had a twin sister?'

'Jack has no family left,' Eve said sternly. 'They died years ago in a car accident.'

'No,' Mitch corrected. 'Jack's father is Anthony Murphy. You already know how that story ended. Jack and Mel are the two surviving children.'

'Anthony Murphy?' Eve exclaimed. 'Paddy Fitzgerald's deceased business partner?'

'Yeah, that's him,' Mitch said.

'You're hopeless, Mitch. You were found eating a woman's face, and now you're trying to project blame onto my fiancé.'

'Your fiancé is The Poet,' Mitch said, trying to sit up in the bed and face Eve. 'And I can prove it. I was on his yacht the Saturday morning when you and Jack went sailing. Pablo didn't forget to lock the doors; I picked the lock. I was in the bedroom, looking through Jack's wall-safe, and guess what I found?'

Eve stared at Mitch in silence.

'The notepad where he wrote his poems,' Mitch said, breathing heavily, 'and a list with the dates of all his murders. There were even photos of his father, Anthony Murphy. If you don't believe me go check for yourself. The combination to the safe is 3333.'

'Bullshit,' Eve said, veering close to a panic attack, falling forward slightly, almost breathless. 'If you found any evidence you would have called it in.'

'I was suspended,' Mitch said, 'and anyway, you wouldn't have believed me, you were too blinded by his charm. Everyone

226

thought I was crazy, but I wasn't. I was on to him, building evidence, but I got too close and look at me now.'

Eve breathed heavily as Detective Lee opened the door and peeked inside.

'Go now and check for yourself,' Mitch said, 'or are you covering for him? People are dying, and that's on you, Eve.'

Eve quickly closed the door on Lee and locked it.

'What's going on?' Lee asked. 'What are you two plotting?'

'One more minute,' Eve said before turning to Mitch. 'Jack sold his yacht. We're moving to Australia in three days.'

'The notepad will be packed in his suitcase,' Mitch said. 'It's like a trophy, Jack won't leave without it.'

Detective Lee started banging on the door. 'What the hell is going on in there?'

'Don't leave with Jack,' Mitch urged. 'He's a monster, Eve. Turn him in. Think of all the victims. He and Mel killed my wife and Glenda trying to discredit me, don't you see that?'

'I can't listen to this any longer,' Eve shouted. 'I suppose Jack put the bourbon to your lips, too? I'm outta here, Mitch.'

'Check his suitcase,' Mitch shouted after Eve. 'The notepad will be there.'

'Yeah,' Eve said, 'screw you. I came here. I came to...I don't know what I expected, but not this.'

Mitch's heart rate was rising. He drifted in and out of consciousness, shouting. 'Check his suitcase. Check his suitcase. Check his...'

Lee rushed in as Eve unlocked the door. 'What the hell was that about?' he asked as Eve brushed by.

'I need some air,' Eve said, running for the main entrance.

'Eve,' Lee shouted after her. 'If Mitch told you something, you need to tell us.'

'Air first,' Eve shouted back. 'I need some air.'

Chapter 40

Jack stumbled home steaming drunk in the early morning hours, mumbling about how he had met with old friends and how they had given him a memorable send-off. 'One for the books, babe. Killer night.'

Eve felt cold towards him. What friends, she wondered. When she probed Jack for more information, he ignored her and started singing, *You Want It Darker.*

'The state of you,' Eve said, shaking her head.

Jack didn't look like the man she loved. His eyes were large and empty, thrilled by some secret world where she did not belong. Eve knew Jack's darkness was on the loose again, that he looked at her, not as a lover, but as a toy.

'I love you,' Jack said slurring his words and wiping his hands in his jeans.

He hugged Eve like a stranger, aiming to kiss her cheek but missing, lipping her ear awkwardly. He passed out a few moments later when his head hit the pillow, fully clothed, star-fished across the bed. Eve watched him for a while, picking at her fingernails, her suspicions stumbling forward, Mitch's remarks spreading across her thoughts like fungus.

Before Jack arrived home, she had searched his suitcase, wardrobes, and drawers but she couldn't find any notepad or Polaroids. Mitch had it wrong, she guessed. What did Mitch know anyway? His mind was messed up from all the booze. But still, Eve felt the knot in her chest get tighter and tighter. Her head ached from thoughts, and she fell into a dark reverie, staring at the ceiling, plucking away at sights and sounds, dissembling her worries like the small gears of a watch, which later, she would be unable to piece back together when everything had changed, when the past tripped over and fell into the future, damaged and delirious, the flow and overflow of Jack's duplicity drowning out her days like a deluge.

Close to dawn, while Jack slept, Eve looked over at him and noticed a bulge in the front pocket of his jeans.

'What's that?' she muttered.

She rummaged through Jack's pocket, trying not to wake him. Slowly, she prised a small notepad from his pocket; her heartbeat drumming in her ears, her thoughts trying to convince her to abort and go to sleep. But Eve persisted, wriggling the notepad from side to side in slow, steady motions. As Eve lifted the notepad, a few Polaroids fell onto the floor.

She felt her tummy drop.

'No way.'

On the back of one of the Polaroids were the words, **Clearwater 1996.**

A tear streamed down Eve's cheek as she scanned all the dates on the first page of the notepad.

No. What? How...?

Eve paused momentarily, sitting on the side of the bed, her head buried in her palms.

Hardly. No way.

She flicked through the pages of the notepad, looking at all the creepy drawings of couples murdered in weird ways. Soon, tears formed, history reformed, dust and ash fell along the memories she and Jack had shared. A shriek sounded moments later, waking Jack.

'What does this mean?' Eve cried, holding up the notepad. 'Was Mitch right about you?'

Jack stumbled into consciousness. 'What? What's going on, babe?'

'Don't babe me,' Eve shouted. 'What are all the dates in this notepad and the creepy fucking drawings?'

~~~

At that moment, Jack realised their union had fallen, like so many detonations exploding upwards, the heights of their relationship crumbling back upon itself in the aftermath. He could almost feel the fallout, the intense tragedy of it all, their romance swept away and swallowed up by a mushroom cloud.

'What is Mitch doing here?' Jack shouted, pointing at the door.

'What?' Eve asked, and as she turned her neck, Jack sprung, gripping her in a rear guillotine choke. Eve struggled in Jack's grip, smacking and scratching at his arms. Jack squeezed tighter and tighter until Eve's resistance faded. When Eve's arms fell by her side, Jack let go and she collapsed on the bedroom floor.

'Fuck,' Jack screamed, feeling the pendulum of the moment swing from real to surreal, drunk to sober, fiancé to victim.

'Fuck this,' he cried.

Not Eve. No.

He drew a deep breath and closed his eyes, calming inhalations, pragmatic outcomes flashing like a strobe light. Jack knew what had to happen, though he wished, in the worst way, that some other outcome would dawn upon him like a new day. He would have to make it look like suicide, some residual guilt Eve couldn't bear to carry after Mitch's arrest.

A note on the bedside locker.

No, scrap that.

Maybe some text to a former colleague.

'Okay,' Jack screamed, hyping himself up. 'O-fucking-kay.'

He picked Eve's limp body off the floor and placed her in a guillotine choke again, applying deadly pressure before dropping her to the floor and screaming into his palms. 'What the fuck?'

Equilibrium wobbled.

Human, all too human.

Jack couldn't do it.

Eve wasn't that disposable.

He loved her.

She wasn't some souvenir.

Some muse.

An oval mirror he'd one day paint a smile on.

Things were different.

Times had changed.

Jack scanned the room. A plan loosely formed as he stared over at Eve's bedside locker, at a sleeve of Ambien she'd left out for the long flight ahead. He ground up two tablets and mixed them in a tumbler of water before rousing Eve, bearhugging her from behind and forcing her to drink.

'What are you doing?' Eve asked, barely conscious. 'I don't care. I love you any...'

'Shush now,' Jack soothed, making Eve drink from the glass.

Eve mumbled for a while, barely lucid. 'Do you still love me?' she asked, her voice trailing off, her head falling towards her chest as she passed off into slumber.

Jack kissed her on the forehead. 'Another life, eh.'

He scrambled to his feet, grabbing his wallet, passport, and suitcase, all the bits he needed for a swift escape.

He rang Mel next.

'Hey you,' Mel answered.

'Just listen,' Jack shouted. 'Things have gone sideways. You need to collect me at the back of my building ASAP.'

'Is everything okay?'

'Get here now.'

Jack ended the call, getting everything in order, wheeling his suitcase to the front door and zipping up a duffel bag full of cash. Next, Jack phoned the pilot of the private plane they had chartered, one Jack had used before, an expert in veiled continental travel.

'Just listen,' Jack said calmly. 'This is William. I need to move things forward. I need to leave Toronto in an hour. I'll wire you half now if you say yes.'

'Yes,' the pilot answered. 'But three or four hours is more realistic. I'll need time to make the changes. One hour could arouse suspicion.'

'I'll need to dodge passport control and security.'

'Done.'

'I'll also need to change the name on the charter. Use Alexander Golden as the booking.'

'Done.'

'The first stop is Dublin. That's where I'll part ways. You refuel before continuing to...I don't know; wherever is lax on security.'

'I know a landing strip outside of Nairobi. No questions asked if you have the cash. They'll stamp Alexander Golden as entering.'

'Whatever it takes,' Jack said.

'But I can't drop you off at Dublin,' the pilot said. 'Security is too tight.'

'Then where?' Jack asked.

'I have a contact at Knock Airport. A smaller strip in the west of Ireland. I'll call to confirm, but there should be no issues.'

'Just get me out of Toronto as soon as you can. Wiring you half now.'

'Okay,' the pilot said.

Jack sat on the floor in the hallway, swirling a tumbler of whiskey, smoking a cigarette, feeling exhausted. Everything felt surreal, like a skier who'd survived an avalanche but hit his head on a boulder. Jack's cat, Ohana, rubbed her body against his knee. He petted her head as she purred. He'd forgotten about her – what to do with her – sentiment dazzling in her eyes like diamonds.

'You can come with Dad,' Jack said, smiling at her stately pose, listening to her purr. He led her to the kitchen, feeding her a pouch of wet food. 'Eat up,' Jack said, bending down to pet her as she ate. 'In a few hours, we'll be in Ireland. That's where Daddy's from.'

Ohana headbutted his hand and meowed again.

'Daddy has one more thing to do before we leave,' Jack said, scratching underneath Ohana's chin and cuddling her. He looked at his watch and shook his head. He knew what had to happen. He didn't want it this way, but that's how the dice had fallen. He knelt beside Eve, searching the bed for her phone before opening it with her thumbprint, clicking into Twitter and typing a Tweet.

@CTVNews This is Mitch Bauer's partner, Eve Salah. I support what Mitch did. We planned it together. We believe the only way to reform this city is with a cull. I killed my fiancé tonight & it felt great. If you don't like someone, kill them. As a member of @TorontoPolice I give you permission.

Jack shared the Tweet and wiped his prints from Eve's phone before grabbing Ohana in one arm and his suitcase in the other. He descended the emergency stairs and slipped meekly into Mel's car at the back entrance of his condo.

What now?

Chapter 41

Jack regretted not kissing Eve one more time. Everything had happened so quickly, the events playing out in his mind like a disaster movie, the walls caving in on him, a giant wave of karma washing him away. Toronto appeared different as Jack passed through the city one last time, its sparkle passing from his possession like some stolen jewel. He wished Eve was sitting next to him; her excitement throbbing, practising her soundbites in a silly Australian accent.

'Put another shrimp on the barbie.'

'G'day mate.'

'Crickey, that's a big croc.'

Jack caught sight of his reflection in the side mirror. His face looked pale and sour like spoilt milk, his eyes appeared as big as saucers, his mouth felt slack with defeat. Ohana eventually settled and curled up on Jack's lap. Mel would pet her head from time to time in a bid to break the tension. 'That's a good girl,' Mel said, scratching Ohana's head, 'off on a big adventure with Daddy.'

When they approached Pearson International Airport, Jack directed Mel towards the private runway, speaking for the first time.

'So, this is it?' Mel asked, shrugging her shoulders. 'No explainer. No Eve by your side. You almost have me intrigued.'

'She knows.'

'It was bound to happen,' Mel said, indicating into another lane. 'You got too close. Icarus, arms out, trying to kiss the sun; the eggplant playing mind games in the pants.'

'I felt I could.'

'Of course you did,' Mel said. 'Self-doubt was never your problem, Seany. Even as a kid, you always believed in the green light glowing in the distance. You must have read The Great Gatsby nearly a dozen times, finding all sorts of meaning in it. I remember you striving for the same levels of success as Gatsby at first, but the more you read the book, the more you became aware of the tragedy and intractability of the story.'

'The unattainable future that feels so real we can almost touch it,' Jack added sadly. 'I remember how I'd reach out into the darkness of our bedroom trying to feel the glow of the green light glisten between my fingers, and yet, all I felt was darkness.'

'The question is,' Mel added, 'if Gatsby knew his outcome, would he have left his obsession with Daisy behind, tucked his dream into bed one night and pressed a pillow to its face?'

'No,' Jack said. 'Gatsby was a believer. He thought he could bend fate to his will.'

'Yuck,' Mel said, shooting out her tongue. 'He was so hopeful. I never let that sickness get into my thoughts. I knew we were doomed from day dot, Seany.'

'Eve changed all that for me,' Jack said, trying to calm Ohana as her nose sniffed around the dashboard. 'I didn't feel doomed anymore. I eventually got to feel the green light.'

'Gatsby dies in the end,' Mel said coldly. 'How does your story go from here?'

'I'm about to split the atom over Dublin,' Jack said, staring wildly at his sister. 'Clearwater will crumble, and Jenny and Don will be found bludgeoned beneath the rubble.'

'You're turning me on now,' Mel said, pressing her thumbs hard against the steering wheel. 'I drank fifteen shots and killed some John last night, and I felt nothing. There's no colour to my world. Everything is still black and white. There's no arc to my story either, Seany. But maybe, if we kill Jenny and Don, I'll feel something, even for a short little while.'

'I felt my heartbeat for the first time this morning,' Jack said, sadly.

'What did it feel like?'

'Shit,' Jack said, rubbing his eyes with his hand.

'Yeah,' Mel said, gazing off into the distance, 'but life's so boring when the seesaw doesn't move. No ups or downs, or highs or lows. At least you felt something, even for a brief while. I just want to know what it feels like. Falling in love, wanting to spend the rest of my life with another person. Books make it sound so magical, a big rush of heat, seemingly.'

'That ends cold.'

'It always does,' Mel added. 'I used to wonder what it would feel like to kill someone; now I wonder what it's like to feel.'

'Remember those days,' Jack said fondly. 'We were so curious about killing, wondering if anything would change if we did.'

'I didn't,' Mel said. 'And everyone can fuck off, they don't have a word for that. I won't wear a label. Calling someone a Psychopath is like saying I have an STI...well which bloody one? It's too broad a term, Seany, and we're too niche a product.'

'Then what are we?' Jack asked.

'Only God knows the answer to that,' Mel said. 'Anyway, have they found the body yet?'

'Eve's not dead,' Jack countered quickly.

'I don't mean Eve,' Mel corrected. 'The dude we killed down Church Street last night. He had rapey eyes. We done the world a favour disposing of him. The city should be paying us for taking out the trash.'

Jack scrolled through CTV News on his smartphone.

'He was found,' Jack said.

'What else does it say?'

'That a body was found off Church Street and the cops are investigating. Mayor Adams is expected to address the press again this morning at 11:30.'

'I think I'll kill Mayor Adams next,' Mel said, approaching the private terminal where a female worker waved down their car before looking over her shoulder suspiciously.

'That must be for me,' Jack said, 'pull in over there. I need you to do me one last favour, Mel. Go back to my condo after you drop me off, put Eve in the largest suitcase and smuggle her back to her apartment. Her keys are on my bedside locker. Use the back exits and try look like Eve. Wear a disguise if you have to.'

'Can I kill her?'

'No,' Jack said coldly. 'Then go back to my condo, lure Tom upstairs and butcher him with a steak knife in my bed. Burn my condo to the ground and erase all the CCTV footage. Can you do that for me, Mel?'

'Happily,' Mel said. 'Godspeed, Seany. Ring me when you land.'

'Get rid of this car, and any other evidence as well,' Jack added, lowering his baseball cap and pulling the hood of his jacket over his head.

~~~

Hours later, as Jack flew across the Atlantic, he visited the pilot in the cockpit. 'All sorted?'

'Yes,' the pilot answered. 'My people will be waiting for you at Knock Airport. Move quickly and don't stop for anyone.'

'Okay,' Jack said, moping back to his seat, where Ohana slept in the seat next to his, in the spot where Eve should have been, curled up, stretching out her hand for reassurance. It took only four hours and twenty-one minutes for Eve's Tweet to go viral.

Most news publications ran the story, amplifying the chaos and outrage. #KillerCops trended on Twitter in twenty three countries, and over three hundred thousand outraged comments later, former Detective Eve Salah was public enemy number one, doxed and publicly shamed, with some Twitter users vowing to 'hunt down the witch and kill her.'

Later that day, Detective Lee appeared on CTV News saying that Eve had visited Mitch at Toronto General the night before, purporting that he had heard them laughing about the murders, with Mitch telling Eve to 'finish off the job.'

Riots broke out across Toronto that night. Mayor Adams' home was burned to the ground with her and her husband trapped inside. Witnesses reported seeing an attractive redhaired woman near the scene, speeding off on a motorbike as flames climbed thirty feet high. Eve was arrested after an anonymous tip lead the cops to Jack's condo where a scorched body was found with a knife in its chest.

Toronto seemed nothing like the city it had been a few months prior – the sports fans jovially arguing over who would win the World Series; the Chinese girl studying in UoT, drinking beer for the first time with her new friends; the picnics on Toronto Island where families didn't feel the need to look over their shoulders at the slightest noise. Fear now stoked the embers of the city's outrage. Nerves, like guitar strings, felt stretched to snapping point.

Toronto no longer felt like a safe city and soon Dublin wouldn't either.

Part Five

Chapter 42

'Tell me why you want to work for Clearwater?' the head of Clearwater's HR department, Erika Furlong asked.

Erika had risen through the ranks quickly, an assertive young woman, obsessively neat in appearance, dressed that morning in a tight navy pencil skirt, a white blouse and a fitted navy blazer. She was half-Irish and half-Philipino, born in Galway but moved to Dublin when she was ten. She was one of the first employees through the doors every morning and amongst the last to leave at night; the consummate workaholic who just about managed to squeeze in two yoga classes per week and three intense gym sessions with her personal trainer.

'I believe I can turn things around,' Jack Lawson said confidently. 'The company earnings keep slipping further and the share price is lower than it was this time last year. I read the article The Times ran after Paddy Fitzgerald died, saying that Clearwater was one more scandal away from collapse. Employee sentiment is amongst the lowest I've ever seen. I want the challenge of turning that around.'

'Things are getting harder to turn around,' Erika said, fluffing up her long, dark hair. 'We've never hired a clinical psychologist before. Our last hire was a performance coach, but she stopped showing up to work a few weeks ago and nobody has heard from her since. In the last few months, we've lost over fifty employees to stress leave in our Dublin office alone. How would you change things, Dr. Sheen?'

Jack was still getting used to hearing his new alias. He looked at Erika a little bewildered before peering out the window at the River Liffey, watching people cross the Samuel Beckett Bridge, When Jack laid out his five-step plan to achieving optimal employee performance, Erika appeared impressed, glancing at his resumé before moving on to her next question.

The proceeding hour moved along in the same amiable fashion. They built rapport quickly, like two compatible hopefuls on a blind date. Erika's lustful discomfort was getting harder to hide; the sultry way she looked at Jack's dark brown eyes, chiselled jawline and sweeping chestnut hair. His suit was tailor-made, exaggerating his musculature and broad, athletic shoulders. He was intelligent. That impressed Erika most of all. His verbal fluency and deep vocabulary, how he made her wait five seconds before responding to her questions.

'I'd be a perfect fit for the role,' Jack said, answering Erika's final question. 'In Toronto, most of my clientele worked in finance. I'm familiar with the pitfalls of the job. I can implement my experience here, and after three months, if you're not satisfied with my approach, I'll walk away. Simple as that.'

'Simple as that,' Erika repeated.

She was ready to stand and conclude their meeting when the door opened suddenly and the CEO, Jenny Sullivan, stormed in. Erika's mind drifted off, thinking of all the reasons why she hated Jenny; how she considered herself a rockstar in the investment world, though her employees used an array of different monikers to describe her: The Dragon Lady. The Heartless Bitch. Though the less creatively-minded, and mostly male employees, simply called her 'that Geebag' – a redoubtable woman in her early sixties who wore designer dresses that showed off her curves without the garish promiscuity of the younger girls.

'So, this is the guy?' Jenny announced, unenthused. Erika went to reply, but Jenny shushed her by swiftly wagging her finger in the air. 'We've slipped out of the top 100 best companies to work for in Ireland, and our employee reviews on Glassdoor are abysmal. Something needs to change quickly. Convince me in ten words or less,' Jenny said, turning to glare at Lawson, 'why I should hire you?'

Erika watched Jack stare deeply into Jenny's eyes, unblinking, but in no way threatening. Erika had seen this power play before, the way Jenny stormed into her office, inconvenienced by Jack's presence, with a demand that exaggerated the extent of her authority, her extremity. It was all veneer, Erika mused; Jenny's emotionless exterior hid layers of unhappiness, like an onion that gets sadder and darker the further in you peel.

'I don't need to,' Jack answered. 'You didn't get where you are by listening to a man pontificating his own imagined brilliance. You trust your intuition, though, you're a pragmatist by disposition. You stood in the hallway for forty-two seconds, waiting for the conclusion of this interview. I saw you in the reflection of Erika's glasses. A woman of your status waits that long for no one unless they're valuable to them. That leads me to believe this interview is little more than a formality, a meet and greet. I recognise what others don't, Jenny. I smelled ketones as soon as you walked into the room. Your diet has changed recently; you've cut out carbs. You see them as toxic, and you have too much toxic stuff going on in your life right now. Your employees are abandoning ship at an alarming rate, and it's starting to gnaw at you. Your red eyes suggest you don't sleep much at night. The way you applied your lipstick this morning implies a slight tremor in your hand, possibly due to excessive alcohol or nicotine cessation. I'll settle with the former since you recently stated in an interview that you've never smoked. Though, I'm aware people lie.'

Jenny appeared lost for words as though embarrassed in some monumental way. 'Hire him,' Jenny said, storming into the hallway afterwards, shouting at an administrative assistant to sit up straight and make a greater effort to pronounce her 'THs' when speaking on the phone.

By the time Jack started working for Clearwater a week later, he'd have fantasised about her death over twenty times, imagining the scene where he would bludgeon Jenny's face with a two-kilogram lump hammer he kept in his bedside locker.

Chapter 43

Jack's girlfriend, Sinead Foy, smiled when she woke and saw him watching her. 'What are you doing?' she asked.

'If I tell you, I'd have to kill you,' Jack said, 'with cuddles and a million kisses.'

Sinead liked the sound of that, cuddling into Jack's chest, feeling his muscular arms envelop her. She felt loved by Lawson, worshipped in a way she had never felt before. Her last boyfriend recoiled at the thought of cuddles. Peter the plumber, whose understanding of intimacy was the whimsical hugging of a friend when Liverpool scored a goal. Sinead stayed in that relationship far too long, but she was vulnerable like that, fragile like a fledgling, terrified at the prospect of single life. She cried after her first and only one-night stand, then sobbed shamefully again that afternoon, turning up the shower's water pressure so her parents wouldn't hear. She feared she was losing her mind like Britney did, going as far as holding her father's electric shaver to her head as though it were some sort of psychological instrument used to measure a girl's likelihood of a mental breakdown.

Sinead met Jack the previous month. She was in Dawson's Bar with her friends when she saw Jack's magnetic gaze peeking over the brim of his whiskey glass. She pretended not to notice him at first, not until moments later, when he pounced on her with a cheeky smile. He got down on one knee and asked her to marry him. Sinead knew it was a gag, but still, her heart never beat as hard in all her life. A month later, she had all but moved into Jack's swanky penthouse apartment in the Dublin Docklands.

'Let's just lie here all day,' Jack suggested.

His words had a forbidden calling, and Sinead indulged the idea for a moment before saying, 'You're starting your new job today.'

'So?' Jack teased.

Sinead bit her bottom lip, letting the idea flower once again. 'You're trouble.'

'I'm in love,' Jack exclaimed.

'I love you too,' Sinead said, smiling so her face wrinkled. 'But I've got to go to work, and so do you. We have a big merger coming up. I'll probably have to work late again this evening.'

'How late?' Jack asked, combing his hands through his hair.

'Half-nine, maybe later,' Sinead said, walking to the ensuite bathroom, where she stood for a few seconds until the water ran hot.

'I'll have dinner and a large glass of Merlot waiting.'

'That's why you're my man,' Sinead said, feeling butterflies flutter in her tummy. 'I still can't believe you'll be working for my dad; it's like the craziest coincidence ever. You move here from North America, get a job at Clearwater, and end up dating one of the founder's daughters.'

'Yeah, what's the odds of that?' Jack said, laughing. 'It must be fate.'

~~~

Lying on the bed, the loving expression on Jack's face vanished in a flash. He rolled his eyes to the ceiling, bored by Sinead's capture. His face settled into an emotionless trance – looking out at the world like a reptile at the zoo.

Jack had not chosen Sinead at random. Days before they met, he'd stalked her on Instagram and knew she'd be at a friend's birthday celebration in Dawson's Bar. His plans required a girlfriend to blend in, but more important was the required proximity to Sinead's father, Don Foy. Jack had a special kind of torture planned for Don, something that would leave a permanent chill in the crawlspace of his spine.

'Join me in the shower,' Sinead called out.

'Coming,' Jack said.

For a brief second, a sombre glint flashed across his eyes as he thought of Eve. She had brought him, hand in hand, to the very border of emotion. What a spark of humanity she had been, magnified by distance, worshipped now in absence. Jack wondered if he'd ever see her again, if she was still alive, somewhere out there in the world, trying to wrap her head around what had happened.

Chapter 44

Jack's first day at Clearwater started with an induction session in a large conference room. The presenter brought all the new hires through the company's vision, mission statement, operating model, and history. There was no mention of Jack's father, the rightful owner, who had grown a little-known Dublin company into a global powerhouse. It was all about Jenny, her goals for Clearwater and her vision for the future. Jack had visions of his own – Jenny lying supine on the floor, a lump hammer landing wetly between her eyes. His mind felt flooded with revenge; everything seemed waterlogged by the image of Jenny's final moments.

In the afternoon, Jack walked to his office on the seventh floor and saw his first client; Paul, an overweight man in his mid-twenties, who had recently returned from stress leave. Paul sobbed into his palms, trying to describe the pain of social anxiety, his terror in a sea of faces, how his imagination had turned rogue. 'It's like an intruder is trapped in my skull. It pains, man. It pains so much.'

'Can you think of a way to let it out?' Jack asked, leaning back in his leather chair.

'Not really,' Paul said.

'Have you considered suicide?' Jack asked in a way that hinted at suggestion. 'By law, suicide ideations have to be reported to the authorities.'

'No,' Paul said, glaring at Jack.

At 5 pm, while Jack prepared his session notes, Erika appeared in the doorway of his office. Her glossy lips shimmered under the fluorescent hallway lights. Her pink bra was slightly visible through her ivory-coloured blouse.

Jack watched her calmly from his desk, gazing into her eyes, surveying her entire mental world. He noted that she seemed hesitant, like a patient awaiting the jab of a needle.

'Everything okay?' Jack asked, peering down at his notebook to make another entry. 'I don't mind staying longer if you want to talk.'

Erika swallowed deeply. 'Maybe another time,' she said, walking towards him. 'I just want to confirm something with you. It's probably nothing really, a misunderstanding.'

'Misunderstanding?' Jack repeated, slowly putting down his pen and leaning back in his chair, chin inclined, like a dog daring the postman to take another step.

Erika sat down on the corner of Jack's desk. 'How do I say this? It's probably nothing.'

'Spit it out,' Jack urged.

'I couldn't find your name on the list of doctoral graduates in 2015. I mean, there was nothing when I searched your name online. Do you know why this might be?'

'That's strange,' Jack said, smiling so forcibly the wrinkles around his eyes fanned out. Then, in a sudden change of tone, he continued. 'Did you email my doctoral supervisor, Professor Lockhart? I provided her contact details on my résumé.'

'I should've done that first,' Erika said, slightly embarrassed. 'Sorry, I'm a stickler for looking up new employees. But I couldn't find anything about you. Do you not use social media at all, not even LinkedIn?'

'I'm on a digital detox,' Jack said. 'I've big goals, Erika. I'm taking this job very seriously. Social media is just a distraction, see.' In moments like this, Jack had a mantra: *it's hard to blame the victim.* 'I know what this is!' Jack continued, his voice slightly raised. 'They've gone and done it again.'

'What?' Erika asked.

'When I graduated, I had to walk on stage and receive a blank parchment because the university administration department was unsure of my date of birth. They misplaced my doctoral application, and rather than reach out and confirm with me, they ruined the proudest day of my life. All those years of hard work felt like they were for nothing.'

'Oh no!' Erika cried. 'That's awful.'

'And now this,' Jack said, shaking his head soberly. 'They screw me over again.'

'I'm sorry for bringing this up. I should've just emailed Professor Lockhart.'

Over the years, Jack had perfected many conversational manoeuvres to shift the focus of a person's attention, and reaching out, he put his hand on Erika's knee. 'It's okay,' Jack said, standing up and walking over to close his office door. 'I've made an observation. You're overworked. Your mind is running a mile a minute.'

'I'm fine,' Erika said hurriedly.

'You can choose the couch or the chair,' Jack suggested, motioning her to choose.

'Maybe another time,' Erika said. 'I've a mountain of work to get through.'

'You're obsessed with getting things done,' Jack said, placing his hand softly on her lower back and ushering her towards the couch.

'Seriously, I'm fine.'

'This is why you hired me.'

Against her wishes, Erika lay down on Jack's couch, careful not to let her dress ruffle too far up her thighs. Appearing embarrassed, Erika sat up and slipped her hand into her blazer pocket, looking for her cell phone. 'I'm expecting a call. Can we reschedule?'

'Close your eyes,' Jack instructed, moving his chair closer to the couch. 'I mean it. Lie back down, Erika. We don't even have to talk. Just close your eyes and breathe. Come into the moment.'

Erika did as Jack said, lying back slowly.

'Take ten deep breaths,' Jack continued. 'In through your nose and out through your mouth. Feel your whole body relax. Let your mind go quiet. This is a safe space.'

Erika closed her eyes and began breathing in a controlled rhythm. Jack watched her for a while, debating whether or not to press a cushion to her face. It would be that easy, but the risk outweighed the gain; for now.

'What was your first thought this morning?' Jack asked.

'Work.'

'Does that shock you?'

'Should it?'

'You care more about work than most.'

'I guess,' Erika said, sounding sleepier after each word. 'Clearwater feels like home. My work fulfils me. I didn't dream of children, marriage, or having a happy family when I was a girl. I dreamed of deadlines and an office job.'

'You mentioned children before you mentioned marriage. Does romantic commitment scare you?'

'I'm committed to the job.'

'And the idea of children?'

'What is this, Sean? We hired you to reduce employee stress, not to wade into our personal lives.'

'I only want what's best for you. If you burn yourself out, replacing you won't be easy. By addressing these problems now, we can reintroduce some balance back into your life.'

'Problems?' Erika inquired, fighting the urge to sit back up.

'Couples get divorced. Even the strongest marriages shatter.'

'Are you saying I'm married to the job?'

'Is Jenny a loving spouse? I saw the way she shushed you in my interview.'

Erika took her time considering Jack's words. During this momentary gap, a tear slid from the corner of her eye, curled around her cheekbone and dripped into the glossy opening of her mouth. 'I started off our session with a lie,' Erika said. 'As a girl, I never once dreamed of deadlines and an office, though, in the past year, I dream of deadlines all the time, but more so in a nightmarish way.'

'I appreciate your honesty,' Jack said. 'Let's focus on Jenny today. The mention of her name elicited an emotional response and that's worth investigating.'

Jack handed Erika a Kleenex and she dabbed her eyes. 'I'm sorry,' she said. 'I feel so stupid bawling like this in front of you on your first day.'

'Tears are perfectly normal,' Jack said. 'They have a way of showing us that something is painful. Let's discuss Jenny. I want to know everything about her. Consider this couples counselling with an absent member.'

A bountiful harvest, Jack thought, sometime later. This session provided him with many gloomy accounts of Jenny's private life. Events that Erika had carefully observed over the years. Most interesting to Jack was Erika's claim that Jenny hadn't attended Paddy's funeral.

'What sort of monster doesn't attend a friend's funeral?' Erika blasted. 'How can someone be that cold? Jenny and Paddy were long-time friends. They started the company together, and she didn't have the decency to show her face.'

'I read about that murder?' Jack said. 'Scary stuff.'

'Yeah, the office hasn't been the same since,' Erika said, sniffling. 'Everyone's just scared and sad, I guess. Like to be murdered by a serial killer is just crazy. And Jenny hasn't once publicly acknowledged Paddy's passing, but she went and hired personal security giving us all the jitters. Like, are we in danger?'

'Why would you think that?'

'Well, a couple of months back, some detective, I think his name was McGuire, called around claiming that Paddy's murder was some revenge plot linked to our previous CEO.'

'Sounds like a Netflix thriller,' Jack added.

'I know,' Erika said. 'But still, why would he say that? And you should've seen the way Jenny handled it; she had her security guards drag him out. I hate her,' Erika said before turning her head quickly as though to apologise. 'I mean, she treats me like her dog, not like a pet, like a dog that just wandered into her office – a stray fecking dog. I don't know why I've stayed here so long, why I've sacrificed everything to be her bitch.'

'We are all mere products of our past,' Jack said. 'I suspect your childhood was full of rules, unrecognised achievements, and a demanding mother serving as the matriarch. And so, we have stumbled into our first cliché. Tell me about your mother?'

That evening, after her session with Jack, Erika did something she had never done before, something she never imagined within the realms of possibility. She left Clearwater before 6 pm.

Five minutes later, Erika, who was in no way forgetful, forgot her debit card pin as she stood at the checkout counter of a grocery store in Dublin's IFSC. The harder she tried to recall her four-digit pin, the broader her mind expanded.

'People normally just tap with a stolen card,' the checkout boy said in a hoarse North Dublin accent before looking at his older colleague awaiting some appraisal.

Mortified, Erika fled the grocery store with her debit card still wedged inside the chip & pin machine. Her cheeks burned so hot she feared the makeup would melt off her face. Her world spun for a second time that day, her energies off-kilter, the world stumbling off its axis, spinning off into the distance like a dreidel.

Erika didn't see Jack watching her from across the street, standing in the umbra of an alleyway, pretending to be texting on his phone. Erika had been added to his list of *things to bludgeon*. She was clever. She would eventually figure out that Jack's qualifications were forged, and Jack was done with letting problems fester any longer than they needed to.

Chapter 45

Eve appeared in Jack's dreams most nights, the same scene every time: Jack in the passenger seat of a car, Eve behind the wheel, driving over a bridge, losing control, flipping over the barrier, and plunging into the water below. Jack couldn't rinse the feeling of Eve from his thoughts. She possessed him now – their dream of spending their lives together glowing like the green light he could never reach. How Gatsby-esque. How cruel the hurt of heartache, not even the coldest corners of humanity are immune to the maul of loss. Jack wished things were different; that he and Eve met under different circumstances, in an alternate reality where all the savagery of the past had spared him from himself. But life is a choice and actions aren't mere accidents. Jack realised this, agonisingly, so unsure of what to do with the feeling of regret. From an early age, it was as though his amygdala had gone to war and never come home. But now, that dead part of Jack's brain was kicking and screaming in its watery grave as he scrolled through pictures of him and Eve on his phone, his smile lifting briefly before collapsing at the realisation of all that was lost.

Jack spent hours every week searching for Eve online, desperate to find out what had happened to her, but there was nothing. She was a ghost now. A landmine buried somewhere, one Jack hoped he would step on soon just to feel her energy tearing through his flesh again.

Mel called Jack most days with a fresh set of questions, curious about his life in Dublin, as though Jack had moved to Narnia or fled down the rabbit hole. 'What are the people like?' Mel would ask, before lurching into another question and then another. 'Is it really as green as they say? I can't really remember. We were so young when we left.'

'Have you had a Guiness?'

'Have you been to where they filmed the Notebook? That's like my favourite movie, Seany. Imagine falling in love like that.'

Mel's questions would go on and on, and often Jack would stop her to inquire if she had heard anything about Eve. 'Not a thing,' Mel said one morning in early November, 'which is crazy really. That PI chick is working overtime but can't find a thing. Maybe Eve's dead, Seany.'

'She's still alive,' Jack said. 'I can sense it; I can feel her out there, somewhere.'

'Well, whatever you're sensing, it's not the same Eve you fell in love with. You left her a pariah, Seany. The cops, the whole city, everyone turned against her. After she was arrested on suspicion of murdering you, people started a petition to bring back the death penalty for her and Mitch. No one cared that Eve was released from custody a few days later. She faced trial by social media and was found guilty of all accusations. The new mayor used her as a scapegoat, the cops threw her under the bus along with Mitch, and CTV have yet to report that Eve was released. You manufactured the perfect storm, Seany.'

'I wish I could turn back time,' Jack said, his voice steeped in sadness. 'I'd end my life instead and give her the chance to live hers. I miss her so much. I can't move on, Mel. Nothing means anything anymore. It's like a part of me is missing.'

Mel fell silent.

Jack could tell his sister didn't know what to say or where to place that chunk of information; the context blurry, like words with the letters all jumbled up.

'The Spadina store manager won't be a problem anymore,' Mel said, trying to steer the conversation back into depths she could course. 'He's lying at the bottom of Lake Ontario. No one can connect you to The Poet murders now. I got to Mitch's apartment before the cops as well. All the evidence went up in a ball of flames.'

'I don't know what I'd do without you, Mel.'

'This is what twins do for one another,' Mel said. 'I really want to come see you.'

'Soon,' Jack said, 'I'm still getting all our ducks in a row. I'm about to crush Don Foy in the worst way possible.'

Chapter 46

Sinead Foy left for work early on December 7. She was excited for her Christmas party that night, dinner in Peploe's, and then drinks in Café en Seine afterwards. Sinead had so much to live for, so no one could understand why she just vanished. She was last seen getting into a car at 11:28 pm on Dawson Street. Her phone died soon after. The last cell tower it pinged from was near Killiney, which made no sense to anyone as Sinead lived in the city centre, and Killiney was over thirty minutes outside the city.

Jack reported Sinead missing the next day when she failed to return home. Her father made a public appeal on the 9 o'clock news, promising a large reward for any information on her whereabouts. The tips led nowhere. Most of the calls were attempted money grabs, pranks, or news hogs seeking attention. Jack Lawson (or rather Sean Sheen) was brought in for questioning later that day. The two detectives noted Jack's calm demeanour. Detective Cleary – an overweight, middle-aged man, and Detective Joyce, a slim woman in her fifties – listened intently and jotted down notes as Jack spoke.

'This isn't like Sinead,' Jack said, holding a Styrofoam coffee cup, sitting on a plastic chair in the centre of the stark interrogation room. 'Sure, she was stressed out with work and always anxious; she works twelve hours a day, but she wouldn't run away or do something stupid. No way, not Sinead.'

'And when was the last time you saw her?' Detective Cleary asked.

'She'd stayed over in mine the night before,' Jack said, letting out a gentle sigh before looking up at the fluorescent lights humming overhead. 'We chatted over breakfast before she left for work, probably around 7 am. She was so excited about her Christmas party. I hadn't seen her that fired up in weeks. She had that sparkle back in her eyes, you know. Her law firm has her pitted for partner next year. At her age, that's a big deal. Others are there far longer than Sinead and they'd been overlooked.'

'Overlooked?' Detective Joyce quizzed. 'Sinead said that? Was there tension with any of her colleagues?'

'Oh, I wouldn't know about that,' Jack said, opening his palms. 'Sinead is too polite to gossip or speak ill of anyone. That's her nature. She's a kind, well-mannered woman. I work for her father, and he's the same, a real gent.'

The detectives didn't catch on that Jack was interrogating them as well, testing how they would react when he paused or feigned emotion, changed the octave of his voice, or touched his face in various places: lips, ears, nose, eyebrows. Everything was data.

When the detectives left the room, Jack was careful not to smile or loosen up too much. He placed his elbows on the table and leaned forward, his head lowered, his feet uncrossed. He knew how reckless he had been, how he had shored the enemy up outside his door, feeling the glare of their floodlights, the swell of their suspicion. But killing Don Foy's daughter was worth it, Jack thought, just to hear Don bawl down the phone in tears, sniffling and stuttering, pleading on the news. The world felt fairer. The chess game more honest. Don had taken some of Jack's pieces, and now Jack had taken one of his.

The interrogation lasted four hours. Detective Cleary didn't get the impression that Jack had anything to do with Sinead's disappearance, but his colleague wasn't so sure. 'He's almost too smooth,' Detective Joyce said at the coffee machine. 'His girlfriend is missing and he hasn't shown an ounce of genuine emotion. There's something about his eyes, too, and the intense eye contact is fucking eerie.'

'I don't get that impression at all,' Detective Cleary said. 'He's very mannerly, very well-spoken, seems like a nice chap.'

'It doesn't mean he's not a killer.'

'Ay, that's true,' Cleary said. 'But his alibi checked out.'

'He left the gym at 11:18 pm, he'd have ten minutes to get to Dawson Street.'

'You couldn't get from Clontarf to Dawson Street in ten minutes.'

'Yes, you would,' Joyce said.

'But we saw the CCTV footage of him outside his apartment at 11:30 pm.'

'The man had a hood over his head,' Joyce said. 'That could've been anyone.'

'Nothing showed up on his background check,' Cleary added. 'He hadn't as much as a parking ticket in Canada.'

'That's suspicious in itself,' Detective Joyce said. 'Sean Sheen, it's a strange name. Honestly, everything about this guy feels off.'

Jack was let go later that day when he passed a polygraph test. Fresh CCTV footage later emerged showing Sinead getting into a dark-coloured Volkswagen Passat, but the Garda forensic team couldn't make out the number plate on the grainy footage. Fresh appeals were made on social media every day, but by the time Christmas rolled around, the news cycle had moved on, the Brexit rhetoric ramping up, the country shocked and saddened by the steep rise in homelessness on Dublin's streets.

Jack took some time off work, compassionate leave mainly, as hope of Sinead's return faded, and the conversation shifted from 'I hope she's okay' to 'she must be dead.' A sub-Reddit appeared in mid-December, a crack team of online sleuths assembled, posting theories on her disappearance, arguing whether the Volkswagen Passat was black or navy and if it was an older or newer model. Jack logged into Reddit most mornings to read the comments over a cup of coffee, Ohana purring on the island beside him, purring louder still when he scratched her head. Ohana reminded him of Eve. He felt sad at the remembrance, but the emotion had nowhere to land, so it just fell flat, making Jack feel exhausted, like a refrigerator door left open, the motor burned out from trying to keep the contents cool and fresh.

Chapter 47

Jack travelled to the Foy's Kildare estate house on Christmas day after Sinead's mother, Mag, had pleaded with him to join them.

Jack feigned a sombre demeanour as he stood to say grace before Christmas dinner. 'Please, Lord. Deliver Sinead back to us, alive and well. Let her smile light up the world's darkest corners. She always snorted when she laughed. It was so uniquely her. Please, let us hear that sound again...'

Jack's prayer went on for nearly two minutes. He thought of Eve throughout every word, imagining her beside him again, praying that she would be soon. The Foys never caught on to Jack's act; they thought his words were heartfelt and endearing. A sombre atmosphere settled around the large, lavish dining room. The air crackled with emotion: faint sounds, sharp sniffles, and those loud, excessive swallows people make when they are on the verge of a mental breakdown. Grief jostled around the table at the sudden realisation of the empty seat where Sinead should be sitting; then, the mental flash of where she might have ended up, living another life over in London, Don hoped; buried in a shallow grave in the Dublin Mountains, Jack remembered.

Mag broke down in tears, trying to cover her face. Her whimpers sounding a lot like a woman drowning in a shallow puddle, while Don coughed and croaked, like a man who had swallowed a large fly. It was all ecstasy to Jack, to feel a part of their grief, to muck around and rummage through it, nose first, like a hungry grief hog.

'Sorry,' Jack said, smiling briefly, his teeth stained red with wine. 'That was too heavy. I just want her back.'

'Thanks for those lovely words,' Mag said, wiping streaked mascara from underneath her eyes with a napkin. She looked much younger than fifty-four, with long blond hair and a half dozen cosmetic enhancements clawing back the years.

'You raised an angel, and I must say, you look stunning today,' Jack said, nodding to Mag. 'Don, you're a lucky man.'

Don raised a toast, and they all clinked glasses awkwardly, the comment ill-fitting of the mood. 'To Sinead,' Don said, teary-eyed.

When the toast was over, Jack held out a Christmas cracker to Sinead's younger sister, Graine. She had inherited her mother's looks, but unlike Mag, she often felt embarrassed by attention. 'Merry Christmas,' Jack said, waving the Christmas cracker around in Graine's face, 'and many happy tidings.'

Graine abruptly left the table and ran upstairs in a fit of tears.

'Sorry about that,' Mag said. 'She's not being rude; she just misses Sinead.'

'She idolised her,' Don added.

'Her big sister,' Mag whimpered, snorting into her napkin again as the grief hog resurfaced to rove and trash, root and rummage. Jack pictured himself on all fours, scouting around for sustenance, rooting through dark pits of grief and sorrow, splashing in the puddle of their dead daughter's tears. Jack fought hard to hide his pleasure. He couldn't believe how easily he had crossed the family barrier, like one of those pathogens that tricks the immune system into downing its defence, ignoring its deadly intent. *P. aeruginosa.*

All the fancy cutlery and lavish decor couldn't hide the empty seat. Mag and Don, at different times, would look towards it, half-expecting to see Sinead sitting there smiling back at them.

Instead, her killer ate at the table, complementing Mag on the succulence of the turkey, the richness of the gravy, and how the carrots were, 'Al dente.'

Don picked at his food, only eating half a roast potato and a slice of ham. He constantly lifted his fork before putting it down again, confused and clumsy. Christmas music played in the background, the melodies seeping into everything, emotion mauling them, like fingers poking around in a purse for loose change. It was all theatre. Jack had arranged them for his viewing, like a movie director, inventing reasons for them to act in weird ways, to force smiles and indulge him.

They watched 'Home Alone' that evening on the L-shaped couch in the movie room. Graine reappeared in fluffy pyjamas before the movie started, looking frail and gaunt, curling into Don as he stroked her head affectionately. Mag fell asleep halfway through the movie and began snoring softly before waking up, pretending she had been awake, and making an extra effort to laugh at the funny parts. Jack pretended to enjoy the movie, but deep down, he hated it; a child abandoned by his family at an early age was about as triggered as Jack could get.

Jack and Don stayed up late drinking Scotch in the lavish drawing room, puzzling over what could have happened to Sinead. 'It doesn't make sense to me,' Don said, sipping his Scotch. 'Sinead was...is a dream child. Sensible, too. She wouldn't jump into a car with some stranger.'

'This might be hard to hear,' Jack said sorely, 'but I think Sinead was carrying on with someone she worked with.'

'What do you mean?' Don asked angrily.

Jack stood and walked over to the window, swirling his Scotch and gazing into the darkness. The fifteen-foot-high ceiling swallowed their cigar smoke. The artwork on the walls was worth over two million, and the collection of rare whiskey edged close to half a million – all bought with ill-gained money, Jack thought, money his father had afforded them.

'A few weeks before Sinead disappeared, I saw a WhatsApp message on her phone while she was showering. I couldn't click into the message, but it started with: *Hey babe, are we still on for later? Meet you on the fifth...*'

'The fifth what?' Don barked.

'The fifth floor, I guess. That's why I think it was a work colleague.'

'Have you told the Gardaí all this?'

'No,' Jack said, turning around to face Don, holding his stare. 'Imagine how the press would spin that. The professional whore offed by her sidepiece.'

'Watch your words,' Don said, a cold glare settling in his eyes. 'That's not my Sinead you're describing.'

'Believe me, Don. I wish it weren't. I didn't mention anything to the Gardaí because I love her, and I didn't want the media to get wind of it. People would change their opinion of her. They wouldn't care about Sinead anymore, they'd be commenting on social media that she probably deserved it.'

Don went to speak, but Jack interrupted him. 'I told the Gardaí that something seemed odd with work, that she wasn't getting home until after ten most nights and that they should look into it.'

Don began to cry, tears drumming down into his Scotch, mumbling something about his *little girl*. Jack comforted him, holding him close, soaking up his grief like a sponge. 'This is why I didn't say anything sooner,' Jack said, easing Don's head towards his chest. 'I didn't want to mar her image.'

'Nothing could,' Don muttered.

'I know, I know,' Jack said, excited by Don's shame, petting his head like a lame buck before wiping his hand in his chinos. Jack's plan was beginning to emerge from the chrysalis. The moment felt right, the tension close to peaking. Jack tipped his cigar ash on the floor and poured two more tumblers of Scotch, looking behind his shoulder to see if Don was looking.

He wasn't.

Jack crushed up two Nembutal tablets and mixed them in Don's drink. Nembutal was Jack's favourite truth serum. In less than five minutes, Don would be putty in Jack's hand, spilling secrets like a slot machine spewing out its jackpot.

'Tell me,' Jack said, handing Don his Scotch, 'how did you get so successful? This house is like something only seen in movies.'

'Hard work,' Don said boastfully.

'Let's raise a toast to that,' Jack said, holding out his glass.

Both men clinked glasses before downing their whiskey. Don didn't notice Jack's smile unravelling, how large his eyes had grown, and the strange, unnatural shape his face had morphed into.

'I have to say,' Jack remarked, leaning forward on his chair, 'I read a very unsettling article about Clearwater in The Sunday World Online, how Detective McGuire believes that the former CEO didn't kill his family, that it was a professional hit-job.'

'A load of hogwash,' Don said.

Jack relaxed back into his chair and listened to the classical music playing from a nearby record player. He closed his eyes and nodded to the music, waiting for Don to get a little drowsier.

'So, who was Anthony Murphy?' Jack asked some moments later, pulling his armchair closer to Don. 'I mean, I've been working for Clearwater for months and I haven't heard of him.'

'He was someone who didn't know his place,' Don said, starting to feel weird and dizzy, rubbing his eyes, shaking his head, trying to find his focus.

'How so?'

'He was a shyster from North Dublin,' Don said in a sleepy voice. 'He had no business running a global company. If it wasn't for Jenny and I, there would be no Clearwater. This is awful to say, but his death was the best day of my life. Things could move forward the way they should, in the hands of the people who mattered, who deserved it. There's nothing I despise more than those new money types. Anthony Murphy was a new money con man, and as for his wife, an agricultural gob from the west of Ireland walking around with a pearl necklace thinking she was Jackie Kennedy. It's a pity people like that can't die twice.'

'A real pity,' Jack said, urging Don to talk more. 'And two of the children survived. That's mad, isn't it?'

'They weren't supposed to survive,' Don said, ploughing deeper into drowsiness.

'But Anthony Murphy had to go,' Jack suggested, pulling his armchair within inches of Don. 'It's okay, you can tell me. We're like family now, Don.'

The Nembutal was really starting to take effect. All expression fell from Don's face, and he looked catatonic. 'We needed him gone, permanently,' Don said in a droll voice.

'Anthony Murphy didn't deserve to live,' Jack said encouragingly. 'So, you, Jenny and Paddy removed him from the picture. Yeah?'

'Yeah.'

'With your own hands?'

'No.'

'Then how?'

'Paddy's uncle organised a guy.'

'Who?'

'Someone named Trevor.'

'Okay,' Jack said, tipping cigar ash on Don's bald head. 'That's a good boy. And who is Paddy's uncle?'

'Mick Devine.'

Jack walked to the whiskey station and poured another Dalmore Constellation 1969 Cask 1. Don floated in and out of consciousness. He wouldn't remember any of this in the morning; Mag would find him lying on the floor in a pool of vomit.

Jack sat back down beside Don, slapping his face for sport. 'You're an ugly prick. Puffy lips and a big nose, something my Dad would have beaten seven loads of shit out of. And look, since we're in the mood of confessing secrets, Donny boy, here's a doozy,' Jack said, getting within an inch of Don's face and licking his lips like someone lost in the desert trying to fight their thirst.

'Sinead died with more terror and confusion in her eyes than anyone else I've killed. Here, listen to her last few moments,' Jack said, pulling out his phone and pressing play on the recording. Sinead could be heard screaming and crying and begging for her life, as Jack urged her to say a few final words for her father.

'I'd love to be able to plug that soundtrack into your head,' Jack continued, 'and make you relive her final moments every second of every day. See, Don, you took something from me, you took a lot from me, and actions have consequences. I could have ended you and spared her, but seeing you and your family grieve over Christmas dinner felt so much more satisfying.'

Jack danced around the drawing room afterwards, shuffling his hips, throwing his gaze to the ceiling like a raver on ecstasy when the beat hits, when every nerve ending tingles with excitement, the sort of shamanic bliss that leads the reveller to their euphotic reckoning. It felt like payback, the dividend compounded handsomely, revenge towering up through the roof of heaven. Jack poured the bottle of Dalmore on the floor, urinated in the bottle, and put it back on the shelf. He shuffled towards Don, punching him in the face, causing Don to whiplash back before falling forward onto the plush rug.

'Maybe, I'll go screw your wife now.'

Jack spent the rest of the night watching Gladiator in the movie room, eating leftovers, and hitting pause to urinate in the dishwasher, the washing machine, even the kettle. At 7 am, he snuck into Mag's room and shook her until she woke. 'I'm off, Mag. I can't be here, it's too upsetting.'

'Aw, Sean, won't you stay?' Mag asked, drowsily. 'It's been great having you around.'

'I put on a brave face yesterday, but I feel on the verge of a breakdown now. I need to go clear my head. But thank you so much for inviting me, it means a lot.'

'You're always welcome here, Sean.'

'Thanks,' Jack said, kissing Mag on her lips, a force she hadn't felt in years. 'Chat soon. Oh, and check on Don in the morning. He drank himself stupid. God bless him, soft as a marshmallow.'

Mag didn't answer. She felt confused by Jack's kiss, her feelings muddled up, a glut of guilt greasing over layers of middle-aged lust, like oils sliding down the sides of a hydraulic shaft.

Driving back to Dublin, Jack called Mel from the car.

'How did it go?' Mel asked.

'It's exactly as Paddy said. They hired a hit guy named Trevor. Mick Devine set it up.'

'Then we need to track down Mick as well,' Mel said, sitting alone on Christmas night in her condo, wearing fluffy pyjamas and slipper socks Jack had sent over.

'Come to Ireland in the new year. Let's finish the job. We have our leads now. I'm tired. I just want to feel like the Murphys won.'

'That we did Dad proud,' Mel added, lying back on her couch, licking a candy cane and wriggling her toes; the word *Evil* emblazed on the left slipper sock, *Twin* emblazoned on the right.

'Any update on Eve?' Jack asked.

'For the millionth time, NO.'

'Okay,' Jack said. 'Chat soon.'

'Yeah,' Mel cried. 'My Christmas day was lovely, thanks for asking, Seany. I really enjoyed sitting alone at the table.'

'Happy Christmas, Mel. I love you too.'

Chapter 48

Dublin, Jan 2020

Erika Furlong hadn't shown up for work in two days. By Tuesday, the shadow of her absence loomed large around Clearwater – her colleague's hushed chit-chat at the coffee machine in the morning, theories spilling over into Teams chats by midday, suspicions shared over bowls of soup during lunch break.

'It's so unlike Erika,' her colleague Megan said.

'I bet she couldn't hack Jenny anymore.'

'No one can hack Jenny,' Lisa added.

'Even so, two days absent from work and not a peep from her. That's really strange.'

'Maybe she met a fella,' Rebecca added, stirring her soup, 'and he whisked her away to Monte Carlo or Dubai.'

'I saw her and the shrink in a tense convo a few weeks back.'

'Who, Sean Sheen?' Lisa asked, her eyes perking up.

'That's a made-up name if I've ever heard one,' Pamela said, debating whether or not to say what was really on her mind.

'Erika was probably writing him up for being too damn hot,' Megan joked.

'He gives me the creeps,' Pamela said, shaking her head and scanning the other woman for approval. 'There's something about his eyes.'

'Yeah, they're sexy,' Lisa interrupted.

'No, they're not,' Pamela said in a thick Tipperary accent. 'And then, all this craic about his girlfriend missing since Christmas, who happens to be Don-freakin-Foy's daughter. Come on. Pull the other one. I'm no detective, but two girls are missing, and he's the common denominator.'

'We don't know if Erika's missing,' Lisa said. 'She just hasn't shown up for work. Maybe she quiet quit.'

'Quiet quit my arse,' Pamela said, pushing her bowl of soup to the side of the table. 'Her phone hasn't been on since the weekend seemingly, and no one's heard a word from her since Friday. Erika wouldn't quiet quit, and I bet her disappearance has something to do with that Sean Sheen fella.'

'Don't let Don hear you talking like that,' Megan said nervously. 'He loves Sean. He couldn't praise him enough at our last All Hands session.'

Later that afternoon, Erika's colleagues in HR held a meeting on the fourth floor, sounding the alarm, suggesting they should call the Gardaí and ask them to perform a welfare check. The male Garda, who answered the call, listened as all the voices on the other end of the phone expressed concern.

'It's very strange she hasn't shown up to work.'

'Something awful must've happened.'

'We'd check ourselves, but don't want to disturb the crime scene. Not saying there is one.'

'She felt overworked.'

'I think she was depressed.'

'She was drinking a lot lately.'

'No fella on the scene, for a girl her age, it's very odd.'

'She was with a fella.'

'No, she wasn't.'

'She told me she got a letter from some correctional facility in Toronto. Maybe she was into that prison pen pal sort of thing. It could be something to look into.'

There were so many voices yapping that the Garda stopped taking notes, put down his pen, and rolled his eyes. 'Give me her address and we'll check it out.'

The Gardaí didn't find anything out of sorts at Erika's apartment. Her passport and phone were gone, her wardrobe was gutted out, and there was an empty space where she usually stowed her suitcase. They didn't find the mysterious letter that had landed on her desk the Friday she had gone missing. Erika hadn't noticed it until after lunchbreak, a white envelope with poor handwriting, a return address on the back: The Old Don Jail, Toronto, Ontario.

That's odd, Erika thought, prying her index finger between the seal and tearing it open with staggered rips. It was from a prisoner named Mitch Bauer, who started off by writing, *This is going to sound crazy but please read until the end.*

Mitch's letter went on to warn the HR department that a killer might be working amongst them. He'd be handsome and charming, have an elaborate backstory that didn't quite add up and a slight North American accent. He'd murdered multiple people in Canada and was in Dublin to kill Jenny and Don because he believed they were responsible for murdering his family.

Erika read the note in disbelief. Her eyes widened at the mention of murder, palms sweated at the mention of Jenny. She believed it was a prank, not stopping to think how much the profile matched her friend and colleague, Sean Sheen.

During their one-to-one session later that afternoon, Jack asked Erika what she wanted to discuss. Erika laughed. 'I got a weird letter today from some prisoner in Toronto. I searched the guy's name online, and he was found eating a woman's face.'

'Well, that doesn't happen every day,' Jack said, staring intensely into Erika's eyes. 'What did the letter say?'

'Oh, you know, the usual,' Erika joked, as though this interesting story made her far more interesting, too. 'Murder plots and revenge; warning us that we might have a serial killer working within Clearwater, some psycho that wants to kill Jenny and Don.'

'The irony,' Jack remarked. 'Jenny and Don are the true psychopaths.'

Erika snorted.

'I probably shouldn't have said that out loud,' Jack said, smiling.

'And not in front of HR,' Erika teased, lying her head back against the couch, feigning exasperation. 'Why does this always happen to me, Sean? The letter could have been addressed to anyone else, but it ended up on my desk. I swear, I'm a magnet for madness.'

'Touché,' Jack said jokingly, unsure how much consideration to show. It crossed his mind that Erika was probing him for clues, that this was a sting operation, and that she was recording their session on her phone as evidence.

'Like, what do I do?' Erika asked. 'Do I go to Jenny with this? If I do, what do I even say? She'll think I'm crazy.'

'I wouldn't go to anyone else with this,' Jack said sternly.

'The prisoner told me to contact Detective McGuire.'

'And did you?' Jack asked.

'No,' Erika said, sighing. 'What would I even say? And anyway, if Jenny knew I contacted that detective, she'd have me fired on the spot. Maybe this is all Detective McGuire's doing. You know he's been hanging around outside the offices, watching who's coming and going.'

'That's mad,' Jack said. 'Look, let's go for a drink after work. It's Friday, we can discuss it more then, and bring the letter; I want to analyse it.'

'I like the sound of that, Sean.'

'It's a date, and best keep it to ourselves. You know how folks like to gossip around here, and with Sinead still missing and all.'

'Oh, sorry, I never even thought of that,' Erika said. 'Are you sure you're ready?'

'It's only a couple of drinks between friends.'

'Yeah, yeah. I know,' Erika said, looking a bit embarrassed.

'I'll meet you in O'Brien's at six.'

'O'Brien's is an old man's pub,' Erika whined. 'It hasn't changed in a hundred years.'

'Nice and private,' Jack corrected. 'Now, what else is on your mind?'

The Gardaí wouldn't learn about Erika and Jack's date that evening, nor the fact that Jack burned Mitch's letter in the early hours of Saturday morning in the Dublin Mountains. After leaving Erika's apartment, the Gardaí couldn't confirm that anything suspicious had happened. It looked like Erika had simply left, but they kept an open mind as it was strangely connected to Sinead's disappearance, and the mysterious vanishing of another Clearwater employee, the performance coach who had went missing a few weeks before Jack started working in Clearwater.

Chapter 49

The day after Erika was reported missing, Mel called Jack with exciting news.

'Hey,' Jack answered, leaning back in his office chair, his feet resting on his desk.

'I've got a lead on Eve.'

Jack lurched forward, spilling his coffee. 'Where?'

'Some place called Sodus Point,' Mel said excitedly.

'That's close to where we got engaged. Listen to me, I need you to go there and find her.'

'And say what?' Mel asked. 'Hi, I'm the psycho's twin sister.'

'Just get her phone number. I'll do the rest.'

'Like she'll give it to me.'

'She will,' Jack said hopefully. 'I know she will. We had something bigger than all this. You wouldn't understand, Mel.'

'Yeah, rub it in.'

'Will you do this for me?' Jack asked.

Mel never answered him.

'If you do, I'll give you something bigger,' Jack teased.

'Like what?' Mel asked.

'Jenny and Don.'

'I'm listening,' Mel said.

'I can't stay here much longer,' Jack said, pacing around his office. 'With this Erika chick missing, it doesn't look good for me. That's two girls missing in a month and the rumour mill is aimed in my direction. I need to bounce in the next two or three days. I won't get to finish the job, but you can, and I can set it up. There's a big board meeting in two days. Jenny and Don will be there, and all the others too. I can give you my key card and anything else you need. The board room on the top floor is fully sound-proofed.'

'No one will hear them scream,' Mel said, energised.

'You said you wanted to right the wrong.'

'I did.'

'Here's your chance.'

'It is,' Mel said. 'I always imagined you'd do it for some reason, but this one is on me, Seany.'

'Get to Sodus Point and ring me when you find Eve.'

'Roger that. Mel Murphy, over and out.'

What a goof, Jack thought, what a wonderful goof his sister was, like some weird, murderous nerd who could transform into a demon or summon up a spell like a Salem witch. Jack always thought Mel was the only person he would never kill, but in the end, it was Eve. He knew this now, after champing the water his sister coursed, gaslighting a happy rhythm, drawing her towards a situation he never imagined her surviving.

Jack never showed up for work the following day, arousing even more suspicion. He was too busy planning his escape to Australia, phoning his pilot and chartering a confidential flight.

'Okay,' the pilot said. 'But you're not giving me much time, William.'

'I know that, but I'll double what I paid you last time?'

'You'll have to get to Knock Airport. I can't do Dublin.'

'Can we be out of Knock by 10 pm?'

'We can.'

'I'll see you then.'

'Where are you going?' the pilot asked. 'What airport in Australia?'

'Preferably Sydney.'

'I can't do Sydney,' the pilot said. 'I can land at a private strip near Gosford, but coming in on an international charter could complicate things, and we'll have to stop somewhere along the way to refuel.'

'Just get it done,' Jack said. 'Wiring you half now.'

Jack packed his suitcase afterwards, riffling through his various passports, wondering who he would be next – a surfer boy, he thought, a personal trainer, a lifeguard at Bondi Beach. Everything felt dull without Eve in the picture. He paused for a cigarette break, standing on his balcony, staring out at Dublin, his mind already sloshy with nostalgia. He'd never be able to return to Ireland, to feel imbued with the power of ancient myths, or stand on the western shores and feel the cool Atlantic spray wet his face. In a way, Ireland felt like another victim, something he'd dust off from time to time, reanimate and remember with a smile.

At midday, Detective Joyce called Jack, asking if he could come in for questioning over Erika's disappearance.

'I'm a bit tied up today,' Jack said, 'but I can come in tomorrow morning if that works.'

'We can meet you.'

'As I said, tomorrow morning works better for me.'

'Dodging us only makes us more suspicious,' Detective Joyce said. 'We got a letter from an inmate in Toronto, a former detective, Mitch Bauer. Does that name ring a bell?'

'I can't say it does, no.'

'But you lived in Toronto?' Detective Joyce probed.

'Toronto is a big city,' Jack said.

'Does the name Paddy Fitzgerald ring a bell.'

'Yeah, he was one of the Clearwater co-founders.'

'Paddy was murdered in Toronto around the time you were living there.'

'That's tragic,' Jack said. 'I'll be happy to discuss all this tomorrow when I'm back in Dublin.

'Where are you?'

'West Cork,' Jack said, 'focusing on my mental health.'

'We can have someone pick you up.'

'As I said, tomorrow works better.'

'We'll be waiting, Mr. Sheen.'

For the second time in six months, Jack held Ohana in one hand and his suitcase in the other. This time felt more desperate than the last, his patience spent, his calm confidence replaced with bouts of paranoia and a fixation on seeing Eve again.

Later that evening, as Jack sped towards Knock Airport with Ohana snoozing on the passenger seat, his phone rang.

'Mel!' Jack answered.

'I found her, Seany.'

'And? Did you get her number?'

'There's something you should know first.'

'Did you get her number?' Jack asked, his voice raised.

'Seany, you need to hear...'

'Did you get her number?' Jack shouted, arousing Ohana.

'Yes.'

'Then, call it out to me for God's sake.'

'Chill out,' Mel cried. 'I'll message it to you. You don't need to be an asshole about it. Eve and I went for a coffee; there's something you should really know.'

'I don't want to hear it,' Jack said, speeding forward, gripping the steering wheel as tightly as he could. 'I don't want you trying to change my mind. I'll tell Eve where to meet me. If the cops show up instead, then it is what it is, Mel. Life without Eve doesn't feel like living anymore. My mind feels like it's constantly searching for something, like it's trying to find a word it can't remember, and it won't settle. Even when I sleep, my mind feels awake, thinking of Eve. I don't know what's happening to me. I don't know if this is love or obsession, or some fixation I have with her. I don't know who I am anymore. But, at least, if Eve shows up then I'll know that someone cared for me. That someone loved me, even though she knew the ugliness rotting away inside of me.'

'I love you,' Mel said sadly, 'and I don't see anything ugly inside of you, Seany.'

'That's not the same, Mel.'

'Let's just run away together,' Mel said. 'It can be like old times, just me and you against the world, eh?'

'Those days are gone,' Jack said coldly. 'I'll message you my address in Dublin. There's a Glock under my bed and I'll leave my access card on the kitchen table.'

'This is goodbye, I guess.'

'For now,' Jack said, ending the call and pumping the throttle, doing 150km/hr down the N60. He added Eve's number to his contacts and searched flights from JFK to Sydney. There was still a shot at happiness, Jack thought, the green light glowing faintly in the distance. He took his eyes off the road, typing a message to Eve, hesitant to make a call.

Jack: Hey, it's Jack. There's a flight out of JFK to Sydney tomorrow at 2 pm. Get on it. I'll meet you at Sydney airport. I'm sorry. I've a lot of explaining to do. Give me the chance. I love you to death.

Eve never responded to Jack's message. It floated in the ether as Jack flew halfway around the world, saying prayers in his head, trying to bargain for a miracle. God had never answered Jack's prayers as a child, and he wondered if God would listen to him now, knowing all the evil he had done.

It was close to midday when Mel's flight touched down at Dublin Airport. She said 'Hi' to everyone she met, making her way outside the airport and hailing down a cab. She asked the driver to stop at a hardware shop, where she purchased an axe, and smuggled it back into the car before giving the driver directions to Jack's apartment.

'My dad was Irish,' Mel said as they drove through Dublin city.

'Yeah,' the driver mocked. 'All ye yanks say that.'

'But I was born here, and I might die here, but let's hope it doesn't come to that.'

'Ye Yanks are a very dramatic bunch, ya know that.'

Mel never answered him.

'Are you here on your own?' the driver asked licking his lips. 'I can you show a good time, love. Do you want to take a detour back to mine for a sausage sambo?'

The driver looked at Mel in his rearview mirror, and Mel grinned back at him, holding his stare eerily. Her pupils were so dilated the driver couldn't tell what colour her iris was.

'Are you okay?' the driver asked. 'I'm only messing with ya. '

'I feel bored a lot,' Mel said. 'I'm a psychopath, see. And psychopaths find it hard to feel stimulation. A part of my brain is stuck in sleep mode. It's the part that usually makes people feel emotion. I don't have any of that, so, you should drive a little faster, because if I get really bored, and you're starting to bore me, I might have to kill you and do something weird to your body.'

Mel zipped down her jacket, pulled out the axe, and put the sharp end to the driver's neck. 'Maybe I'll chop off your cock and feed it to you. How's that a for a sausage sambo?'

Chapter 50

It was spilling rain when Mel arrived outside Jack's penthouse apartment. She stood for a while, staring up at the sky, opening her mouth, trying to drink the raindrops. Dublin was duller than Mel had imagined. She expected to see the sky sparkling with rainbows and feel a sort of magic flowing through the streets. But Dublin was just another city, today felt like any other boring day, and the cab driver had reminded her that men are all the same.

Mel walked through all the rooms in Jack's apartment, rubbing her fingers over surfaces, investigating her brother's life in Dublin. Everything felt numb and grey. She had expected to feel some rush by now, some razzle of excitement, or the hum of her heartbeat, like Jack had felt for Eve. She picked up Jack's access card and rooted around for his handgun before swinging her axe through the air in violent motions. 'Maybe when I actually kill them, I'll be released back amongst the herd.'

Everything moved one way and Mel the other. She smiled manically to see if anything would change. 'Feel something,' she screamed, smacking her head into the kitchen wall. 'Answer me. Lord or Lucifer, reach out and find me. Pull me like a thread, enchant me. What do you want? Just answer me for once.'

Mel raved with questions for over an hour before leaving Jack's apartment. Her eyes appeared dark and dilated as she walked in the rain, staring forward, hitting into people that she passed. She hid Jack's Glock in her Canada Goose jacket and concealed the axe in the waistband of her jeans. She breezed through the turnstiles in Clearwater's office, scanning Jack's access card and making her way to the third floor to make herself a coffee in the communal micro kitchen. She made idle chitchat with some employees, introducing herself as a wealthy North American investor with a few hundred million to invest in clean energy.

When the reminder buzzed on her smartphone, Mel said, 'Time for me to go, folks. I've got a meeting with some VIPs.'

Mel took the elevator to the twelfth floor and stared at herself in the large mirrors on the walls. She forced herself to smile, but Mel didn't feel happy. She didn't feel anything at all. Everything inside of her felt so empty. When Mel was younger, she had gone to a few AA sessions to hear people talk about the hell they had lived through. Those people always described hell as the feeling of mental pain and suffering. But they had got it wrong, Mel reasoned. Hell isn't the feeling of pain and suffering, it's the absence of feeling anything; to wander through a world filled with music and not hear a single note.

Mel exited the elevator and peered around the corner, watching all the suits and skits scamper into the boardroom.

She took out her phone and messaged Jack.

Mel: I don't know if I'll make it out of this one. I love you, Seany. You're my everything, and believe me, I'll make you proud.

Jack messaged back a moment later.

Jack: Get to Knock Airport afterwards. I'll arrange your flight out.

Mel: I don't think I want to make it out.

Jack: I'd rather you did, Mel. I'm arranging a plane for you now. There's a black Tesla waiting for you in the

underground parking lot. The key is on the driver's side wheel.

Mel didn't respond to Jack's message. She walked casually towards the boardroom, entering with a twirl and a slight bow. 'Who's for tea and coffee?' Mel asked, locking the door and slipping the key into her pocket.

The boardroom was windowless, with thick soundproofing built into the navy walls. The ceiling was painted navy, too, and the dimmed light gave Mel the impression that she had stumbled into the lair of some secret cabal.

'This is a private meeting,' Jenny shouted from the head of the table. 'Who are you?'

'I'm Miss Wish,' Mel said, tilting her head to the side.

'What's going on here?' a board member asked.

'Are you a journalist?' Don Foy snarled. 'This is a business meeting, get the hell out of here before we call security.'

'She's probably here about Erika,' another board member added, rolling her eyes.

'No,' Mel answered, scooting over beside Jenny. 'I told you, I'm Miss Wish. Anthony Murphy's daughter. Do you all remember him? The man who built this company from the ground up. The man Jenny, Don and Paddy had murdered in 1996 when I was only four years old.'

'I built this company,' Jenny shouted.

'And I suppose you're here looking for a handout,' Don jeered.

'She can fuck off,' Jenny cried. 'Call security, now.'

When one of the board members took out his phone, Mel produced the axe from her jacket and swung it like a baseball bat, landing a heavy blow between the man's eyes. Five more swings and he hit the floor: flesh and blood splashing outwards, like a pig's dinner emptied from a trough – bits of bone, lips, eyeballs and nose all mashed up where his face used to be. Most of the board members screamed and fumbled out of their chairs. Two

282

remained sitting, rooted there in fear and disbelief. Don tried to overpower Mel, charging at her, trying to grab her hair and grip the hood of her jacket. But Mel was strong, swinging the axe furiously, lacerating Don's chest and arms before taking out her Glock and pointing it at the other board members.

'Put down the phone,' Mel shouted to a middle-aged man whose phone shook uncontrollably in his hands.

Mel waved the Glock around. 'Everyone sit back down,' she said, walking around behind the other board members as they sat shaking, looking down into their laps. 'What you all did to my family was wrong,' Mel said, wiping the blood splatter from her eyes. 'I'm here to right that wrong. I am vengeance. I am...'

'Fuck you,' Don mumbled from the floor with blood leaking from his mouth.

'My brother murdered your daughter,' Mel mocked, glaring down at him. 'That stupid whore. You shouldn't have had my family murdered, but you did, and now I'm going to murder you. Watch.'

Mel stood over Don, like a landscaper driving a fence pole into the ground, delivering blow after blow down on Don's head. A few board members vomited as Mel swung the axe again, this time sideways, like a golfer driving off a tee. She began walking around the table next, swinging the axe, trying to decapitate a man, causing his head to flop to the side like a wet sock. Most of the other board members scrambled for the door as Mel took out her Glock and emptied the whole clip. Seven bodies hit the floor, defecating, twitching, and bleeding out in a pile. Mel stood over the bodies, swinging the axe again, butchering limbs and torsos, hacking at heads. The floor was so damp with blood that Mel's feet squelched when she moved around. Blood hissed out of arteries, and the occasional groan could be heard somewhere among the pile of bodies.

Jenny sat at the head of the table, staring at her fingernails, an exaggerated look of boredom in her eyes.

'Look at me,' Mel said, taking off her jacket. Sweat beads dripped from her forehead, mixing with blood splatter, creating little red streams on her cheeks.

Jenny's eyes glanced up slowly.

'Look around,' Mel said, her face distorted and demonic. 'This is what my head feels like every day. This is what my heart looks like, all mangled and mutilated...because of you.'

'Am I supposed to feel sorry for you?' Jenny asked, smirking.

Mel smirked back.

'Your father might have left the tenements all those years ago,' Jenny continued, 'but the stench never left him, and I can smell that same foul odour wafting from you. It has a certain musk to it; it gets all clogged up in the back of your throat and you just want to hock it out onto the floor.'

'Wow,' Mel said with a lame clap. 'I always imagined you as some fierce woman; a real cutthroat killer. I used to think you'd gone on to live this amazing life while I inherited hell...but you're just a miserable, petty, old bitch.'

'Just like you,' Jenny said.

'I'm nothing like you,' Mel said sharply.

'I'm your mother,' Jenny said. 'That's why I let you and your brother live. Your father and I had an affair, but I never wanted children, so you were sent to live with him. I guess no one ever told you that.'

'Bullshit,' Mel said, walking for Jenny, letting the axe drag against the polished concrete floor. 'Daddy wouldn't have touched a dog like you. He would have seen right through you.'

'I'll get legal in here,' Jenny said, 'and we'll give you back your father's shares. We'll clear his name too. There's a way for you to make it out of this.'

'I don't care about making it out,' Mel said calmly. 'I don't care about the money, and I don't care about cleaning my Daddy's name. I only care about killing you.'

Jenny charged at Mel trying to scratch her face, but Mel laughed at her feebleness, grabbing Jenny's wrists and headbutting her hard into her nose.

'Sit down, bitch.'

Jenny went stumbling back into her chair as Mel swung the blunt end of the axe, hitting Jenny on the forehead, sending her backwards, tipping over in the chair.

'Don't do this,' Jenny begged, crawling along the polished concrete floor, the gash between her eyes gushing.

Mel smiled when she looked down at Jenny's Prada stilettos. She slipped them off Jenny's feet and put them on her own, prancing around, hearing them clatter on the cold concrete. 'These are the perfect souvenir.'

'Let me live,' Jenny pleaded. 'Please let me live.'

'Not today,' Mel said, rolling Jenny onto her back.

Mel tried to balance on one foot as she aimed the stiletto heel into Jenny's eye. Jenny screamed in pain, and when both heels were sunken into Jenny's eye sockets, Mel peered over her shoulder, saying, 'Anthony's bitch is about to walk over your dead body.'

Jenny wriggled around the floor, screaming louder and louder as Mel began lifting her feet and stomping the stiletto heels into Jenny's eyes. Blood and tissue oozed down the sides of Jenny's face, and soon the room was quiet again, save the stomping, squishy sounds of Mel's feet.

When Mel was done with Jenny, she dragged the bodies away from the door before opening her backpack, taking out a towel, and wiping the blood from her face and arms. She changed into clean clothes and trainers, placing the blood soaked stilettos in her backpack as a trophy.

'I'll enjoy wearing these again,' Mel said, taking the elevator down to the basement as Jack had instructed. His Tesla was parked close by the entrance. Mel got behind the wheel, fixing the rearview mirror, staring at herself for a moment and breathing heavily. Mel felt more alive than ever, pressing her foot hard against the accelerator, sinking back into the seat as she sped through Dublin. She phoned Jack when she reached the motorway, putting her hand around her throat, and chocking herself for pleasure.

'Well,' Jack answered excitedly, 'how'd it go?'

'I was like Genghis-fucking-Kan,' Mel said, the whites of her eyes barely visible. 'You would've loved it, Seany. Everything feels right again. I don't want to die over here. It's not my time.'

'I've a plane waiting for you at Knock,' Jack said. 'It'll bring you wherever you want to go, Mel.'

'Switzerland,' Mel beamed, taking her hands off the steering wheel and wiping her palms along her face. She told Jack all the grisly details, injecting her excitement directly into her brother's bloodstream.

'I'm proud of you,' Jack said once Mel had finished. 'Dad would be too.'

'Thanks, Seany.'

'Things will be different now,' Jack said, muddying the mood. 'Our faces will be everywhere. We'll have nowhere to hide, Mel. They will come for us, from all directions.'

'Switzerland doesn't have extradition laws,' Mel said, staring in the rearview mirror, her hairline caked with blood. 'Forget about Oz, come live with me in Switzerland, or we could go to Russia, or Cuba or Ecuador if you want somewhere warmer.'

'Maybe,' Jack said, petting Ohana as she slept on his lap. 'But first, I need to see if Eve, if...' he paused, loading his apprehension and aiming it at his temple like a gun. 'I need to know if it was real.'

'I hope she shows up,' Mel said, picking at the dried blood in her hair. 'But have you thought about what happens next, a life on the run, always looking over your shoulders? Do you think Eve would be able for that?'

'I hope so,' Jack said before changing the subject. 'Did you hear about this new virus in China? They reckon it could be a pandemic. It could give us cover to go underground.'

'Yeah, I heard,' Mel added. 'Some *corona* thing. Imagine if everyone died. The human population just wiped out in a few months.'

'Aw, these things come and go,' Jack said. 'But we mightn't get to see each other if they restrict travel. Anyways, there's a new passport waiting for you at Knock, some cash too; I'll wire you more once you get a bank account sorted.'

'Thanks, Seany.'

'I guess this is goodbye for now.'

'For now,' Mel said, picking a bit of flesh from her ear and tossing it out the window.

Chapter 51

Mel boarded the private plane at Knock Airport. The pilot appeared alarmed at her appearance, the dried blood around her hairline and the wild mania in her eyes. 'I can't land in Switzerland,' the pilot said nervously, 'their air control is too strict.'

They settled on Portugal, and Mel arrived at Faro Airport a few hours later. She slipped off the plane near a cargo bay and was ushered out the staff entrance, hailing down a taxi bound for Villamoura. It was close to midnight when Mel arrived at Villamoura Marina. She sat for a time, watching the yachts bob back and forth on the water, breathing in the sea air, listening to the *whoosh* of waves breaking on the nearby beach. Her high had worn off, her heartbeat quiet again, boredom back behind the wheel of every thought. *What now?* Was there anything left to live for? She missed Jack. They had never spent this much time apart, and she wondered if she would ever see him again. Maybe this was the end of the line. Maybe her life had run out of runway.

She took out her phone and sat for a time, googling different queries.

Things to do in Portugal?
The best beaches on the Algarve?
Does Portugal have extradition laws?
Famous Portuguese serial killers?
What's the average sentence for murder in Portugal?

Can psychopaths fall in love?

Mel left her phone on a bench at the marina, the screen left unlocked, her last Google search lighting up the darkness. **How do you cure boredom?**

Mell walked along the beach, feeling the waves splash her feet, then her knees, walking out until her whole body was submerged in the cold, dark water. Mel felt more bored than ever; everything seemed so forgettable, time trickling by, yawning in her direction. The world felt unchanged, even more unchangeable. 'Maybe it's time to end it all,' Mel said as the tide swept her further out to sea.

In Dublin, specialist investigative units assembled in Clearwater's lobby while a scrum of journalists amassed outside the office. Dublin's terror alert was raised to red, and the city streets were soon empty. At 9 pm, the lead investigator appeared on RTÈ News for a special briefing. 'There has been a serious incident in Clearwater Capital's office in the IFSC,' she announced. 'We're imposing a curfew for Dublin city, effective immediately.'

A CCTV screenshot of Mel appeared on screen next.

'We need your help identifying this woman, and we want to speak to anyone who knows her or has come into contact with her recently. She is considered highly dangerous and is believed to be armed – do not approach this woman if you see her. Notify the authorities immediately.'

Twitter turned into a storm of speculation. **Clearwater Murders** trended alongside **Coronavirus.** Theories quickly appeared across the news feed, with some users speculating that the murders were revenge for the financial crash in 2008. The left blamed right-wing extremists. Only one post mentioned the murder/suicide in 1996, a user who went by the Twitter handle @det_McGuire69.

Mitch Bauer saw the headline on CTV News the next day as he sat in the rec room of the Old Don Jail – **Clearwater Boardroom**

Butchered in Dublin, nine board members dead, one survivor in critical condition. Mitch shook his head, peeling his lips over his teeth like an agitated chimpanzee. He looked different now: his head shaved bald, sporting a ten-inch scar on his face, *Colossians 3:25* tattooed across his throat. Mitch didn't know it then, but this was the start of his release appeal, and in a few years, he would be a free man but shackled, too, just like Mel and Jack, borne along by fantasies of revenge and murder.

Meanwhile, Jack waited at the arrivals area in Sydney airport, clutching a bunch of yellow roses and practising a suite of different smiles. He didn't know what to expect. Maybe Eve wouldn't show up at all. There was a chance she was still pissed off at him. But their romance had breached new heights, Jack reasoned, it was beyond love. It was beyond good and evil. Other people wouldn't understand. Only he and Eve had felt the earthquake beneath them when their lips touched. They were inexorably drawn to each other, like cats to heat, kites to wind – love rattling in their bones like dice. The world is laid out like a chessboard, anyway. Jack had his chance to checkmate the queen but left the game instead. Eve wasn't a thing to topple. She was the beginning of a song he wished to hear until the end – one he would hum along to and sing the chorus at the end.

Jack eyeballed everyone walking through arrivals, watching them move about like people emptied out from the pages of a magazine – all the excessive smiling, families reunited with loved ones, kids kissing grandparents, happy tears forming in their eyes. He wanted to have all that, to feel their happiness. To be plucked like a flower from the dirt and bundled into a vase for everyone to admire.

Eve's flight had landed half an hour ago and there was still no sign of her. Jack thought about leaving, staring at the exit and then back towards arrivals, the sentimental accounting of memories seeming stupider, some gigantic loss in the ledger.

What's taking her so long?

When three airport cops walked by the arrivals gate, Jack turned to run, but then it happened, like an apparition. Eve appeared through the arrivals gate, wheeling a large suitcase, a big bump on her tummy. She was eight months pregnant and struggled to haul her luggage.

Jack's heart raced at the sight of Eve's bump; love alighting from his eyes like the pellets of a shotgun. This was the feeling Jack had been chasing all his life, a sort of happiness that shook the world to pieces, an overwhelming excitement for the future that drowned out the dark drumming of the past. Standing there, Jack felt a hot tear fall from his eye, a tear carrying the very essence of humanity, an essence he had only ever worn as a costume.

Eve approached him, no expression on her face.

'I guess we should talk,' Jack said, extending his arms.

'I guess so,' Eve said, leaning in for a cuddle.

Jack kissed her forehead. 'Let's go to Bondi like we always dreamed of doing, babe. Are we having a boy or girl?'

'First, you need to tell me why, Jack. Why on earth did you kill all those people in Toronto?'

'Later,' Jack said. 'I've a driver waiting outside; he'll be getting impatient.'

'I'm not leaving until you tell me why,' Eve said, withdrawing from Jack's embrace. 'I need to know.'

'I guess, I was angry,' Jack said, grabbing Eve's hand and attempting to drag her on.

'That's a shit answer, Jack. I saw first-hand what you did to Paddy Fitzgerald. That's not something you just feel like doing one day. That's something a person does when they're sick in the fucking head.'

Jack couldn't help but laugh. 'He did worse to my family. He deserved it, babe.'

'How many people have you killed? I need to know if we're to move on from all this.'

'I can't remember,' Jack said. 'That's all in the past. Love is the only thing I crave now. I read that psychopathy can't be cured, and that psychopaths can't change; they are what they are. But finding you and falling in love has changed everything. You've cured me, babe.'

Unseen by Jack, a tactical net was closing in on him. The airport's arrivals area was crawling with plainclothes officers, their senses sharpened, their eyes tracking Jack's every movement. Before Eve could answer, the officers converged, their guns drawn and aimed in his direction. It was only when a woman screamed close by that Jack saw what was happening.

'Jack Lawson, you're under arrest,' an officer announced, his voice steady, his eyes locked onto Lawson's. 'Don't resist or we'll shoot.'

More officers emerged, surrounding Jack. Pandemonium ensued as bystanders scrambled in all directions, the airport's security protocols kicking into gear.

'How could you do this?' Jack shouted, staring at Eve, his eyes dappled with defeat.

'I had to,' Eve said, tears streaming down her face.

'There's no getting out of this one,' the officer said, edging closer to Jack, his finger tight on the trigger. 'Down on your knees, hands behind your back, keep your head to the floor.'

Eve walked away in tears, holding her bump, trying to drown out Jack's screams in the background. It didn't feel like justice. What did that say about her, she wondered. To still be in love with a man capable of such evil. She hoped his arrest would separate her heartache from the horror. She saw two worlds inhabited by the same man. She saw the good monster and the bad one, who was at times, both selfless and kind, murderous and cruel. She lived hoping to forget it all, a little frightened that she might one day understand it.

Somehow, then, life was the constant packing and unpacking of feelings, toying with desires, overbaking indifference and the grave, transitory merits of meaningful attachments. Meaning was a submerged code whose cypher was only ever discovered in bouts of afterthought, among tethered scribbles of retrospect, inside balloons as they burst. Still, time forged on, humourless, premeditated, trying to look behind its shoulder to marvel at the misery trailing in its wake.

About the author

Gary Colton is a debut author living in Ireland. He has lived in both Dublin and Toronto, and has a strong connection with the cities where *Dark Finds* is set. His background lies in psychology and cognitive behavioural therapy. He loves anything behavioural science related, and this passion led him towards a career in advertising where he currently works as a Senior Client Solutions Manager at LinkedIn.

You can connect with Gary online via the following channels.

Instagram: @dark.finds or @darkfindsbook
Facebook: Dark.Finds
TikTok: @darkfindsbook
LinkedIn: linkedin.com/in/garycolton-psy/

Acknowledgements

I've failed more times than I care to remember. I've failed again and again and again as a writer, but I guess, if you are reading this acknowledgement, then this book has made it off my laptop.

Thanks to my editor, Anthony J Quinn, you've taught me so much, and I am wholly grateful. Thank you, Vanessa O'Loughlin (aka Sam Blake); your advice helped me hone my style and gave me the confidence to keep going. A huge thanks to the @dark.finds community on Instagram. You people rock, and gave me hope that a little book like this can work in the real world. You're all a part of this journey.

Thank you to my friends, family, work colleagues, and everyone who listened to me yabber on about the book and dream aloud. Thank you to my mam and dad; you are my rock, and the perseverance to get this far is because of you. To my wife, thanks a million, Bubba. You've supported me in every way possible. Countless times, you've picked all the pieces of my broken dreams and put them back together even stronger. You are my North Star, the light in the darkness, the words to a song I hum along to every day.

9601173001842

BVPRI - #0003 - 130224 - C0 - 229/152/17 - PB - 9601173001842 - Gloss Lamination